THE BOY WHO

~ LOST ~
FAIRYLAND

by Catherynne M. Valente

with Illustrations by Ana Juan

SQUARE
FISH

FEIWEL AND FRIENDS
NEW YORK

For all my brothers,
those with whom I was a child
and those who are children still.

An imprint of Macmillan Publishing Group, LLC
175 Fifth Avenue
New York, NY 10010
mackids.com

THE BOY WHO LOST FAIRYLAND. Text copyright © 2015 by
Catherynne M. Valente.
Illustrations copyright © 2015 by Ana Juan.
All rights reserved. Printed in the United States of America by
LSC Communications, Harrisonburg, Virginia.

Square Fish and the Square Fish logo are trademarks of Macmillan and
are used by Feiwel and Friends under license from Macmillan.

Our books may be purchased in bulk for promotional, educational, or business use.
Please contact your local bookseller or the Macmillan Corporate and Premium
Sales Department at (800) 221-7945 ext. 5442 or by e-mail at
MacmillanSpecialMarkets@macmillan.com.

Library of Congress Cataloging-in-Publication Data

Valente, Catherynne M.,
The boy who lost Fairyland / Catherynne M. Valente;
illustrated by Ana Juan. pages cm.—(Fairyland)
Summary: "A young troll named Hawthorn is stolen from Fairyland by the Red
Wind, and becomes a changeling in our world, a place no less bizarre than Fairyland
in his eyes"—Provided by publisher.
ISBN 978-1-250-07332-7 (paperback)   ISBN 978-1-250-07279-5 (ebook)
[1. Fantasy. 2. Trolls—Fiction. 3. Changelings—Fiction.] I. Juan, Ana, illustrator.
II. Title.   PZ7.V232Boy 2015   [Fic]—dc23   2014042417

Originally published in the United States by Feiwel and Friends
First Square Fish Edition: 2016
Book designed by Elizabeth Herzog and Barbara Grzeslo
Square Fish logo designed by Filomena Tuosto

6 8 10 9 7

LEXILE: 950L

Dramatis Personae

HAWTHORN, a Troll

THE RED WIND, a Harsh Air

IAGO, a Panther

BENJAMIN FRANKLIN, a Postmistress

SEPTEMBER, a Girl

THOMAS ROOD, a Boy

GWENDOLYN ROOD, his Mother

NICHOLAS ROOD, his Father

A BASEBALL

MAX, a Schoolboy

HUMPHREY!, a Desk

MRS. WILKINSON, a Schoolteacher

MR. WOLCOTT, a Substitute Schoolteacher

MR. GRANBERRY, a Gym Teacher

TAMBURLAINE, Perhaps a Girl, but Perhaps Not

BLUNDERBUSS, a Wombat

SCRATCH, a Gramophone

CHARLES CRUNCHCRAB, King of Fairyland

THE SPINSTER, a Strega

BESPOKE ESPADRILLE, a Walrus, but Additionally, a Shoemaker

PENNY FARTHING, a Changeling

BAYLEAF, also a Changeling

HERBERT, a Changeling as Well

SADIE SPLEENWORT, a Sour Girl

THE OFFICE

MADAME TANAQUILL, a Prime Minister

FOUR VICIOUS ALBINO MOOSE

SATURDAY, a Marid

A-THROUGH-L, a Wyverary

AUBERGINE, a Night-Dodo

SIR SANGUINE, a Redcap

THE MARQUESS, Former Ruler of Fairyland

GRATCHLING GOURDBONE GOLDMOUTH, a Clurichaun and Former King of Fairyland

SUSAN JANE, a Mechanic

OWEN, her Husband

MARGARET, an Aunt

CHAPTER I

ENTRANCE, ON A PANTHER

*In Which a Boy Named Hawthorn Is Spirited Off
by Means of a Panther, Learns the Rules of the World,
and Performs an Unlikely Feat of Gardening*

Once upon a time, a troll named Hawthorn lived very happily indeed in his mother's house, where he juggled the same green and violet gemstones and matching queens' crowns every day, slept on the same weather-beaten stone, and played with the same huge and cantankerous toad. Because he had been born in September, and because he had a scar on his right cheek, and because his hands were very small and delicate, for a troll, the Red Wind conspired to cause mischief, and flew to the creaky old well that served as the chimney of his underground house one evening just after his first birthday. She was dressed in a red breastplate, and red hunting boots, and a red gown, and a red bandit's mask.

It is very dangerous below the banana trees, in the Rhyming Jungle where the Red Wind hides her secrets.

"You seem a sweet and pliable enough child," said the Red Wind. "How would you like to come away with me and ride upon the Panther of Rough Storms and be delivered to a great desert that lies in the midst of a strange and distant land? I am afraid I cannot linger there, as Parched Climates do not agree with me, but I should be happy to deposit you upon the Wild and Walloping Wastes."

"No, no," cried Hawthorn, who deeply loved his green and violet gemstones, and also his huge and cantankerous toad. He began to wail in his whale-skull cradle.

"Well, then, come and be a good boy, and do not thrash about too much, nor pull too harshly on my Panther's fur, as she bites."

The Red Wind held out her arms, shimmering in red gloves, and Hawthorn, for a moment, was dazzled. He could not help it: He loved anything red. Leaves, some moons, rubies, ragelilies, blood, wine, apples (both poison and not), toadstools, riding hoods. Red was dark and fascinating. You couldn't deny red things. He once saw a Redcap dancing on a wild moor all tangled with beautiful poison berries and had never wanted anything so much in his life. He would have named it Walter and fed it fresh white rats. His mother said rats would never be enough for a Redcap and besides the little fellow would certainly murder them all in their sleep the first chance she got. Hawthorn had sighed with longing. He kept a few mice in a willow cage by her bed from then on, just in case.

Hawthorn's eyes got so full of the Red Wind that he could see nothing else. And so, even though he knew he oughtn't, Hawthorn reached out and took both the beautiful scarlet hand of the Red Wind and a very deep breath.

The Panther of Rough Storms picked up Hawthorn in his soft mouth just as any cat might do to a naughty kitten. The great black cat lifted the troll out of his whale-skull cradle, out of his lovely familiar nursery with its wallpaper of garnets and big, blue, long-lashed eyes, out of his underground house, leaving a parlorful of untidy green and violet queens' crowns with enchantments still clinging to their prongs by the skin of their teeth.

One enchantment had been cast by Hawthorn's father, who, at that moment, lay sleeping in a long mulled-wine-colored magician's cloak, snoring smoke-rings in his bed of green butterflies with a wand clutched in his arms like a teddy bear and gleaming things on his sleeping cap. It was meant to keep his son safe from marauding pirates, of whom he had an irrational fear.

One had been cast by Hawthorn's mother, who, at that moment, was bending over an overturned church bell full of leprechaun teeth in a distant midnight meadow, her arm muscles bulging. It was meant to keep her son safe from marauding disappointments, of which she had too much experience for any one troll.

One had been cast by a cabbage-gnome a hundred years ago. It was meant to wilt the leaves of anyone who forgot the gnome's birthday. Of these enchantments, one missed its mark, one bided its time, and one had no effect whatsoever, as trolls have very few leaves.

"Now," said the Red Wind, when she had Hawthorn firmly in hand upon her glittering ruby saddle, "there are important rules in your new home, rules from which I am entirely exempt, as Hot Air is the friend of all bureaucracies. I am afraid that if you trample upon the rules, I cannot help you. You may be ticketed, or executed, or elected to high office and given a splendid parade, depending upon the fashions of the day."

Trolls are quick learners and quicker growers. They speak as quickly as a newborn giraffe can walk and sprout up like pumpkin plants who have heard Halloween means to come early. Hawthorn was only a baby still, but tall as a table already. He had made friends with all manner of words and some cracking good ones at that. But at the moment, the poor creature was far too terrified to use the better ones on the red-cheeked lady who had burgled him up as though a troll-child were no more than a very fine hat in a shop window. Or her wildcat. All he could make out of the howling air all around them, the last shreds of his sleep, and a troll's blue tongue was:

"Is it so terrible there?"

The Red Wind frowned into her dark crimson hair. "All countries are terrible," she admitted finally. "But this one, at least, has some lovely scenery."

"Tell me the rules at least?" Hawthorn said uncertainly. His father had taught him when he was quite small that if one finds oneself captured by pirates, politeness pays better than sass, and Hawthorn had begun to feel that his current situation might share a drink or two with piracy.

"Firstly, no magic of any kind is allowed. Customs is quite strict on this point. Any charms, enchanted beans, grimoires, or talismans you might have on your person will be confiscated and sold as Christmas ornaments. Second, the practice of *physicks* is forbidden to all except young ladies and gentlemen with Advanced Degrees."

"But I like *physicks*!"

"It is certainly possible you may grab hold of a Degree," winked the Red Wind, "but I am afraid I do not know where to find their nests. Third, aviary locomotion is permitted only by means of Balloon or licensed Aeroplane. If you find yourself not in possession of one of these, kindly confine yourself to the ground. Fourth, all traffic travels on the right, except where it doesn't, and no signs will be posted. Fifth, shape-shifting and glamours are restricted to October the thirty-first of each year. Sixth, all children are required to attend School, which is like a party to which everyone forgot to bring punch, or hats, or fiddles, and none of the games have good prizes. Seventh and most important, you will find that several things are extremely dangerous to your person, namely: iron, eggshells, fire, and marriage. You may in no fashion allow any human to call you by the name your mother gave you or pass beyond the borders of Cook County, or else you will either perish in a most painful fashion or be forced to sit through very tedious sessions with doctors in thick glasses. These laws are sacrosanct, except for visiting demigods and bankers. Do you understand?"

Hawthorn, I promise you, tried very hard to listen, but though his mother had taught him brownie backgammon as soon as he could whack two hazelnuts together, he always forgot when you were allowed to turn your opponent into a raccoon, and he certainly had no hope of remembering such ugly and foreign rules. The rushing wind stopped up his ears and blew his silver-green hair into his face. Its strands wrapped his chin like woolly scarves.

"Obviously, the eating or drinking of human foodstuffs constitutes a formal and binding agreement to become mortal and never return, releasing Fairyland and all her subsidiaries, holdings, and most particularly, ahem, *representatives*, from all liability concerning your behavior in Lands Beyond."

"What? What does that mean?" Hawthorn had every intention of eating and drinking until he was sick the very moment this ridiculous cat put him down. A goodly size moose might do nicely. Perhaps a polar bear. And a side of basilisk, roasted, not boiled.

The Red Wind tightened her bandit mask. "That means: Off to bed and no supper for you, wicked Changeling child!" She laughed like the hot, heavy wind of summer crackling before a storm. "Sour and hairy, strong as sherry, the dark of my starry sky!"

The Panther of Rough Storms yawned up and further off from the cobblestone chimneys of Skaldtown and the green mountains of Fairyland, to which Hawthorn could not even wave goodbye. The Red Wind hugged him so tightly he could not even waggle his thumbs. And a good thing, too! Babies are forever rolling off of beds and ottomans and changing tables and Panthers. If their mothers do not take care, they might keep on rolling and rolling until they get all the way to the ocean and are forced to learn boatbuilding and the language of walruses. Though babies are generally quite bounceable, it does not pay to take chances while at cruising altitude.

And so Hawthorn could not say farewell to his house, or his mother's trusty church bell, puffing clouds of luck far below. He could not wave goodbye to his father, dreaming of quick, silent, clever pirates hiding around every shadowy corner. You and I might be well pleased about all this, having read a great many books that begin in such a fashion and end marvelously well for everyone. (Except, naturally, those who end up in red-hot shoes or locked in a chest at the bottom of the sea.) But Hawthorn had not had a chance to read any books without pictures yet. He did not know that to be spirited away by means of jungle cat means that one may reasonably expect a heaping helping of adventure, a pot of daring feats to dip it in, and a hunk of wild coincidence to mop it all up. He did not know that trollmothers and trollfathers only worry when they think their little adventurer has been running about with poorly designed bridges of ill-repute. Once they discover he's simply been meddling mischievously with humans, everything is forgiven. He did not know that he was headed, at the breakneck speed of flying folklore, toward the Province of Poorly Designed Bridges, the Land of Quiet Libraries, the Kingdom of No U-Turns, the Country of Shops Closed On Sundays. He did not know what was going to happen to him.

But he suspected that he was at the beginning of a story.

Hawthorn looked up into the deepening sunset clouds. *I shall be as brave as my Toad,* he thought, *for my Toad never hides under the bed when she is afraid of lightning or bats. She sticks out her tongue and eats them.* The troll stuck out his tongue at the whipping, glowing wind. He buried his fists in the Panther of Rough Storms, whose pelt was soft and dark, and listened to the beating of that huge and thundering heart.

"If you don't mind my saying, Miss Wind," said Hawthorn, "where are we going? After awhile we shall certainly pass Pandemonium and the Autumn Provinces and the Perverse and Perilous Sea and simply come round to my house again."

The Red Wind chuckled. "I suppose that would be true, if I did not know a great deal more about geography than you."

"I'm reasonably sure you know more about everything than me. For example, you seem to know that it's perfectly all right to kidnap poor trolls in the middle of the night. Who taught you that? You must have had a very bad mother."

The Red Wind snorted red clouds through her nostrils. "*My* mother could blow a hurricane out of one nostril and thump your mother at cards, boxing, and every one of the maternal sports! I have a Receipt made out in very fancy writing indeed which entitles, nay, *orders* me, to collect one Changeling and deliver it safely in accordance with local conservation laws. You should feel honored! I chose you! Out of all the trolls in Skaldtown, all the hobgoblins of Spleenwort City, all the satyrs of Tusktug. I chose you for the Changeling life—my Panther and I promise you'll like it, and a cat's promise is . . . well, it's as good as old milk, really. But old milk makes a splendid yogurt, my lad! Doesn't it just! And when a *Wind* promises you a rollicking time, hold on to your skirts and your hats and your billowables! Now, hold on tight, I've got to duck the gravity interchange or we shall indeed come round to your house again, which would be awkward for all of us."

The Panther of Rough Storms gave a shattering roar. Several fogbanks slunk gloweringly out of their way.

"Well, *I* think you're no better than a pirate. My father says pirates are the worst things in the world after Kings and centipedes."

"And what would you know? That might hurt my feelings if we went on holiday together every year and belonged to the same Blustering Society. But we have only just met! One cannot really be bothered by insults from strangers. Might as well cry over the tide coming in! Besides, without pirates, the sea would be an awfully boring place. If I am a pirate, pass me the grog! Poor lump. It's all right if you feel a bit cross with me and want to thump me on the skull. That's only to be expected from a Changeling."

"What's those?" asked the little troll.

"A Changeling, my dear, is rough and wild, vaguely *unhinged*, a bit of a *riddle*, a bit of an *explosive*, and altogether maniacal when its fur is stroked the wrong way, which is always! Think of it as an academic exchange program, my belligerent belladonna. Like the banshee apprentice your uncle Monkshood hired when you were just born."

"How did you know about Uncle Monkey?" exclaimed Hawthorn. The clouds gobbled up his cry.

"I happened to be performing my summer ablutions just then. She had on a suit of birchbark armor; you were all swaddled in salamander skin. She and your industrious uncle built quite a sturdy windmill that day." The Red Wind scowled darkly. "Harsh Airs have excellent memories for things that have tried to capture them."

Hawthorn looked out into the brilliant ruby clouds of the skies between Fairyland and the Other Place the Panther meant to take him.

"Fairyland is not unlike your cradle," said the Red Wind kindly, her maroon eyes flashing behind her mask. "We are going to climb over the railing while no one is looking, and when we have slipped the bars and snuck out the nursery door, we shall be in another place entirely, which is to say, the human world. It won't be long now."

"What's a human? Is it like a toad? Can I ride one?"

The Red Wind pondered. "A human is a know-it-all ape who got so good at magic, it thought there was nothing special about the way it behaved and then forgot magic ever existed in the first place. And you should most definitely try to saddle one up."

"But what if I want to go home?"

"Don't worry, my little lump of rock. Everybody gets a chance to choose. Or else where would irony come from?"

And indeed, in the rippling red clouds above everything, a great number of treetops began to peek out. They were all very tall and very lush: great umbrellas of glossy leaves, lacy branches twisting and toppling together, cupolas of orange and fuchsia flowers, obelisks of braided beanstalks, huge domes like the ones Hawthorn had seen in his picture book about Pandemonium, but made of climbing roses and hanging bananas and iridescent turquoise bubbles that would not pop, even when they tumbled into thorns. Just the sort of place where the wind stills, grows sleepy, turns around in a few lazy circles, and settles down for a nap in a sunbeam. Everything was hot and wet and alive, like the inside of a summer raindrop.

"Welcome, Hawthorn, dear as vino and veritas, to the Rhyming Jungle, where the Six Winds spend their holidays."

Hawthorn thought his Toad would very much have liked the place. He liked it himself, but decided not to tell.

The Red Wind and Hawthorn entered the Rhyming Jungle smoothly, the Panther of Rough Storms being extra careful not to jostle the landing. They soared down the Sestina Shunpike, where wide-winged haiku-hawks darted and sang: five trilling notes, then seven, then five again. The Panther of Rough Storms purred and snapped his jaws at them. Sunlight rushed and rippled down the paths of the forest the way rivers run through the cities you and I have seen.

"Why is it called the Rhyming Jungle? A jungle can't rhyme," Hawthorn said sullenly, refusing to give the Red Wind the satisfaction of being impressed.

"Look around you, little blind mouse! Everything rhymes! There's the Guava Grove on the edge of Lava Cove, the Savannah of Bananas, beaches full of peaches, moonflowers growing in the evening hours. And look there! The pink-backed snake basks in the shade of the ink-black mandrake, the cuckoos in the bamboo, the wide-mouthed frogs in the seaside bogs, the crocodiles sleeping in the hollyhock isles, the ocelots among the apricots, the mistletoe twists round branches of pistachio, the plum trees gossip with the gum trees, dryads tango through the mangoes—and when night falls, the fruit bats and the muskrats and the wildcats and the wombats hold their wild sabbats on their thorny ziggurat! If you look closely at the world, you will see that it is made of nothing but interlocking verses. For everything that is, there is a mirror and a match, a rhyme and a rhythm. Ask me instead what does *not* rhyme? That would be easier."

Hawthorn looked down at the seething poem beneath him.

"But . . . but there's a herd of elephants eating cashew leaves. And capybaras with their cheeks full of sarsaparilla roots. Kumquats next to cinnamon trees and an avocado grove with mosquitoes and coconuts and tapirs and orchids mixed in. Those don't rhyme at all."

"The Jungle enjoys a spot of free verse from time to time. Don't nitpick, it's a very unattractive trait."

The Panther padded down softly and trotted off into a thicket of coffee berries and rosy cherries. They were heading for a shimmering clearing at the end of the Shunpike, so thick with ferns and wild purple flowers that Hawthorn could not see right away that the ground beneath was not green, but a bold, cheerful blue. As they drew nearer, the little troll looked down upon a lovely strange sort of painting in the earth: Grass and vines and fallen fruits and old leaves and gnarled roots and wet, clayey mud grew and corkscrewed and scattered and fell and twisted and squelched in a hundred colors—a map of the world made of the world itself. The blue grasses made a flowing ocean; little heaps of papayas and tangerines clustered into continents, great red tree roots showed safe sailing routes, and a thousand brilliant flowers floated in the grass like islands in the sea. Across the middle of it all lay a path of perfectly even, flat, glistening obsidian stones. Hawthorn could see his face in their black, glassy surfaces, broken into a dozen other Hawthorns.

"What are *those*?" he whispered, entranced by the stones and the boy trapped inside them. The continents looked nothing like his book of maps at home. His book was gigantic and red, and therefore one of his favorite toys. Best of all, if you stepped on a page and said the right words, you could go right into the talking desert or candy-cane towers it showed. His mother hadn't shown him the word yet, but Hawthorn felt certain she was keeping it in the high kitchen cabinet he could not reach, behind the baking soda and the belladonna. Pretty soon he'd be big enough. But this! This map had so much ocean! And all the land looked like a great broken puzzle, as though if you squeezed them all together they would fit precisely, shore to shore, and make a picture of something else.

"*Those* are the Equator, my dulcet demon. And we can't get very far without an Equator, so do stop gawping at them." The Red Wind dismounted with a gallant sweep of her leg and lifted the troll from the Panther of Rough Storms, letting him squish his toes in the blue mud. She looked him over. "Do see to your hair. It's sticking up dreadfully in front."

Hawthorn blushed—trolls blush a very fetching shade of chartreuse—and squashed his forelock down hurriedly with one hand.

"But that's not right! Everyone knows the Equator is a great fat serpent who lays around the whole world and bites her own tail and keeps us all safe from marauding meridians," he spluttered quickly, embarrassed. He did so love to be right. It was his third favorite thing, after fire and his mother.

"Don't be silly, child. The Equator is a dotted line on a map. It marks the widest part of the earth, midway between the North Pole and the South Pole. Serpents! Why, I've never heard such a thing!" But her dark eyes twinkled, and her red mouth quirked as though she was, somewhere deep inside, laughing at him. Perhaps the snake was hiding off further in the Jungle, smirking too, holding her giant breath to keep from being discovered.

Hawthorn felt quite shy in front of the mossy map. Being a troll, he loved the earth. A troll's love for the earth is a peculiar thing—it is something like the way you and I love our parents and our dogs and our favorite novels and the stuffed rabbits we have had since we were in our cradles and the very best thing we have ever done with our own two hands, all smashed up together in a rough, enormous ball of feeling the size of a planet. But this wasn't *his* earth. He felt as though he were being introduced to the beautiful cousin of his best friend. All his skin flushed and tingled. He felt faint. Perhaps it was only that he hadn't eaten anything since supper last night and the Jungle was so wickedly hot and wet and close. Being a Changeling was, so far, very tiring work.

"Are they going to come alive?" Hawthorn peered closer at the dark stones. "Or grow legs and dance? Or tell us fell secrets from the deep and loamy vaults of lizard-time?"

"You're going to have to start a sort of backward, old-fashioned sort of thinking, I'm afraid." The Red Wind picked at her sleeve shame-facedly. "Not everything is going to be always alive the way you and I are. Not everything has a dance or a secret or a song locked up inside it. Where you are going, a map is just a map. If it has any magic, it is a simple one: A map shows maybes. Maybe you will climb the Himalayas or sail the Mississippi. Maybe you will see Paris; maybe you will eat wolf stew in Siberia. A map shows the way to everything. No more and no less. But it cannot choose between Annapurna and Missouri. That is your job. If you want the job, that is."

The Red Wind turned to him with a very serious expression on her lovely face. She crouched down so that they could look each other in the eye directly, troll to wind. "When you make a choice," she said, "how do you do it, my stroppy, surly, splendid lamb? Think of all the things you have chosen in your little life, from porridge or parrot pie for breakfast to whether or not to bother with learning to walk. How did you pick the pie and the trip-trapping upon the bridge?"

Hawthorn shuffled his large, mossy, bare feet on the brilliant blue grass of the blooming map. "Well . . . you start with fretting," he said finally. "If you don't give a thing a proper fret it'll never come out right.

I know that from my own belly, which always makes a feeling like falling when it doesn't know what to do. And then . . . well, my mother says everything in the world is a boxing match in your heart, between Boldness and Not-Boldness. You let them holler inside you and wallop each other with Arguments For and Against. Then you end by betting on one or the other and that's how things get decided." He thought about it for a moment. "If you're my father you bet on Not-Boldness, Being Safe, with a bridge over your head and a good beefy riddle in your pocket. If you're my mother, you bet on Boldness. Mummy says a choice is a bet you make with the world, and a gambler drinks better than a spend-thrift. And all the while it's happening you have a stomachache."

"And who do you take after?"

Hawthorn thought back to his garnet nursery, his great toad, his father and his hat, his mother and her pot, the family bridge, with its good, creamy mortar and nice thick stones and new riddles every year. He thought of everything that had ever happened since he had been born, which was really not so many things, but to Hawthorn was the whole of the universe.

"I don't know!" he cried. "I mostly take after my Toad, I think."

The Red Wind grinned, her red lips curling under her red mask. She looked as though she had been given a present just specially for her, all wrapped up in red. "Oh, my darling stumpy mushroom-lad! Quite so! And a toad means *adventure*. A toad means starting out a nasty clammy little thing and turning into a prince. A toad means sticking your tongue out as far as it can go and gobbling up everything it touches. A toad means golden balls and wells and cursed princesses and archery contests and swelling music and flowers falling from towers and the en-chanted bowers of fair maids! Choose, Hawthorn, the Toad's True Son—a life in the tourist industry, sticking close to home, trip-trapping poor backpackers who never harmed you, or a life of strange lands, wild wandering, splendid machines, and deeds of daring?"

Hawthorn hopped from foot to foot, quivering and sweating and furrowing his brow. He could feel his fret starting up in him like a sour green balloon, slowly filling and growing. He could see the gorgeous land the Red Wind spoke of on one side of his heart, opening up like a book of many colors, like his book of maps, wonderful, new—and on the other side he saw his beloved whale-skull bed and the opal porridge his father boiled up on Thursday mornings and the dear, familiar shops of Skaldtown all lit up for the holidays. The Equator glittered beneath his feet. Each stone seemed as deep as the sea, as a dark, dark door, a tunnel, through which the troll knew he would find another Hawthorn, a boy he could not even imagine right now, who had chosen adventure and towers and flowers and whatever bowers were, who had a gleam in his eye like a lad who had placed his bet and won.

Hawthorn wanted to meet that boy *awfully.*

The Red Wind gently pulled a strand of Hawthorn's mossy hair free of his nightclothes. "A choice is like a jigsaw puzzle, darling troll. Your worries are the corner pieces, and your hopes are the edge pieces, and you, Hawthorn, dearest of boys, are the middle pieces, all funny-shaped and stubborn. But the picture, the picture was there all along, just waiting for you to get on with it. Now, grab hold of that bit of grass. That one there, under the guavas. Get your nails underneath, that's a lad."

Hawthorn, his fret still squeaking and swelling, did as he was told. He squooshed his thick fingers into the Jungle earth. It was as soft and sweet as warm chocolate. He felt a hard lip and hauled on it—the edge of the blue grass, the edge of the map, came up in his hand. The Red Wind had snatched up a stretch of canteloupe-continent, and as Hawthorn watched, she heaved it up, up, up, over her head. The Panther of

Rough Storms bit a pale swath of moonflower-arctic in his black muzzle and yanked it free. The troll gritted his sharp teeth and pulled harder, hardest, until his scrap of sea came up as well, and they all three tripped and tumbled toward each other, dragging the grass and flowers and stones behind them like capes, until suddenly all was dark. The boiling sun was gone. They crouched together, breathing fast, huddled inside the bundle of the world like a fort of blankets. The rich smell of flowers and roots and soil and growing, living, rhyming things swirled and danced in the shadows. Hawthorn's fret popped in an emerald burst. He peered at the Wind and her Panther with great bright crimson eyes like nursery-garnets and Redcaps and poison apples.

"There isn't really a choice, is there?" he whispered. "Adventure cheats. It's so much shinier and louder than Not-Adventure."

Solemnly, the Red Wind held out her free hand to the troll in pajamas. With the other hand, she held the world together.

"Aren't you the cleverest thing," she said, and pulled him in close to her scarlet side, to her Panther, to the Equator, and the infinite sea of maybes she clutched in one strong, red fist.

How to Send a Troll by Post

*In Which Hawthorn Chooses Between a Variety of Attractive
Packaging Options, Meets a Certain Benjamin Franklin,
and Receives a Commemorative Stamp*

I have told you three times that the world is a house—and everyone knows a thing you say three times must be true. But now I shall tell you how the world is shaped for the fourth time.

Fours are a funny business. No one ever gets four wishes from a genie in a great brass coffeepot. Nobody demands you perform four tasks to be done in order to win the heart of a rhinoceros, or accepts four gifts from the suspiciously overeager witch at the bottom of a well. A joke repeated three times is a satisfaction, four tires the patience and the jaw. I have never heard hide nor hair of the fourth blind mouse, nor what the fourth little pig might have found left over to build his house with when his brothers had done. The fourth wish, the fourth gift, the fourth mouse—they live outside the story of stories, outside the rules. Anything might happen to that poor white-eyed creature nosing in the dark. She might find herself crowned Queen of the Kingdom of Drywall and rule with an iron paw. One simply cannot know what to expect. Not even me—and I know quite a lot of things concerning stories, as well as the care and keeping of royal mice.

But we are seasoned travelers, you and I. We have gone together every which where: into the front parlor of our own dear planet, full of diamonds and dinosaur bones and Canadian geese and the Cathedral of Notre Dame and ballpoint pens. We have crept up into the lush, painted bedroom of Fairyland and bounced upon the bed until feathers flew. We have slipped through the cluttered closets between worlds, down into the dark cellar of the underworld, up onto the roof to see the lost baseballs and fallen stars and astronauts left all about. We have sailed and spelunked and flown hand in hand—we have even walked on the Moon. How wonderfully expert we have become at the whole business! We know just where our traveling socks are kept. At the drop of a page, we polish our passports and pack our overcoats and turn up the collars on our rather fetching matched luggage. We shall go to the Country of Four together! What fun it shall be! The Country of Three is such a safe place, after all. It is so comforting to know that the third house always stands fast, no matter how the wolf blows. But the fourth? Who can tell?

This time I shall not lead you into a new corner of the house of the world. We know it so well by now, after all. We know where the Fairies live and where the shadows fall, where the cobwebs really ought to be cleaned up if anyone ever gets around to it, where a window is loose, where a door creaks. We are annoyed by the stove that will not light, by the weeds in the garden, by that ungodly mess in the closet. A thing too familiar becomes invisible.

It is time for us to Go Out.

But do not fear, even if it is colder outside than you might prefer, if Spring has been once again rudely tardy, if the trees only have a breath of green at their tips like a fine lady's jade rings, if the sun is pale and high and makes you squint, if the wind, for there is always wind, bites and pierces deep. Tug up your best coat round your neck and tie your longest scarf tight. You may hold my hand if you like. I promise, it is good for your health to step outside the house of the world. After all, we are not going far.

Only so far as the mailbox.

When one wraps oneself up in a blanket of earth, one expects, quite rightly, to find oneself underground when all is wrapped and done. But when Hawthorn opened his eyes (which he had scrunched up tight in case of a frightful rush of air, a bang or a flash, any jostling or walloping that might accompany a crossing of, or indeed a burrowing into, the Equator) he stood outside, on a pleasant, clipped lawn, with a number of respectable hedges and flowerbeds about. The sun sparkled in a cloudless sky; a brisk breeze ruffled rows of several-colored tulips in neat beds. Hawthorn shaded his eyes, dazzled. Before him rose quite the largest building he had ever seen. Troll architecture is mainly accomplished by having a good long talk with a hill or a swamp about the marvelous advantages to be found in doors, windows, and indoor plumbing. But this was a palace. Twelve black columns rose up, all tangled round with golden moss and briars bursting into deep violet roses and deep violet quill-pens, their feathers drooping elegantly toward the grand steps. A great triangular roof capped the columns. Beautiful carvings danced upon it, a parade of dashing daredevils: Peasants and princes and spriggans and salamanders, fairies and firebirds and fauns, maidens in armor and maidens in chariots, strange, smartly suited folk with plain faces and more buttons on their coats than anyone needs, horses and dogs, clerks with sharp pens, all laughing as though they had heard the same excellent joke. All passing parcels and letters between them, some secret and furtive, some open and glad. And below this stone gathering, bright blue letters read:

GREATER FAIRYLAND POSTAL SERVICE
STATION NO. 1
NEITHER ROUGH STORMS NOR GLAMOURS
NOR FIREDRAKES NOR GLOOMY NAIADS
WITH THEIR DRESSES OFF
STAYS THESE COURIERS FROM THE SWIFT-ISH
COMPLETION OF THEIR APPOINTED ROUNDS

A great rush of folk hurried in and out of its grand doors. Some carried bundles under their arms, some letters, some nothing at all. A Fairy boy with blinding orange wings clutched a sheaf of papers to his chest and wept. A manticore tore joyfully into a bushel of toffees wrapped in brown paper right there on the steps. The Red Wind and her Panther gazed up at the post office with a certain sort of familial fondness.

"Are we going to post a letter?" asked Hawthorn wonderingly. He plucked at the sleeve of his nightdress, feeling suddenly very shabby. He would have dressed up if he'd known he was going to meet the post office.

"In a manner of speaking," chuckled the Red Wind, and prodded him up the long, shining path through the grass. It was cobbled in brass plaques, most worn and faded by foot traffic. Hawthorn peered down—they were postmark plates, for a few familiar places and a hundred thousand cities the troll had never heard of. Cockaigne, Brocéliande, Seattle, Buyan, Pandemonium, Lilliput, Chicago, El Dorado, Paris, Norumbega, Tain, Odessa, Melbourne, Almanack, London, Johannesburg, Addis Ababa, Omaha, Walghvogel—and there! Skaldtown! Hawthorn squeaked with glee. He longed to stay and read them, every one, the wonderful names and the plain ones, home and far-off. But the Panther of Rough Storms nipped at his heels until they were jogging along much too fast to get any more good looks. And as they drew close to the great palace of post, he saw that the black columns and walls were not smooth stone as he had thought, but thousands and millions of brimming inkwells packed together like bricks, their dark ink rippling safe within or trickling out or oozing from cracks in the round glass globes. By the time they reached the top of the gloriously dizzying staircase, Hawthorn's feet had gotten quite soggy with purple-black ink. The Red Wind turned aside the door: a leaf of parchment paper as thick as a girl's arm. For a moment the troll worried about tracking ink inside—but the damage had already been done. The floor of the post office was the color of closed eyes.

A bright, piercing bell chimed and a deep, pleasant voice announced: "Now serving number thirty-four." Overhead, a throng of glowworms rearranged themselves to display a glittering numeral 34 in the air.

A long counter perched at the head of a vast ballroom full of customers, velvet ropes and brass bannisters, buskers playing harps and hurdy-gurdies, stamp sellers in colorful waistcoats calling out their wares like fresh fruit: *Vintage Mallows, ten for a Kiss! Commemorative World's Foul Airmails, no two alike! Black-Mail stamps straight from Fairyland-Below, Still*

Ripe! A bright blue-and-yellow theatre mask grinned down from the polished teak of the service counter. A long, slow ticker of numbers peeled out of its mouth like the bow-tied tail of a balloon. A little gnome with spiky hair hopped up and ripped one off, grimacing at what must assuredly be a number quite estranged from thirty-four before taking her place in the queue.

"Shall I fetch us a number?" said Hawthorn shyly.

"Certainly not," replied the Red Wind. "Rules are for those who can't think of a better way. Imagine! A Changeling waiting in line!"

The Red Wind shuffled in the pockets of her wild ruby gown and came up with a magician's fan of tickets, each with a merry little number written upon it.

"Let's see . . . 12? 21? 122? 697? No, no, I know I've something in the forties here."

"Miss Wind," Hawthorn said as she shuffled through the underside of her breastplate and boots searching for more tickets, "I want to ask you a question, and I want you to answer me seriously and not call me any baby names or make fun of me."

"Hmm? Oh, of course, my . . . Hawthorn. And you can call me Red. Formalities irritate the skin and cause nearsightedness, you know."

"Why did you take me out of Skaldtown? Do you take very many children? Are they all trolls? What *is* a Changeling?"

Hawthorn was quite certain the Panther of Rough Storms laughed at him.

"That's rather more than one question. Therefore I think it's only fair I give you rather more than one set of answers." She cleared her throat dramatically. "One: Skaldtown is a frightfully dull place with nothing at all to do on a Wednesday night. Two: Goodness, I couldn't possibly remember. Winds have the beastliest jet lag, you simply can't imagine. Three: See above. Four: A Changeling is a little bomb dropped by Fairyland upon the human world for fun and profit."

Up ahead, the glowworms called number thirty-eight, and a throng of young ladies in short black capes bustled forward, smoothing their hair so as to impress the mail.

"I said no making fun," said Hawthorn.

"One: I was bored. Two: I have been known to spirit a child or two away, I shan't lie. It is in my nature to Swoop In and Make a Mess of the Garden. Three: Trolls make excellent Changelings as they weigh quite a lot and enjoy violence. Four: A Changeling is the sort of child who climbs out of his crib at night just because he sees something shiny that he wants. If you were not already a Changeling, you would have told me politely that you like bridges and porridge and your father's snoring and to please be on my way."

They took their place in line. Everyone towered above Hawthorn—but do not worry, little love! When you are a grown troll no one will tower over so much as your left elbow.

"You said I was sweet and pliable! Was that why you chose me?"

"One: There is a department in the human world entirely devoted to receiving young boys and girls of Fairy extraction so that their supply of a certain kind of tale will never run dry, even when modernity comes and no one can remember what a spindle is. Two: See above. Three: Trolls, being mostly dirt and stone and moss with a bit of blood mixed in, are prime candidates. It's like sending a piece of Fairyland itself on vacation. It's much harder to talk a Wyvern into flying about on a Panther. After all, they have their own wings, and besides, they don't fit very well into a Changeling suit. Might as well try to cram a forest fire into a handbag." The Red Wind crouched down and touched Hawthorn's face ever so gently. Her eyes grew large and soft. Tickets fell out of her coat onto the floor all round her. "Four: The mass of Fairyland must remain constant. A Changeling is a deal struck with the second law of thermodynamics. Spit on the palm and shake."

Hawthorn curled his fists. He tried very hard not to cry.

"Red! Stop it! I just want to know—"

"One! Because you were born in—"

"What's going to happen to me," finished Hawthorn, halfway between a whisper and a squeak. "In stories, when someone appears in a cloud of red veils and asks the son of two magicians to go away on an adventure, it's because he's the best man for the job, because he's secretly a prince or has a birthmark in the shape of a train engine, and can invent unsolvable riddles and call the lava from the deeps and defeat the Unicorn Queen of the Electric Mountain, but I don't think they have any of those things in this human world you keep talking about. I don't even know that I'm as sweet as all that, if sweet is what you need to survive there. I'm not *mean* or anything; I know about runes and shapeshifting and I can fix the chimney by talking to it in a winsome way when Mother is busy with her leprechauns, but what I mean to say is: Maybe I won't make a good Changeling. Maybe you don't want to tell me what one is because it's something awful, and anyway I only weigh half a ton, but my father says I'll grow."

The Panther turned his heavy jet-black head and looked at Hawthorn with large, solemn, yellow eyes.

"A Changeling," he growled, "is a Fairy child brought across the border and exchanged for a human child so quickly and secretly that no one knows it's happened at all. Like sweeping away a tablecloth and leaving all the glasses standing. You go there, the human comes here, and between the both of you the world has such a lot of fun it nearly passes out."

"But what am I meant to *do*?"

The Panther wrinkled his muzzle. "You don't have to tell a Changeling to do anything. They *do* it the way the sun *does* daytime."

"Here we are!" the Red Wind crowed. "Yes! Forty-six! We oughtn't make it too obvious, you know. The best cheat is the one that looks like fair play."

And in hardly a moment, the glowworms scattered into tiny fireworks and settled back down into a broad, proud number 46.

"NEXT!" boomed a deep, severe voice, which echoed all over the post office. That great bellow blew them straight back into the folk who had silently joined the line behind them. The party in front of them, all severe cheekbones and graceful deer-legs, protested as the Red Wind, along with her cat and her troll, sailed past them toward that tall counter half buried in flurries of paper and clanking machinery.

At the top of the towering teak desk, more like a judge's bench than a shop counter, loomed an enormous and terrifying creature. It took all of Hawthorn's strength not to hide behind the Red Wind's skirts. The thing had one head, and that was well enough, and two arms and two legs, which is a more or less average number in Hawthorn's experience. But such a plain face! Such a tiny mouth! And no wings or antlers or bits of jewel peeking through the skin. No mad, curving nose, just a snub, button affair stuck onto the middle of the creature's face. It was a lady-creature. She had long brown hair tied up in a braid around her head, anyway. And spots of rouge on her cheeks. Her hands looked scrubbed and clean, but the troll would eat his own heart if they had ever held a wand or a sword or even a crystal ball. Such things leave marks. Hawthorn himself already had a splendid callus between his thumb and his first finger where his wand (a bone rattle with red ribbon and a silver bell in) had begun already to settle snugly into place.

"PARCEL?" the creature barked thunderously.

"What *is* that?" whispered Hawthorn.

The Red Wind smiled slowly, her whole face filling up with wicked delight. "Why that, my excitable little emerald, is a human. I should get acquainted, if I were you. I daresay you'll be seeing more of them."

"Can I touch it?"

The human scowled. "I've never heard the like!" she snapped. "How would you like it if I asked to touch you?"

Hawthorn shrugged. "You can touch me if you want," he said softly. And reached up his hand.

The human narrowed her eyes. She puffed out her cheeks like a great fish. Then she gave a short, hard laugh like a stamp marking a form and touched his fingers with hers. Her skin was soft and warm. His was hard and cold as stone—but for a troll, as hard and cold as stone is just the warmest and most wonderful thing to be.

"Pleased to meet you," said the human. "I am the Postmaster General for the Commonwealth of Australia. You may call me Mr. Benjamin Franklin. Everyone does."

"You don't look like a Mr. Benjamin," Hawthorn ventured.

The Postmaster General shuffled several envelopes together and tied them with twine before chucking them behind her into a large canvas bin.

"Long ago," the Red Wind explained, "a wizard called Benjamin Franklin became so powerful, by means of a magical lightning-wand and an excellent wig and a fell familiar in the shape of a kite, that he was made Postmaster of a vast kingdom. Using his monstrous magics, he, the kite, and the wig founded the Grand Society of the Golden Postilion, of which all Postmasters are members. That is why they are called

Masters, you know. Each and every one of them is a great Master of Questing Physicks. How else could a magical sword find its way to the bottom of a lake just in time for a little baby kinglet to wander by? Or a coat of many colors to a shepherd's shoulders, or spinning wheel to a locked and hidden room, or a girl in the shell of a hazelnut to an elderly couple longing for children? The Post is how the end of a story gets shipped safely to the beginning."

"Couldn't *you* do it?" Hawthorn asked bashfully. The Red Wind scowled.

"Sure, if you want your pretty English sword to end up stuck in a stump in a Louisiana swamp and the poor croc who signed for it wondering what to do with the enclosed glittering samite gown and Welsh dictionary," chuckled the Postmaster. "Nobody knows a neighborhood like a Postman. If you let Fairies handle their own shipping and handling you'll end up with the whole world marked Return to Sender, Cash on Delivery, Fragile, Sorry About That Broken Pyramid, There Was a Dog, See? and dropped on the doorstep of some poor blighter in Perth who thought he'd ordered clothespins. Fairyland loves human rubbish as well; don't let them tell you it's all a lot of dull junk. They'll murder you flat for a pair of boots or a good mirror. S'how I got my limp, you know. And God help you if you're a clever nipper! They'll tear the sky down for a strand of your hair. Believe me, it's better for us to sort it ourselves. Someone has to make sure the mail flows freely. And despite Miss Wind here's breathtaking grasp of history, she's got it half right. Possibly one-third. You see, young parcel post, very few humans know about Fairyland—the heart is a Tidiness Engine when it comes to the task of Knowing and Unknowing, and it tends to clear out anything that doesn't fit with what they've read in respectable newspapers and heard from people wearing glasses come springtime. Now, getting boffed in the face with a bolt of lightning tends to bludgeon a man's ability to dust his brain-shelves properly. But it does polish up the windows! So Mr. Franklin the First acquired both a speech impediment and the ability to see through space and time, which is a fairly good bargain when you think about it. He saw a mess of swords and spinning wheels and children flying back and forth with no rhyme or reason, post haste, post hoc, post modern, post-post! The old man set up a system to handle the volume and here we are. All the Postmasters of all the nations take a shift. You're lucky enough to get me today, not to big-note myself. Canada's in on Thursday and he's a bear before his coffee. We keep the secrets—the Postal Code is sacred. But Fairies live as long as planets, and we all look alike to them. They call us all Benjamin Franklin so they don't have to remember that my name is Agnes Robinson and I have never worn a powdered wig nor electrified a kite nor earned myself even one goiter. I do believe that's plenty of natter for you, young man. Step up here into the Postal Ruler, please?"

Hawthorn frowned at the enormous rusty slab of half-painted metal that appeared suddenly before him in a puff of stamps, dwarfing the counter. It had several slots cut into it of different sizes with all manner of things written over them. The letters had obviously worn away, gotten drawn back on, and then worn off again. He could see Benjamin Franklin's face through one of the slots. Over the slimmest gap, Hawthorn read:

DOCUMENTS ONLY! GRIMOIRES/PROPHECIES/JOKES/CONTRACTS (DEVILS AND OTHER DAIMONIA USE CORRECT CUSTOMS FORM OR YOUR PAPERS WILL NOT BE PROCESSED!)/CURSES

On the next slot, a little longer and wider:

ENCHANTED SWORDS/PENS/CLOTHING (NO SHOES!)/
NOVELS/UNGUENTS/PERISHABLE FOOD ITEMS

The next said:

PORTENTS/WOLVES (MEDIUM)/CHILDREN (SMALL/MEDIUM)/
FOOTWEAR/GOBLINS/TRAGEDIES

The grooves went on, growing bigger and bigger, until they said things like DRAGONS and HENGES (STONE AND OTHER) and REVOLUTIONS. The Postmaster's eyes glinted through CHILDREN (LARGE)/HORSES/EXISTENTIAL CRISES/PLASTICS/FLYING CARPETS/AQUATIC BEASTS/FETCHES.

"Come on then, squeeze in," the Postmaster beckoned. "The Post waits for no man. Postage rates are determined by size."

Hawthorn bit his lip and climbed up, turning sideways, to wedge himself into the slot that concerned itself with children and horses. But it was too large for him, as he was not yet a very big troll. He stepped instead into PORTENTS/WOLVES and found it quite snug, but if he held his breath, the ruler held him.

"Standard Priority Air Mail rate?" Benjamin Franklin asked, noting down something on her pad of paper. She used a beautiful yellow pencil with a pink nub on the end, so bright and cheerful Hawthorn immediately longed to steal it.

The Red Wind shook her head. "Special Handling. Fragile: Excessive Narrative Weight. Changeling Type: Live Troll, Active Exchange."

"Would you like to pay his return postage in advance?"

"Certainly not," snorted the Red Wind.

"Would you like him Wrapped Specially?"

The Red Wind waved her hand in the air. "He can choose—I always find it's funnier when they pick it all out themselves."

The Postal Ruler vanished from the air like butter melting away. Mr. Benjamin Franklin emerged from behind the counter and took him by the hand. Her fingers felt moist and soft; Hawthorn suddenly worried that he might crush her, or any human, if they were all made of this velvety, squishable stuff. The Postmaster led him to a charming little desk on which rested several rolls of wrapping paper, spools of ribbon, and a handsome book of colorful stamps. The Panther padded along behind with his Wind, whiskers twitching curiously.

"It's always nice to put on your glad rags when you're traveling," said Mr. Franklin kindly. Her pale-blue uniform shone with crisp cleanliness. "Where I come from, some people wear fine suits just to ride on an Aeroplane—I suspect they think if they impress it enough it will be sure to carry them safely. Let's get you bundled up!"

Hawthorn looked at the wrapping paper. There was a roll of plain brown, of gleaming gold, a merry green print with foil Ferris wheels and snowflakes and sailboats upon it, and a rosy one with leaping fish and palm trees and umbrellas. Hawthorn wanted the gold, if he wanted anything in this strange place. But when he looked at the snowflakes he remembered Skaldtown and how the snow sounded falling into his old chimney-house. He had no idea on earth what those funny wheels were, but they looked marvelous and shiny and magical and before he knew it he had reached out a tentative finger toward the green paper. The ribbons came in every color he could think of and three that only existed in that singular Post Office and had never been seen by anyone except packages and Postmen. He could only choose his favorite, the long, shimmering, silken red cord that looked so much like the yarn of a Redcap's very cap.

But when he came to the book of stamps, the poor troll was quite overcome by the hundreds of lovely pictures pasted to the pages, some drawn in ink, some in gems, some in nothing more than scents that swirled into his mind, making gentle rectangle-shaped images of popcorn and sunshine and centaurs racing. He looked to Benjamin Franklin for help but found none. Hawthorn sighed. He supposed it mattered little. It was only a stamp. He peeled back one of the biggest and most lurid—a field of Knights with banners fluttering, and before them all a beautiful girl with long, dark hair dancing in an orange dress, holding them all back as they stared at her, fascinated, and the sun set behind them.

"Well met and well done!" cried the Red Wind. She seized the edge of the paper and unfurled a great sail of wheels and snow and boats, spinning it round him before he could squeak. The troll could feel it squeezing him, pressing his skin, making him smaller, rubbing furiously at the jewels that show through a troll's skin. She flung the ribbon over him in long loops and cinched them tight. And now Hawthorn's insides huddled up into a strange little shape, making something different, something new, something not-quite-Hawthorn. His fingers were no longer thick and strong but slim, delicate, pink. He began to panic; the ribbons closed up his throat. But it was the Postmaster herself who lifted the stamp carefully from the book and placed it over his heart. It lay against him for a moment and then slowly, gently faded down into the paper and into his skin. He felt it sinking down inside him. It felt odd and hot, but not unpleasant. Like a new bone settling in.

If there had been a mirror in the Post Office, our Hawthorn would have seen in it a small human child, with dark hair and huge dark frightened gray eyes like the stones at the bottom of an ancient well. Only a sort of green shadow around his fingernails and a nose too big for his face hinted that he had ever been a troll who lived underneath an old well and loved a toad.

"Where will you take me?" he choked fearfully. The voice that came out did not sound like his at all.

The Postmaster smoothed his hair. "All Postboxes are portals. You'll see. Things vanish out of them and appear in them with no notice at all. They're as good as wizards' hats. You'll get where you're going, and just when you need to. The Post is never late. It is only On Time or Fashionably Early for Your Next Life. Didn't I mention all Postmasters are time travelers? How else could we get all our work done? I live in the year Two Thousand and Five. It's nice, if a little excitable for my taste."

"Wait, wait!" cried the Red Wind. "I'd almost forgotten! You must take this with you and keep it by your side. It's a talisman."

Hawthorn tried to catch his breath. The wrapping paper had nearly crept over his face. "But you said talismans weren't allowed!"

"Oh, don't be silly. I wasn't born yesterday. I bribed three elves and a congressman. I wouldn't leave you defenseless! You want this, trust me. In the human world, it's a talisman of great power. It grants strength and manfulness and protection against the twin wights of boredom and bullies. Take it and keep it and guard it and love it or I shall be very cross with you. Hurry along, we've dawdled too long. Someone else is hurtling through the system as we sit around and jaw—you must get on your way."

And the Red Wind put a little pale thing with red patterns stitched round it into a sturdy knot of ribbon round Hawthorn's waist. He did not know what it was, but if we peer between his thick, trollish fingers, you and I should know it right away, without a moment's hesitation.

It was a baseball.

What price the Red Wind paid for Hawthorn's postage he never saw. One can only know the weight and heft of the prices one pays oneself. The costs borne by others are their own, secret and deep and long. He knew only a sudden black rushing, which I shall tell you was the inside of a mailbag, and the trundling, grumbling sounds of a delivery truck crunching the long earth beneath it, and these sounds were as awful and wonderful and strange to our troll as any dragon hawking up fire. Only once in his headlong hurtling did Hawthorn see anything but the dark— off in the distance, so dim it might only have been a dream, he thought he saw a girl in a green coat soaring along even faster even than he, and in the other direction, her hair streaming out behind, riding upon the back of a bright, roaring Leopard.

Hic Sunt Dragones

In Which Apologies Are Begged and Explanations Offered

Being patient and trusting readers, you must by now be awfully worried about the state of your addled narrator. I can hear you across the ineffable miles between my house and yours, twisting your thumbs and whispering: *Yes, Miss, Trolls and Jungles and Postmasters are very nice and all, but have you hit your head on something very hard? This is not what we came to hear! We left September in such a state and you have said not one word about her in two whole chapters! And quite long ones! Won't you please let her come out to play?* And how kind of you to be so polite about it. I'm sure I have not half your manners when books vex me. I shall explain before we go a step further.

A story is a map of the world. A gloriously colored and wonderful map, the sort one often sees framed and hanging on the wall in a study full of plush chairs and stained-glass lamps: painstakingly lettered, re-searched down to the last pebble and participle, drawn with dash and flair, with cloud-goddesses in the corners and giant squid squirming up out of the sea. The maker of such a map will have made it as accurate as she possibly could, for she knew folk would rely on it to travel through a strange country safely. But the troubles of cartography are many. One can never predict when a volcano will explode or a flood should change a coastline, when a silly layabout prince in one tale will suddenly be called to lead a terrible battle in another. Choices must be made: The map must show its splendid country and not another even though an equally splendid nation, just as dangerous and exciting, lies just off the edges, just beyond the borders.

In the map of a story, one follows certain traditions so that mari-ners do not get confused and lost in a storm of metaphors. Heroes get big, splashy symbols, for they are the Capitals of their tales: circles with stars in the center, or magical swords, or a crown stuck all over with jewels. Villains likewise must be marked clearly with serpents biting their own tails or black hats or bold, uppercase letters which read *Terra Peri-colosa.* This is a very old and fancy way of saying *Wrong Way, Detour, Do Not Stop for Tea.* Important Objects, Enchanted Houses, and Plot Twists will have pretty stamps and bear the label of *Points of Interest.* Compan-ions, those stalwart souls who stand beside the Hero as she Does What Must Be Done, often manage only the unassuming dot of a Small Town or Shipwreck, even if they are quite as fascinating, as full of snaggle-streets and dark towers, as the Capital. In mapmaking, too, choices must be made. Paris takes up so much room that poor lovely Calais only gets a brief moment in the sun.

But the truth of the matter is, there are more maps in the world than anyone can count. Every person draws a map that shows themselves at the center. But that does not mean that no other countries exist. Just because most of the maps show Europe in the middle does not make it so. A Capital in one map may be a distant, unknown, misty village in another. A terrible wasteland in one map may be a cozy home in another. It all depends on who is drawing the map, and where they begin.

And in order to get to September, we must journey off the main road for a bit. Don't be afraid. Let us wander in the frightful forests and uncharted islands. Let us find a path through the snow to those little pockets of story which happen while the Hero is off doing other things. The hidden, leafy places where life goes on, even if the *Dramatis Personae* are on the run and incognito and being very *Dramatis* indeed. Let us look, for just a moment, at a little troll lost. Let us stride right up to the part of the map which says in magnificent and mysterious letters: *Hic Sunt Dracones.* For in that same old and fancy way of speaking, those words mean: *Here There Be Dragons.*

And, occasionally, humans.

CHAPTER III
TROLL TO BOY, BOY TO TROLL

*In Which a Troll Named Hawthorn Becomes a Boy
Named Thomas, Meets His Parents (One a Psychologist),
and Hunts a Wild and Woolly Word*

D o you remember being born? Only a few can say they do and not
be caught immediately in the lie, and most of them are wizards. I,
of course, remember it perfectly. Certain benefits are granted to narra-
tors as part of the hiring package, to compensate for our irregular hours
and unsafe working conditions. As clear as waking, I remember your
hands on the cover of the book, your bright eyes moving swiftly over
the pages, the light of your reading lamp, your small laughs and occasional puzzlements. But it is against the rules for a human to recall the
moment of their birth. If people did remember it, they would never agree
to let it happen to them again, and to live in this world is to be born

over and over and over again, every time a new thing happens to your heart, each time more frightening and more thrilling.

Because he will very soon forget it, I shall tell you how a curious boy was born in winter, at night, in a city called Chicago, which is four thousand miles from London, something like a million nautical leagues plus a feral furlong, a shake of the leg, and a stone's throw from Fairyland, but not so very far from Omaha, Nebraska. Chicago at the time owned a lake the size of a sea, several advertising firms, at least six tribes of marauding criminals, healthy herds of sailors grazing free, the first Ferris wheel in all the world, and more wind than it could care for. The boy was called Thomas Rood, or at least he shall be called that shortly. If you squint, you can see him hurtling through the snowy air at the speed of story. At the moment, he is still called Hawthorn. The faster you go, the brighter you get, and Hawthorn glowed so hot the clouds went up in smoke when he touched them.

If you have ever seen a falling star, you have seen a Changeling arriving.

The parcel box outside the home of Gwendolyn and Nicholas Rood, 3 Racine Avenue, received one troll, slightly singed, with a soft sound like an envelope sealing. The Roods were very much alarmed in the morning to find their little boy sitting on the doorstep with snow in his hair, blinking up at them as though he had never seen them before—which, of course, he hadn't, because only a moment ago he had been a troll called Hawthorn. If they'd investigated later, they might have missed him. He just couldn't abide that cramped little box another second and had gotten busy with his escape.

Neither Gwen nor Nicky guessed that their own child was, even then, as they gasped and worried on the front stoop, being bundled into certain red arms, on his way to another world and a much later chapter. How should they guess? The boy on the doorstep with snow in his hair looked just like their Thomas. He made the same gurgling noises and had the same moles and the same round, uncertain gray eyes. Indeed, far from being suspicious, the Roods were secretly a bit proud, as parents often are when their children do something awfully dangerous and at the same time awfully clever. Only a year old and already able to open the front door! What a firebrand our Tommy is! What have you got there, lad? A baseball! A sporting ace in the making! That's our boy!

But this child knew very well that he was called Hawthorn and not Thomas, and was a troll on the inside, not a baby human. It was only that he could not tell anyone—his human mouth was so small and soft! He could not make any words come out of it at all. When he finally managed it, they were just the simplest and plainest ones, none of which were big enough to hold his trollness, or that he had once spoken to a giant Panther, or the wonderful, terrible, burning flight through the clouds. He could not ask anyone about anything, or understand any of the bizarre objects that surrounded him. He could only grab hold of them, and shake them, or put them in his mouth and try to taste what they were. He did not turn his head when Gwendolyn sang out, *Thomas! Thomas, where have you gone, my love?* Because he could not remember that he was meant to be called Thomas now.

Whenever Hawthorn picked up a wooden block or a spoon or a ball, he dropped it at once. He could not seem to keep hold of anything. When one is a troll, one has a fearsome grip, and must handle everything very delicately if one does not wish to pulverize it immediately. Hawthorn's hands still thought they could crush stone by waving hello at it. They still wanted to treat the world as gently as they could. But his new hands couldn't pulverize so much as the corner of his blanket, and when he picked anything up with his careful troll-manners, they slipped right through and clattered to the floor.

His parents began to fear that he had suffered some strange injury during his adventure on the doorstep. Their once-sleepy Thomas suddenly barreled headlong round the house, whacking into walls and chairs and babbling to the chandelier. They did not understand that Hawthorn had been promised an adventure by a very convincing Wind, and intended to have it. He loved the feeling of the silver paisley wallpaper in the dining room when he banged into it. He loved the sound of glass breaking. He loved cutlery, and all the things it could cutler. He loved the way the light jumped and jingled inside the chandelier like will-o'-the-wisps. He was not in the least *babbling* at it. Rather, Hawthorn had begun a concentrated campaign to coax the wisps out of their crystal cottage and down to play with him. He had discovered that though his funny little soft pink mouth could not make human words yet, it could manage some troll-tongue, which is a language rounded like stones at the bottom of a river, slushy as snow melting, warm as an open door. Every morning he stood beneath the chandelier and called up to the wisps he knew must be inside—or else where could all that wonderful light come from? He called up to them in troll-tongue:

"Will-o'-the-wisp! If you come out today I shall give you my whole breakfast pancake!"

"Will-o'-the-wisp! If you come out today I shall give you my brand-new wooden racing car with purple stripes on it!"

"Will-o'-the-wisp! If you come out today I shall give you my mother's wedding ring!"

But the chandelier said nothing. The will-o'-the-wisp did not emerge. No matter—Hawthorn knew it would, one day.

Perhaps you have read stories in which trolls are slow and stupid and made primarily of the same sort of stuff as a sidewalk. While it is true that the difference between a troll and a stone is much like the difference between a human and an orangutan, a stone is not stupid. It is millions of years old, and has more memories and opinions and stories with no endings and fewer breaks for lemonade than even the oldest of your grandparents. Thus, for a troll, learning to talk is as natural as cuddling. Trolls are the best talkers in Fairyland—they make words and sentences and speeches like cobblers make shoes, and with more bells and ribbons and laces and leathers than the wildest dreams of the maddest shoemaker.

But Hawthorn was not a troll anymore. At least, his ears and his mouth were not troll-ears or a troll-mouth. He tried all the tricks a troll has to get his tongue back. He sidled up to English, and petted it, and called it a good language, and a pretty language, and wouldn't it like to come and play with him? But English was not Troll. English loves to stay out all night dancing with other languages, all decked out in sparkling prepositions and irregular verbs. It is unruly and will not obey—just when you think you have it in hand, it lets down its hair along with a hundred nonsensical exceptions.

What a human child must have to get hold of Talk, Hawthorn reasoned, was to go on a Quest. To hunt it down like a pink-horned musk ox. You had to creep along on all fours, hidden in the underbrush, looking for the little words, the weak ones that could be separated from the pack. Then pounce! And quickly, for words were fast and slippery and could get away if you got lazy and unwatchful. *Mummy* and *Daddy* were easy, soft little crunchable creatures he could snap up in his jaws. But Gwendolyn and Nicholas weren't his Mummy and Daddy, and he still knew that, no matter what his name was supposed to be now. So he devoured *Mummy* and *Daddy* quietly in the shadows, told no one what he'd done, and waited for better prey.

It was an important decision: Among troll-kind a child's first word is a kind of spell cast over the rest of his life. Parents hover over their newborn, ready to catch the glittery little thing as soon as it springs free. A boy who said *book* before any other word would surely be a great scholar or monk or journalist. A girl who said *bird* would be a zeppelin pilot or a dodo rider or perhaps an opera singer. Hawthorn the troll's first word had been: *Go!* And this had also been his second and third word. *Go! Go! Go!* But now he had to start all over again.

Hawthorn followed Gwendolyn all round their vast apartment, snatching at the words she used, trying to get them by the tail or the ear. She had a pretty voice and she spoke to him all the time. It sounded to him like the comforting sounds cows and dragons made to their calves. It was a mothering sound. Gwendolyn talked so much and so sweetly that all the words seemed to run together and become a thing more like singing than talking. He understood her well enough, but he just could not make his mouth do the things hers did. He longed to ask her what he considered extremely important questions about this new world he was stuck in: *Why is up up and down down? Why does Father wear that checkered snake round his neck? Why does it keep raining when we all wish it would stop so we can go play in the grass? Why don't leprechauns come out of the church bells when they ring on Sundays? Why do they only ring on Sundays? Why can't anybody fly? What is the point of mathematics when no one likes them? Why is the sky blue? Why won't the stove talk to me? Why won't the teapot talk to me? Why won't the wardrobe talk to me? Why do we use matches to light candles? Why can't we just explain to the candle how much better it is to be lit? Why won't you teach me your magic? Why do I have to sleep? Why are all the trees green when there are so many other colors to be?* But when he tried to ask in troll-tongue, she only gurgled and babbled back at him, imitating his heartfelt noises. Hawthorn made a face whenever she did it—her accent was terrible.

It was not only Gwendolyn's talking which fascinated him: She could also find lost things when he knew, he *knew* they were gone forever and the time had come to weep. She could make music come out of a great brass thing in the parlor that looked like a horn of plenty but wasn't one. She could make blue fire roar out of the stovetop anytime she pleased. She could make hot milk or cocoa or caramel or porridge appear inside a silver saucepan—he never knew which it would be. When his troll-mother wanted porridge, she simply went out to the fields and talked to the oats. Gwendolyn was different. Hawthorn had begun to suspect she was a witch, which deeply excited him. Wherever she went, extraordinary things seemed to happen, and she wore beautiful clothes and had beautiful auburn hair and Hawthorn had only met a witch once but she was beautiful because they all were.

One evening while Gwendolyn was stirring a big copper pot (she had more pots than he had thought existed in all the world) full of beef-and-leek stew, she chirped so prettily to him, telling him that he would grow up big and strong and handsome, and play baseball in school, and go to the same university she and his father had done, and take over his father's practice when he was grown and meet a lovely girl and be so awfully happy.

Hawthorn stared at her. She was stirring up his future. That was witch's work! Yet suddenly he could not think why witches and cook-pots and futures went together hand in hand in hand. What a funny thing to have knocking around his head! And besides, Gwendolyn hardly ever wore hats at all. Thomas drank in everything she said. You had to pay close attention when a witch gave you a quest. Yes, yes, he *would* grow up big and strong! He was a troll, after all; he could hardly help it. But he would also be sly and fast. He knew that his ball, which he kept always nearby, was called a baseball, but he didn't want to *play* anything with it. He knew it was important, somehow, but he could not remember exactly why, or where he had gotten it. It rolled around by itself sometimes, as though it was not content to just sit still like all the other toys. Hawthorn didn't know what it was about—perhaps that was part of the quest! To discover the destiny of the pale orb with its ruby stitching and protect it! Little Hawthorn held up his chubby human arms to receive the blessing of Gwendolyn. *I shall, my lady,* he babbled furiously, reaching for her, willing her to understand him. *I shall Go to the Kingdom of University and Meet a Girl Called Lovely and Practice Psychology Like My Father Before Me! I accept humbly the awesome honor of your prophecy! Have you a great weapon for me, so that I may be your True Knight?*

Gwendolyn looked up from her stew-pot and laughed her singsong laugh. She handed him a pencil from the tight knot of her hair, where she was always keeping things like that, pencils and knitting needles and clothespins. Her hair seemed to be a magical purse in which she could hide anything he wanted. The troll received it solemnly and immediately vanquished the cabinet door with one long, dark scrape across its face.

His new mother was a witch. He knew it in his bones. But the final piece of evidence was this:

Whenever he looked astonished at a suddenly found wooden train caboose or a burst of trumpets from the horn of plenty when there were no trumpeters about or a stream of caramel pouring golden out of the pot when he knew she'd only put a little sugar and cream in, Gwendolyn would lay her finger alongside her nose, and then tap his, and say:

"Magic!"

Then she would laugh and ruffle his hair.

Gwendolyn said it when she produced a new toy that he hadn't seen her making even though he watched her with the intensity of a mountain. She said it when she made all the lights come on at once with one touch of her little finger to the wall. She said it when his wooden train carriages went spinning around their wooden track with no one touching them or saying any eldritch words or coaxing them in troll-tongue with tales of other trains that had loved to go fast in circles just like these. She said it when she knit him socks and scarves and hats and she said it when they played the hiding game. No matter how he looked he could never find her—she would pop up out of nowhere, crying: "Magic!"

Hawthorn tried to snatch up the word in his teeth. He crouched in the shag carpet and pressed his lips together, trying to bite down on an *M*. But the word squirmed and hissed and danced away.

Finally, one day, Gwendolyn set down a cup of chocolate in front of him and kissed his head. Hawthorn moved in for the kill, grinning wildly.

"MAGIC!" he cried.

Gwendolyn laughed with delight. She clapped her hands.

It was a good first word for a witch's son, he supposed.

That was the day that Hawthorn forgot his name. It slipped away from him in the night, as silently as he had snuck up on *magic*. When he awoke in the morning, he was Thomas Rood, and the only Hawthorn he knew was the twisty old tree outside his nursery window.

CHAPTER IV
THE WOMBAT PRINCE OF CHICAGO

*In Which a Boy Named Thomas Talks to the Furniture,
Inquires into the Nature of Marriage, Acquires a Wombat,
and Breaks a Large Number of Household Items*

The childhood of Thomas Rood was full of broken things. Lamps, necklaces, chairs, candlesticks. Cups, saucers, gravy boats, vases. Books with their pages torn out, wallpaper peeled off, paintings cut up with scissors, spectacles with lenses shattered, poked out, cracked, used to burn holes in many exciting objects. No toy lasted long in Thomas's room—he would tear any bear or bunny or dinosaur apart in a frenzy, as if he was looking for some secret thing inside it that only he knew was there. If curtains were drawn he clawed them down. If they were not he wrapped himself in them, turning and turning till the cloth twisted so tight it burst free from the rod and he was left standing in the living room, cocooned in paisley, weeping in fits of frustration. He had even once taken a hammer to the flagstones in the courtyard outside his parents' apartment building, whacking craters into them like naughty moons.

One ought not to judge him: Changelings are all Heart. Their Hearts are so big that there is no room for anything else. They wear their hearts on the outside, like you and I wear our skin. And so all the bravery and headstrong feeling and sweetness and fierceness and wildness and terror and love has nothing to stand between it and the world. Which is why they can hardly bear the touch of the world. Imagine you have fallen and cut yourself, rather deeply, and some awful fellow puts his fingers right into the wound every morning with your toast and tea. That is what it is like to be a Changeling. Everything touches you in your deepest part, whether you asked it to or not. Where human children have years and years in which to grow their hearts and learn to live with them while staying safe from all the troubles a heart hauls with it, a Changeling starts out raw and red and full of longing. Some small ones learn to stitch together a Coat of Scowls or a Scarf of Jokes to hide their Hearts. Some hammer up a Fort of Books to protect theirs. Some walk around naked, though no one can see it but you and I.

Thomas Rood had a naked heart, even when the rest of him was bundled up in hats and mittens in the depths of winter. And it was this naked heart that hurled itself at everything, at lamps and toys and flagstones and draperies. Thomas could not help it. All his life he had known that something was wrong. It was only that he did not know what it *was*. He felt all the time as though there were another boy inside him, a bigger boy, a stronger boy, a boy who knew impossible things, a boy so wonderful he could talk to jewels and make friends with fire. But whenever he tried to let that boy out, he was only Thomas, red-faced, sputtering, gangly, clench-fist Thomas.

This is what Thomas did know, down deep where you and I know about gravity and how good sugar tastes:

The world was supposed to talk to him, and it didn't.

Not just his mother and father and the radio, but *everything*. When he looked at the flagstones in the courtyard, he knew, he *knew* that they should be able to open up their stony faces, showing a mouth that went all the way down into the earth and the rooty loam, and tell him their secrets and jealousies and private jokes. It was the same for the lamps and the teacups and the paintings in the hall. They were supposed to be like him! Alive and real and grumpy! Thomas did feel poorly about breaking those. One of the paintings was his mother's favorite: a dancing girl with wild blue and red silks on and orchid boughs in each hand in the midst of a black and starry wood. He had screamed at it. She should not be frozen in paint! She should hear him wanting her to be real and dance right out of the picture! If the world weren't wrong, if it weren't *broken,* she would do it. He could make it happen with his wanting.

But he couldn't.

The toys were the worst. When he was just a baby, some well-meaning uncle had given Thomas a stuffed frog with fuzzy, brightly colored skin. As soon as he had enough teeth he chewed its head off. Not because he did not love it—he adored the frog and held it so close to his chest that if the poor thing had been alive it would have gotten quite suffocated. He told it everything that grieved him, everything he longed for but could not quite remember, everything he did remember—that some winds could be red, and some cats were as big as horses and could talk, and some wells were really chimneys. And the frog said nothing. It stared back with glass eyes and a pink felt tongue lolling out stupidly and said nothing. Frogs *talked*. Toads talked. That was right, it was! They talked and danced in a funny hoppy thumpy way and liked bouillabaisse for supper. That was a fact as much as *I have five fingers on each hand* or *the stove hates little children and longs to scorch them*. But the frog kept mum and it hurt him like an arrow in his gut. He couldn't bear it. It was wrong, wrong, all wrong.

You might think, given the rather grand scope of the destruction Thomas performed on his house, that he was an unhappy child. But it just wasn't so. For some things *did* talk to him, and these he loved more fiercely than water and red velvet cake. His mother and father, the lovely phonograph in the hall with its great brass bell, certain books in which the author seemed at times to be speaking right to him, other children, the wonderful radio in their little parlor with its staticky growls, the sky when it was full of thunder, the squeaky floorboard in his bedroom that sounded like a whip-poor-will when he bounced on it. And there was one book in particular that Thomas held so dear that he slept with it clutched to his little beating heart. His mother had bought it for him because it had fantastical, wildly colored illustrations. He could not even read it when she first put it into his hands and guided his fingers to the first page. The pictures were enough. Thomas stared at them for hours, at the breakfast table, in his nursery, at the park when other children were playing on the swings, under his blanket at night when he ought to have been sleeping. Even in the dark, he could look at the blackened pages and see the vibrant colors dancing there in shadow.

It was a book about trolls.

Thomas Rood was entranced by them. Their gorgeous *bigness*, their hands like great strong shovels, the way their noses rode majestically on their faces, almost covering their mouths. The way their mouths looked like they could eat anything in the world, and would very much like to. He marveled over the garlands of jewels the artist had drawn hanging over their mountainous shoulders, golden earrings in their long, long ears, their mossy, tangled, rose-twisted hair, their huge, fierce eyes, their skin like birchbark, with bits of gems showing through at their joints, as though a troll was really nothing but a brilliant labyrinth of rubies and amethysts and emeralds and sapphires on the inside.

Thomas wished that he were a labyrinth of emeralds on the inside. Some of the trolls lived inside hollow bridges, peeping out of little golden windows at trespassers. Some were magicians, holding up their heavy, muscled arms to the sky to make the lightning sing. Some could turn into other creatures, mice and dogs and elephants. Thomas could not help it. He was fascinated, enraptured. Whenever he was alone in the house, he went into his mother's closet and pulled out her jewelry, her furs, and his father's fine brown leather coat with the patches at the elbows like flagstones. He put them all on at once. Thomas slipped into the suit jacket so that the sleeves hung down past his wrists like big, strong hands. Over that he put on all the furs at once so that his body looked huge and lumpy and wild and powerful. Then he draped Gwendolyn's jewelry over his shoulders, slung them round his neck, clipped them to the lapels so her pendants and earrings and gold chains and bracelets hung glitteringly down the sleeves, and he looked just the tiniest bit more like the trolls in his book. Thomas laid the book on the floor between himself and the mirror and stared back and forth from troll to boy, boy to troll. His heart wriggled and writhed. He looked into those pictures and some tiny voice in his heart whispered, *But that's me, that's me!*

I shall not be ashamed to tell you that the tiny voice in Thomas's heart belonged to me. And perhaps to you as well—and while we should like to thump him gently and say: *You silly thing, you are a troll and have always been. How could you forget a thing like that? I should sooner forget how to sneeze!* It is not so easy to always know who you are. As we have said, no one remembers being born, even though being born was certainly the most exciting thing that ever happened to us! But it fades into a dim recollection of light and sound and newness, and then melts away altogether. And that is how Thomas Rood remembered being a troll, remembered that he was a Changeling. In the shape of his thoughts, which seemed to be nothing like the shape of anyone else's—a trapezoid tumbling amongst lovely regular rectangles. In his hatred of silence and terrible, urgent longing for jewels and gold and talking frogs. And in the soft flashes of his senses, just before he fell asleep: the scent of a toad's warm skin, the taste of opal porridge with buttercups melting on top, the deep, rumbly, safe thunder of a trollmother's voice, the heat of a jungle where everything, somehow, rhymed.

If Thomas could not, any longer, quite remember that he was a troll, he learned very quickly what he had become.

It was a thing his father called him.

Nicholas Rood said it with a furrowed brow and while he said it he pushed his glasses up onto his nose and scratched the back of his neck. He said it when Thomas ruined the curtains again, or bashed his head against the nursery wall exactly forty-nine times (for any good spell must involve seven times seven and a certain amount of discomfort for the magician) or tore a stuffed dinosaur apart as though he could find its secret cretaceous heart and eat it. He said it often enough that it seemed a kind of title, like Gertrude the Great or Ethelred the Unready.

Thomas was Not Normal.

One evening when Thomas was five, they sat down to supper, all three of them, at the cherrywood table, which Thomas could not help licking when no one was looking. It *ought* to taste like cherries with a name like that. It mostly tasted of varnish and the ghosts of spilled mustards past. But he licked on, in hope. Supper was meatloaf and peas and red potatoes and roasted onions. This was Thomas's favorite, as the potatoes and onions looked like lumps of gold and ruby and the peas like little jades and, somewhere in the back, dusty corners of his troll-brain, the meatloaf reminded him of the rich, spicy taste of manticore. He shut his eyes and slurped up strings of hot onion out of the crispy skins and pretended he was slurping gold out of a mountain. With his eyes still shut, Thomas asked suddenly:

"Why do you and Nicholas live together?"

Gwendolyn quirked her eyebrow. She was long past being startled by her son's strange questions or his odd insistence on calling them by their given names. But Nicholas Rood gave his son a sharp look.

"Now, Tom, that's Not a Normal question for a boy to ask at table, is it?"

"I only mean that you *might* live anywhere. In a Bedouin camp, under the icecaps, on the moon. You *might* lasso polar bears and ride them across the Wild Yukon and write letters to Gwendolyn, who *might* be adopted by a mob of kangaroos and carrying around joeys in her apron. But you don't."

"Heavens to Betsy, Gwen! What's he been reading?"

Gwendolyn shrugged, which might have meant *nothing* or *everything I can't lock up*. Nicholas could never tell.

"Who's Betsy?" Thomas chirped.

"It's because we're married, dear," said Gwen, pulling her hair over to one side of her neck, as she often did when Thomas got on to a curiosity and shook it in his teeth like a dog with a good bone.

"What's married?"

"Don't be daft, Tom," his father sighed. "You know what married is. We fell in love—"

"Is that like falling into a chasm or a canyon or a hole?"

"No. We fell in love and we wanted to make you—"

"What did you make me out of? I think it must have been out of onions and potatoes and Gwendolyn's necklaces and rum because I like those things so much." Thomas beamed and forked another bite of manticore-loaf into his mouth.

"What do you mean you like rum? Who gave you rum?"

"It's the brown stuff in the cabinet that tastes like cake on fire. I gave some to the phonograph and she drank it all up, so I know it's good." Nicholas Rood colored from his neck up.

"It's fine, Nick," Gwendolyn hushed him. "It only warped the Bill Broonzy record; you don't even listen to that one anymore."

Dr. Rood took a deep breath, swallowed the loss of the Broonzy, and plowed on. "We fell in love and we wanted to make you, and the Normal thing to do is to get married, so we went down to a church—"

"Oh! Was it the Wizard's Palace?"

"What? What are you talking about?"

"The Wizard's Palace!" Thomas cried, squirming with excitement in his chair. "On Wabash Avenue!"

"He means Holy Name," Gwendolyn chuckled into her peas. "You have to admit it looks rather spectacular. If I were a wizard, I'd ring up my real estate agent."

"Well, yes, then. That was the place. Your mother wore a white dress—"

"Her witch's cloak," Thomas breathed, enchanted.

"No! For God's sake, what's gotten into you? Your mother is not a witch, Holy Name Cathedral is not a wizard's palace, and you are not made of necklaces and rum! We went to a *church* and Father Lawrence married us and we danced all night under the stars and ate cake and it was beautiful. Now be quiet and EAT YOUR PEAS!"

Thomas held his breath. He picked up a pea and squashed it between his fingers, so hard his fingertips turned red. And he breathed it out all in a rush:

"You fell into a chasm and wanted to make a Thomas and so you went to the Wizard's Palace and put on magic clothes and a Wizard said magic words over you and then you danced in mystical circles so the stars would love you best and you ate the enchanted cake of the Kingdom of Married and it was beautiful and now you eat peas and not polar bears."

Nicholas Rood stared at his son. He pushed his glasses up on top of his nose.

"You could still be married and ride polar bears across the Wild Yukon, though." Thomas went on happily squishing peas, one by one. "Do you know that Redcaps—even the girl-caps!—have nine murder-wives each who only appear when blood is spilt in the homehearth? I've read about it. If you conquered the Wild Yukon, Gwen could have a murderwife and she wouldn't be lonely, so you wouldn't have to worry. I should like a murderwife better than a nanny, I think. And satyrs turn into giant mountain goats when they want mates. I think being a giant mountain goat is better than a white dress. And *trolls*!"

"I won't hear one word more about trolls, Thomas Rood. Or the Wild Yukon or your ghastly murderwives. Why can't you be a Normal child? I'm sure you don't get this from my side of the family. The Roods are not a morbid lot. Now sit up straight and no more chatter or it's to bed with you." Nicholas bit off his words like mouthfuls of mountain.

"But I shan't," mumbled Thomas, and squashed another pea. He hated it when Nicholas said Normal. He could always hear the capital N. It made his skin burn and his eyes tickle like they always did before he was definitely going to cry. "Trolls don't sit up straight. They have marvelous hunchbacks like camels and inside their hunches there's precious gems like pearls in oysters. Hunchbacks are more beautiful than weddings and I want one so I shan't I shan't *I shan't* sit up, not ever!"

Nicholas heaved a great sigh and looked mournfully at his wife.

"Gwen, our Tom is Not Normal. I think I really ought to take him down to the office to see Dr. Malory. He specializes in children, you know."

"No, I am *not* Normal!" cried Thomas, and jumped up on his chair. He was always jumping up on things so that he could be taller, because trolls and other worthwhile things were always tall. "I am Sir Thomas the Un-Normal and all shall bow down to me! If Sir Malory comes near me with his squinty eyes and his stinky pipe, I shall turn him into a toad with my magic pencil!"

So went the song of Thomas Rood. *Something is Not Normal about that boy. Thomas, that is Not what Normal Children do. Stop that racket, Tommy, it's Not Normal!*

Thomas did not have any clear idea what Normal meant, except that it was something Gwendolyn and Nicholas were, and Mysterious Un-named Other Children also were, and possibly Grocers and Teachers and Street Sweepers as well, but that Thomas was not. Despite the awful hurt that capital N did to his raw, naked heart, Thomas was still a little boy—at least, mostly a little boy—and he did not like his father to be sour. He began to collect Normals, so that he could identify them on sight. Anything to keep him away from Dr. Malory and his miserable, smoky, stuffy office where even the bookshelves seemed to frown.

It was Normal to eat your supper all up and go to bed on time and count sheep to get to sleep. It was Not Normal to try to fit your whole supper into your mouth at once because trolls have mouths so big they can swallow basilisks and leap upon the sideboard and holler at the top of your lungs that the Wicked Realm of Bedtime had no power over you and if the vicious were-sheep that ruled there came near you you would slash them all to pieces with your butter knife and pour hot milk over their heads from the battlements. It was Normal to put more wood in the stove if it got cold, or if boiled water was wanted for tea. It was Not Normal to open the grate and feed the bones of the Ravening Oak Golem to the burning red mouth of Jøtun, the King of Fire and Pancakes. It was Normal to take the nice things your mother knits for you and say, *Thank you, they are very nice.* Especially if she has made you a sweater with matching mittens and scarves and a long, oversize hat with a long tail and a pom on the end, blue and orange and red and green, with row after row of polar bears and kangaroos knitted into it, which is quite a lot of work. It was Not Normal to stretch the hat out so you could fit inside it up to your neck and fall down the stairs screaming that you are not Thomas, but Horace the Genie of Ten Thousand Burnt Toasts and you are here to take back all your wishes. It was Normal, when your mother offered to knit you any sort of animal you liked out of all the mismatched bits of scrap yarn she had left over, to ask for a moose or a bear or a lion or a dog and be grateful because after all the toys you've destroyed you oughtn't get another one ever. It was Not Normal to say that mooses and lions and dogs are nothing more than ugly horses and pussycats and lazy layabout wolves and insist on a wombat when your mother has no idea what a wombat is, even though it was obvious to anyone that wombats are the best creatures ever invented because they are muscley and strong and angry and fierce and have square dung and boney rumps and sharp teeth and soft squishy faces and pouches where you could hide all your treasures and if wombats were kings of the world everything would be a lot better than it is now. It was especially Not Normal, when your mother said mooses are also fierce and angry and far bigger than wombats, and live practically next door to

Wisconsin, to tear around the house hollering: "WOMBAT! WOMBAT! ONLY WOMBATS! I AM THE WOMBAT PRINCE OF CHICAGO!" at the ceiling until she relented.

But Thomas did learn. He learned to put on Normal like a hat. When Gwendolyn presented him with his wombat, every color of yarn you can think of, thick and thin and frayed and braided and ribbons and cords, with one red button eye and one brass one and silver cloak-clasps for teeth, he whispered:

"How did you *do* that?"

And she said: "Magic."

Thomas put his arms around her neck. He called her Mother and not Gwendolyn, because these were Normal things to do. And when his patchwork scrap-yarn wombat, who wore a little puff-yarn cocoa-barrel round her neck like a Saint Bernard, did not answer back when he asked her to tell him tales of the marvelous Land of Wom where everything was Biteable and Good, he did not tear her head off in his anguish, though he wanted to, very badly. Instead, he named her Blunderbuss and dreamed of holding her in front of him, wriggling and warm and alive, while she fired passionfruits and horseshoes and whiskey bottles out of her mouth at his enemies. He woke up with a guilty start—Normal wombats couldn't do that. Thomas tried to be good and dream about something else.

Every day, even though it was Not Normal, and he knew it, Thomas Rood stood under the chandelier and whispered:

"Will-o'-the-wisp! If you come out today, I shall give you a kiss!" And after a moment, he added: "Please, please talk to me."

But the chandelier did not want a kiss, and years went by, and the heart of Thomas Rood fired itself at all the quiet, still objects of our world, begging them, pleading with them to come alive.

THE ADVENTURES OF INSPECTOR BALLOON

*In Which Thomas Meets a Book, a Desk, a Mud Puddle,
and a Girl and Fights the Battle of Hastings Over Again*

In the lower left-hand corner of his clothes dresser Thomas Rood kept a notebook whose cover was red and whose pages had no lines. The clothes dresser was called Bruno. The notebook was called Inspector Balloon for the six bright balloons and a big white moon like a magnifying glass painted on it.

Thomas named everything he could put his hands on. After all, he reasoned, nothing could really be real unless it had a name. How awful he would have felt if he had been called nothing at all and had to be summoned to dinner with cries of "Nobody in Particular!" He preferred strange-sounding and thorny names out of his books and his head, and secretly resented every day being called something as workaday as Thomas. He called their cantankerous oven Hephaestus, the laundry tub and washboard Beatrice and Benedick, the chandelier he dubbed Citrine, the standing radio Scheherazade. His bed was clearly an Amalthea; his toothbrush answered to no name but the Ivory Knight. He insisted upon calling their neighbors' cats Henrys I through VIII, though they had their own names to which they had become quite accustomed. Thomas knew they weren't really Patches or Moustache, but eight proud Kings, and he would not be moved on the subject. Names were a serious business and no mistaking. You couldn't expect anything to talk to you if you didn't call it by name.

When he saw the notebook in a shop window, Thomas had gotten very still inside. He recognized it like he would recognize his own hand. He sometimes had that feeling when he saw certain objects—that they were already his, only temporarily and embarrassingly separated from him due to some error in cosmic bookkeeping. He knew instantly what it was for, what it wanted to be when it grew up—a Real Live Book Owned by a Boy. Gwendolyn, thrilled that he wanted something so small and so Normal, had bought him an impressively businesslike silver-capped pen that spat blue ink to go along with it (called Mr. Indigo). The pen, unlike the book, was not cosmically his, but it would do. Thomas had rushed into his bedroom as soon as the door closed behind them, flung himself onto Amalthea, and opened Inspector Balloon to the first beautiful blank page, new and perfect as the head of cream in a glass milk bottle. Mr. Indigo's ink carved thick purpley-blue rivers into the paper, dividing it into a fertile and well-watered countryside, every inch of white fed by those deep, generous streams.

Thomas Rood had excellent handwriting. All trolls are skilled in the Dark Arts of Penmanship, owing to the heroics of Tufa, one of the three Primeval Trolls. Tufa, shortly after solving the mystery of walking upright and making friends with bridges, hunted down a wild Alphabet and made it her pet. Alphabets are one of the longest-lived creatures in all the grand universe. The Troll Alphabet lives still in the Heliotrope Hills, grumbling to itself, devouring passing slang, and blessing, in the small ways an Alphabet can, the folk that tamed it when the world was young.

Thomas could sign his name in such a fashion as to make John Hancock weep.

But he quickly learned that the loops and flourishes of his letters disturbed adults, who did not think a six-year-old should be able to write quite so much like a medieval monk. He owned up immediately to having traced *Happy Mother's Day* out of one of his fairy books even though he hadn't. From then on Thomas wrote only carefully shaky, outsize letters with bad spelling and no punctuation at all.

But Inspector Balloon belonged to him, and where no one could see, he let himself make words as beautiful as pictures, words that would have made the consonants of that wild, ancient Troll Alphabet swell with pride.

In his book, Thomas wrote the Rules of the World. He wrote them down because he did not understand them. Other Children understood them easily. Normal Children. Normal Children grasped the baffling magics of Bedtime, Not Speaking Unless Spoken To, Sitting Quietly When You Don't Want to One Bit, Eating Spinach Which Is Obviously Poison, Understanding Why Parents Serve Poison for Supper, and What Its Effects Will Be. For Other Children, for Normal Children, these things were as easy as dessert after dinner. Thomas's father told him this over and over. *It's just Common Sense, son.*

And yet, Thomas didn't have that Sense. But if it was so Common, he was determined to get it. If he wrote down each Rule as he tripped over it, and wrote it in a way that made sense to him, he would learn them. He would remember that Furnaces Don't Talk and the China Is Only for Guests Even Though It's Prettier Than Our Other Plates and We Never Have Guests.

These are some of the things Thomas wrote:

The Honorable (I Guess) Laws of the Nation of Learmont Arms Apartments (Apt. #7)

If you break something that means it has to be Thrown
   Out, even if you still like the pieces.

Knives and scissors are sharp, but different than swords, and
   you can only use them to fight cucumbers and onions
   and packages from the postman, not Ancient Enemies
   from Beyond Time.

There are no such things as Ancient Enemies from Beyond
   Time.

Hot hurts and cold hurts but hot also feels nice and cold also
   feels nice. Further investigation a must.

If you smile, people smile back and usually start liking
   you. If you scowl, they scowl back and start unliking
   you. This is true even though smiling means showing
   your sharp teeth and even though you can smile
   at the same time as being angry or sad, so I don't
   see why people should want you to do it so much, but
   they do.

Smiling is very complicated. Scowling is better but you are
   not allowed to do it except in private.

Mothers and Fathers have certain Words of Power that cannot be denied. So far, I have collected: Go to Bed! Go Play Outside! You Must Have Your Bath! Eat Your Vegetables! There may be others.

I am not a troll.

I am also not a wombat.

Also I am not a saber-toothed tiger or an ogre or a Wizard.

I am a saber-toothed ogretroll wombat Wizard SO THERE.

I will understand everything when I am Grown-Up. A Grown-Up is a Person Taller Than Me.

The phonograph is off-limits.

Father's office is off-limits.

The cabinets are off-limits, even though there is candy inside.

If something is good, it is off-limits.

I am to Do What I Am Told.

There is no such thing as magic.

Some things are alive and some things aren't but it is hard to tell right away sometimes.

Boys wear trousers and girls wear dresses and I am not allowed to wear a dress even though trousers itch and do not come in very many colors.

In the Nation of Learmont Arms Apartments (Apt. #7), children are taken away from their parents at the age of six and sent to a castle on a hill and this is called the Kingdom of School and if I cry any more about it I shall have no supper.

Thomas's hand trembled a little over the last law. He looked out his darkened window, where a moon as big as the one on Inspector Balloon's cover looked down, examining him with its huge white detective's glass.

And so it came to be that only a little while after taking Inspector Balloon into his confidence, Thomas Rood stood at the iron gates of a wily, dark, enchanted country. He stood bravely, armored to the teeth: On his feet he wore the great and powerful Golden Galoshes; upon his head the Long-Tailed Cap, stitched with protective sigils of polar bears and kangaroos to watch over him with foot and tooth. He sheathed his hands in the rare and precious Carnivorous Mittens, striped like a tiger's paws, complete with black wool claws. He donned his Troll's Mantle about his shoulders: one of his father's old beaten leather jackets that was far too big for little Thomas, hanging as long and billowy as a nightgown. Beneath it, the formidable Houndstooth Suit, which would, if he needed it, tear and bite at his enemies. For weapons he had his baseball and the Magic Pencil, the very one given to him by his own mother so long ago, nestled in the hoary depths of the Secretive Satchel.

Thomas had made himself ready, though his heart quailed within him. He longed to be in his home country—far-off and far-flung!—by his old hearthside with a bowl of soup and a song. The pleasures of home, which he had once disdained, now seemed the sweetest of all possible things. But they were lost to him now. Now was he an exile, a lonely creature on the borders of a foreign and perilous realm.

All around him, folk streamed in through the twisted gate. Giants with pockmarked faces, shrieking maidens with shining hair, and many not so different from him, weeping and gnashing their teeth and covering their faces with their own pitiful, clawless, non-carnivorous mittens. Thomas felt sorry for them. *We are all of us poor exiles,* he thought, though like many of his thoughts, he did not know why he should think of such an odd thing, or be so comfortable calling himself an exile, or even quite where he had learned that word. *I will protect you if I can.*

Thomas had done all he could to prepare himself to enter the barbarian city. He could only hope it was enough. He looked up, through the whipping winds of Autumn and the wild cascade of blood-dark leaves spiraling through his vision. He read what had been writ—by what fell and ancient hand?—upon the gate.

PUBLIC SCHOOL 348

"You'll like school, darling," Gwendolyn said sweetly, tucking the tail of his polar-bear-and-kangaroo hat into his coat.

"Shan't, though," sniffed Thomas.

"There'll be lots of other nice children there, and a desk all your very own, and things to draw with and books to read. And Mrs. Wilkinson is a wonderful teacher. You'll come home all bright-eyed and full of stories."

"Shan't," Thomas repeated. His eyes darkened and his eyebrows waggled. He leaned forward and clenched his fists, and this was Thomas Rood's traditional posture when he meant to deliver a Something Awfully. Gwendolyn had started calling his little tirades Something Awfullies—for it was always Something Awfully Important, or Something Awfully Funny, or Something Awfully Nice, or Something Awfully Wicked that he absolutely *must* tell her *right now.* Thomas never said anything plainly or patiently.

But Gwendolyn knew the signs. She pulled up her son's scarf over his mouth before he could get a breath up under the hundred balloons of his thoughts and bundled him off to that dreadful castle on a hill that grew windows and chimneys and doors the way a briar grows roses.

The boy took a shaky, freezing breath, clenched his fists, safe inside the Carnivorous Mittens, and stepped inside.

The Realm of 348 was divided, Thomas quickly observed, into several smaller districts. His new home was to be in the Underclassmen's Wing, Classroom 4. A thick carpet decorated with a pattern of tiny red flowers covered the ground beneath his feet. Thomas hunched down on his heels, scowling at them. Light as bright and harsh as white paint splashed over everything—the flowers, a herd of slick brown skinny-legged desks grazing in their petals, the shoulders of his coat, the heads of Other Children milling about in small packs. Crushed pencils and crayons and barrettes and hairpins and buttons and pennies and doll eyeballs and bits of someone's ancient lunch crunched underfoot. Pictures of letters and numbers hung on every wall like portraits of their ancestors. A papier-mâché model of the solar system spun, wrinkled and wired and garish, in one corner of the classroom.

Thomas did, indeed, have a desk of his own. He was introduced to it by Mrs. Wilkinson, who had curly hair and wore a necklace of little jade stones. Thomas knew they were jade; he knew the names of all the gemstones just the way I know the names of all my cousins. He looked down at his wooden desk and chair, the slick, brown, skinny-legged creature in the field of red flowers. It had scuffs on the wood and gum underneath it and some time ago someone had carved HUMPHREY! into the bottom-left corner with little lightning bolts around it.

"Hullo, Desk," said Thomas softly. He was charmed to meet it. If something is all your own, you ought to treat it well, like a horse or a dog, and pet it and feed it and take it for walks. Or at least look after it better than Humphrey had. "How old are you, Desk? Have you seen many battles? What do you dream about at night when all the children have gone? Do you ever wish you were something other than a desk? What is your favorite thing to have written on you?"

"Mrs. Wilkinson! Tommy R's talking to his desk!" wailed one of the Others. Thomas was frightened of the Others. The Other Children his father was always wishing he could be. Normal Children. Nice Children. Other Children. This particular Other Child was a boy with yellow hair and glasses and a pen stain on his cheek. He was much bigger than Thomas. His voice wore a sneer like a cap with a feather in it. Thomas had seen him crying into his mother's skirt outside the school. The Other Children giggled nervously, staring at him while Pen-Stain pointed urgently.

"Mrs. Wilkinson! I *heard* him! He was *talking* to his *desk*! You ought to punish him!"

A little thrill went through the Others as they imagined the exciting shapes and colors of his punishment. But Mrs. Wilkinson seemed to be occupied with a little girl who had gotten her hair caught in a stapler and paid little attention to either of them. Pen-Stain, robbed of his chance to make it clear he was better than at least one other boy on the very first day, reddened in frustration. Then his embarrassment turned into a smile—but the kind of smile that shows sharp teeth.

"Fine," he said gleefully. "*I'll* punish you, then. After school. Just you wait, freak-o. I'm gonna thump you."

Mrs. Wilkinson suddenly noticed that her classroom had gone far too quiet for its own good and pealed forth with what was to become her battle cry:

"Settle down, children, settle down!"

Even though they were all quite settled, except for Pen-Stain.

Thomas did not pay much attention to his lessons that day. It hardly mattered, as Mrs. Wilkinson only seemed interested in how to make an *A* and what color was magenta and how to add one and one together. Thomas knew all that. Only that morning, he'd been reading a book full of big, violent illustrations of the Great Battles of Britain with quite a lot of magenta in it. At that moment, the Battle of Hastings came into his mind (he liked it best because it had a bull in one corner of the illustration looking on with a bewildered expression on its brown face. Thomas deeply preferred the bull to William the Conqueror). He wondered if School was a Kingdom like Britain or France. If classes were miniature Hastings and Waterloos. You march out in your best clothes and get hollered at and thumped on all day by knights bigger and better equipped than yourself, who talk roughly and angrily in languages not very much like yours, and if you are not very good, you get walloped and wake up French. Thomas did not know. He had not seen enough of the land yet. But he knew he had to be very good. The only question was: What did good mean in this bizarre country? Only when Mrs. Wilkinson began talking about addition and this many cherries and that many glasses of milk did Thomas notice someone staring at him. A girl at her own desk, her hands folded just the same as his, her eyes large and dark and mildly interested, like a bull who has just witnessed the Battle of Hastings and found it reasonably entertaining.

Beneath his desk, Thomas quietly wrote in Inspector Balloon, so that he would not forget what he had learned so far. The way the boy with the pen stain said *After School* made it sound like a savage, lawless country of its own. Who knew what Sense was Common in that mysterious place? After all, every Nation has its rules. Some are Neat and Prim and Well-Groomed through many years of constitutional congresses and revolutions and having their hair brushed one hundred times each night before bed. Others are Rude and Roaming and Reckless, having sprouted like raspberry thickets and taken root without watering, feeding, or filibustering. A Well-Groomed Law is written down, on very nice paper, preferably using a quill pen—for in the world of humans a pen with a feather attached has certain properties that undecorated ballpoints do not. Anything written with a quill becomes instantly splendid, official, and eternal. This is why clever senators, wedding officiants, and playwrights always keep one close by. A Rude and Roaming Rule is one that no one invented, or carved on stone plates, but that everyone knows, or learns on the double if they know what's good for them.

The Kingdoms of School and After School are full of untamed, unnamed, hungry-hearted rules waiting to pounce upon the unexpected. It was more important than ever to keep Inspector Balloon informed.

The boy with the pen stain, along with what seemed like the whole of the rest of Underclassmen's Wing, Classroom 4 and possibly some of Classroom 3, waited for Thomas beside the jungle gym, a twisted pile of metal girders towering like giants' jaws over the gray stone of the play yard. The Other Boy already had his fists up and looked very much as though he knew what to do with them, so Thomas copied his stance. *I'll be all right*, he thought. *I have my Troll's Mantle and my Carnivorous Mittens to protect me.* He tried not to think of that morning, when Gwendolyn had tucked his hair behind his ear and said gently:

"Darling, you do know that those aren't really tiger paws, don't you? Tell your mother you know that."

He knew what she wanted, but he couldn't make his mouth do it. It was a just a bit of yarn, of course it was. He'd seen her knitting them over the summer. But Thomas couldn't, he just *couldn't* make himself not believe that they would not *become* claws and fur and sinew if only he wanted it hard enough, if only his need was great enough.

"I'm warning you," Thomas whispered to the jungle gym as he brandished his fuzzy orange fists. He wasn't quite brave enough to say it to the crowd of children. "My paws have known the jungles of Sumatra."

"What the devil is a Sumatra?" Pen-Stain boggled.

"It's a place far across the sea where there are tigers and coffee and—"

"Stop talking! I'm gonna hit you now! Hold still!"

The part of Thomas that was human, and thus heir to territorial orangutans and Hastings and Sumatran coffee and assorted other belligerencies, wanted very much to not hold still, but rather, punch the boy in the nose before he could get punched himself. But the part of him that was a troll, and thus heir to the gentlest of woolly mammoths (for they are the extremely-great-grandmothers of all trolls; mammoths, and igneous rock) and the most patient of mountains, knew how to do one thing better than anything else: talk to a thing that does not want to listen.

Thomas fixed the Other Boy with a solemn gaze. He lowered his fists a little—but not all the way. Thomas was not a fool. He made his eyes into deep, endless pools with soft stars in the mud of their bottoms. He didn't know why he could do that lately. He thought he had probably learned it from the glassy, unblinking button eyes of his scrap-yarn wombat. But when he did it, it made people stutter, and he liked that. It was like a magic spell: *Look into my eyes and I'll take your talk.* Thomas put on his best eyes and said in the very softest, kindest, most seductive of voices:

"What's your name?"

"What? Nothing. Max."

"Why are you so mad at me, Max?"

The boy blinked. He tried to look away from Thomas, but succeeded only in looking at his chin.

"'C . . . 'cause you were talking to your desk like a freak. My dad says freaks and hobos are scum."

Thomas opened his eyes wider. The rain clouds above the jungle gym rolled and reflected in them.

"Max! Do you mean you *don't* talk to your desk?"

"N . . . no. Why would I? That's stupid," Max sneered.

Thomas blinked slowly. His eyes shone. "Why is it stupid, Max?"

Max's voice began to shake. "'Cause . . . 'cause they don't talk back, dummy."

"Are you sure? Maybe yours doesn't. Maybe you got a dud. Or maybe it can't talk. But that doesn't mean it isn't lonely and sad because you haven't even said hello to it. My cousin had the mumps when he was little and he can't talk at all now. But he listens and laughs at jokes and he can make signs with his hands so we all know what he's thinking. Just because you can't use words doesn't mean you can't talk. There's lots of kinds of talking. Talking is the best thing in the whole world, I think. Talking is Something Awfully Magic. You can make things happen just by saying the right words, in the right order, at the right volume. You can make your mother bring eggs instead of tomatoes for breakfast or take you to the pier to see the lights instead of staying home and going to bed early. You can make a toy appear in your arms and chocolate appear in your cup."

Max was breathing slow and heavy. The Other Children leaned in, their mouths open, listening fiercely.

"Maybe, if I can think of the right words, I can even make you stop wanting to hit me. I'll make you a deal, okay?"

"Yes," Max breathed.

"If my desk hasn't talked by the time we're out of this school, you can hit me. Twice. And your fist will be bigger then. And if it does—"

"You get to hit me?"

"Sure, if that's what makes you happy. I get to hit you. Sound fair?"

It worked better than Thomas had thought it would. His parents were mostly immune to this sort of thing by now. Max nodded. He looked like he was going to cry. Thomas felt it best to exit while he was still mercifully unpunched. He turned to go, almost tiptoeing, as if he could give them all the slip and vanish like a spy in a comic book. But he couldn't, not in real life. Max came to and flailed out with his foot. He knew he'd been shown up somehow, and no small primate can bear that for much longer than a minute. Max's kick landed and Thomas went sprawling, the Secretive Satchel flying open, his baseball and his pencil and Inspector Balloon skittering out under the toothy mouth of the jungle gym. His mittens did not unravel into real paws. They landed in a freezing, half-dried mud puddle. One of his Golden Galoshes came loose as he landed on the pavement. One of the Other Children snatched it up. His stocking foot soaked through in a moment with filthy, sludgy water.

Goodbye, shoe.

"What's *that*?" one of Max's friends shrieked. "Is that your *diary*, Thomas?"

The Other Children gasped all together at this juicy bit of fresh meat thrown before them. Thomas scrambled for Inspector Balloon, but Max was faster. He seized it and held it up like a hunter parading the head of a vanquished lion. Only then did a snag in his plan seem to dawn in his eyes.

"Well, but I can't read it, though."

Thomas breathed relief. Saved by Mrs. Wilkinson only having

gotten to the letter *L* today. But it was not to be: A girl in the back of the throng trilled out:

"Make him read it!" The voice was only a little thing, strangely flat and soft, but it carried over all their heads and into Max's ear.

Max, triumphant, shoved Inspector Balloon back into Thomas's muddy hands. "Read it or I'll thump you till your mummy won't know you," he barked. "Nice and loud, Bobby's deaf in one ear."

Thomas wiped the rainwater off of his notebook. He shoved the Carnivorous Mittens in his pocket and sniffled. They would hate him forever if he read them his rules. They would stare at him like his father did and tell him to shut up shut up shut *up*. They would know he wasn't Normal. That he had no Common Sense. That he couldn't understand things the way they could understand them. He would be a leper in the Kingdom of School forever. For the first time, Thomas Rood longed for his house full of things that he wanted so desperately to be alive but stubbornly refused. Real alive things were terrifying. And they could pull out *your* stuffing if you disappointed them. But none of the Great Battles of Britain had much to say on the subject of just wanting to go home and have some milk and a sulk.

Thomas tried to make his eyes deep, endless pools with soft stars in the mud of their bottoms. But he was crying too much and his nose was dripping and they just stayed a little boy's red eyes. He tried to make his voice kind and hushed and seductive, but it cracked and shook like a skinny twig in the wind.

"The Laws of the Kingdom of School," he squeaked. "One: A Teacher is the same thing as an Empress only a Teacher wears skirts and uses a ruler instead of a scepter. Two: Be present at eight o'clock sharp or you will be marked Tardy and if you are Tardy enough you will be banished to the Land of Detention, where no food or joy can live. Three:

If you write that you shall not do a thing five hundred times you cannot do it again for your whole life. Only Teachers possess this magic, as
Mother and Father have never tried it. Four: A race of Giants live in the
Kingdom of School. They are the Big Kids and they dwell in the
Upperclassmen's Wing. They must be treated as dragons and never
bothered or they will destroy us, for they know great and terrible magic
as well as how to drive cars. Five: When the clock strikes three in the
afternoon, the power of the Teacher is broken with the pealing of a bell
and all go free. Six: There is a curse called Homework a Teacher may
cast if she longs for her power to continue after the great bell has
rung. . . ."

Thomas stopped. Twenty children stared at him. Twenty children
gawped at Thomas the Un-Normal in the wet, gray play yard. Finally,
Max coughed.

"You got any more?" he whispered.

When Gwendolyn Rood collected her son from his first day at school,
she was surprised to see him surrounded by boys and girls, all smiles
and chatter and *See you tomorrow, Tom! Bye, Tom! My mother says you can
come round for cake if you want, Thomas!* Thomas was surprised to see her
waving in the distance. It had not occurred to him that his exile was not
final and absolute, that he would be allowed visitors—that he would be
allowed to go home and have toast with honey and play with his toys as
though the castle on the hill did not exist at all. He folded this away
with all the other facts he had learned about the fell land of Public
School 348, drawing it into a kind of map he could hold in his head, a
map that showed the classroom and the play yard and Mrs. Wilkinson
and HUMPHREY! and Max and staplers and carpets with little red
flowers on them.

A warm hand settled on his shoulder. At first, Thomas thought it was a teacher, or perhaps, perhaps—the hand felt like something he could almost remember, but not quite, another hand, gloved in red, and how it moved on a pelt of black fur. . . . But the hand did not belong to the Red Wind, nor to Mrs. Wilkinson. It belonged to a girl his own age. It belonged, in fact, to the girl who looked like a bull at the Battle of Hastings.

Thomas turned and saw two curious, hickory-brown eyes dancing before him. The girl was staring at him with acute interest, standing awkwardly, like an improbable giraffe poised to flee through the long grass. She twisted the ends of her hair in her fingers, fine and thick and black. Her skin was darker than his, and in places here and there the fine lines of scars snaked over her limbs. Her skirt had a threadbare hem and she clutched her satchel like it could save her from drowning.

"What happened to your shoe?" she said in a soft, bright voice. He'd heard that voice before, only then it had said: *Make him read it.* Thomas opened his mouth and closed it again. He lifted his sodden stocking foot.

"I lost it," he said.

The girl smiled. It was a smile like a soapbox racer—tiny, uneven, crooked, a smile that looked brand new, as though she had just made it in her cellar and was trying it out for the first time.

"You didn't lose it," she said, letting her soapbox smile run free, careening all the way across her face. "You left it."

She held up one of his Golden Galoshes, rinsed clean and shining.

"My name is Tamburlaine," she offered.

"That's a funny name," Thomas said, and immediately regretted it.

"It's not funny, it's Marlowe," she sighed. "My father is a librarian." She seemed to think this was an explanation.

And she left him to his boots and his mother and his sudden, bursting desire to know who Marlowe was.

• • •

The Kingdom of School is guarded by a peculiar breed of demon-wights called Report Cards. As I have special privileges concerning all the belongings of Thomas Rood, particularly the secret ones, I shall snap my fingers and summon one of these cruel beasties to guide us out of the gates of the realm:

REPORT CARD: THOMAS ROOD, GRADE 1
Mathematics: Good
Language Skills: Excellent
Penmanship: Poor
History: Fair
Science: Excellent
Deportment: Very Poor

Dear Mr. and Mrs. Rood:

I am writing to share my concerns regarding your son, Thomas.

Thomas is a bright and intelligent child, although we might perhaps wish he were _less_ bright and intelligent at the end of a long day with him. We all think your son is going places! However, I have reason to be worried by his classroom behavior. Thomas, as I'm sure you're aware, is extremely talkative and inquisitive, which has become quite disruptive. Last week, when asked the sum of 3+1, young Mr. Rood responded with the following: _When Carbuncle, the Emperor of the Deeper Trolls, was exiled from the Citadel of Gullion, she took with her_

CHAPTER V

three wishes granted her by the Elk-King of
Mottleworst, and only one arrow for her bow of stone,
making her treasures four and her soul bereft.

Thomas is six years old! I haven't the faintest idea
where he gets these notions, and I certainly am not a
cruel enough teacher to have put such words as bereft
and carbuncle on the spelling tests of first graders.
He simply cannot answer a straight question—yet he
blurts out his ridiculous troll trivia without so
much as raising his hand.

More important, the level of influence Thomas has
among his classmates is highly disturbing. On his
first day, I made the mistake of assigning him to a
desk which had a spot of vandalism on it. Nothing
profane, I assure you; boys will be boys and school
boards will be school boards and school boards never
replace anything that can still be held together with
a rusty nail and a prayer. Well, children miss
nothing—they caught him straightaway whispering to
his desk, calling it Humphrey, being generally peculiar,
and sticking out, which is a hard suit of clothes to
wear on your first day, as I'm sure you know.

Now, I felt for the boy. There is always some
sensitive soul in every class who is too imaginative
and gentle for his own good, and I thought little
Tommy was this year's poor lost lamb.

But not a bit of it! By the next week all the
children had found some way to carve a name into
their desk—and not a one their own! I've a classroom

76

full of desks called Genevieve and Victor and Frankincense and Secretariat, and I'll be an old maid in Heaven if I didn't catch Annabelle Bosch whispering to hers during Quiet Reading! What's more, they've all started addressing me as Queen Wilkinson, and I can't say as I like it. Additionally, he is destructive toward school materials when frustrated (please see enclosed bill for the classroom planetarium) and insolent toward his teachers.

Mr. and Mrs. Rood, I think you can agree this is not normal behavior for a little boy. We don't like to use words like "deranged," but what is one to say when a child of six insists that the library is alive? When he convinces other, well-behaved children that the wind is red—Mr. and Mrs. Rood, they believe it so wholeheartedly that when they come in from any stormy recess, all sopping wet and filthy, the whole class babbles on about how "red" they are. Should this behavior persist, I would recommend special schooling for Thomas, as his presence is impeding the progress of other students, who are currently more adept at reciting the genealogy of King Goldmouth the Clurichaun than geometry.

I am trying to run a classroom, and it is quickly becoming a little Bedlam. Please see to your child!

Mrs. May Wilkinson
1st Grade

CHAPTER VI

TAMBURLAINE

*In Which a Baseball Makes a Fateful Decision,
a Boy Makes a Perfect Pitch, a Girl Breaks Her Leg,
and Thomas Sees Something He Should*

In the end, everything that happened happened because of a baseball and a pencil. If not for the pair of them, you and I should be having a lovely chat about old Mr. Rood who lives in the brownstone next door and how his grandchildren are just the noisiest things living but his geraniums are prettier than three sunrises and a baby parakeet.

Whether we ought to thank the baseball and the pencil or scold them remains to be seen.

Come along, then! We must run a little faster to catch up with our boy. We must chase him down through second and third and fourth grade, past fifth and sixth, all the quick years of primary school, which do not obey the usual rules of time and space, as any mother could tell you. School-time runs separately from usual time, like a certain country on the other side of the Equator, or the other side of a dream. School-time spins up and sputters and whirlwinds, all hopped up and in a hurry. Only once Summer comes round again, with its bindle full of adventures and bendings of rules and unwatched, unfettered, unending days in the sun does time return to its favorite pace, slow and golden and warm. But with the seasons, Summer disappears, off on its own wanderings and exploits and love affairs with the Equinoxes.

Let us run, run far and fast over the Summers and Autumns and inches grown until we can catch Thomas Rood at being twelve years old.

Thomas had not yet grown up particularly big or strong. He was thin and dark and looked all the time as though he had just received some secret, grievous wound—unless he smiled, and then he looked like everything in the world turning out all right at once. But he didn't smile often. When you have a smile like that in your back pocket, you learn to use it like a little knife: at just the right moments, when it can do sudden, mortal work.

Thomas walked tall down the halls of the Kingdom of School, still in his Troll's Mantle, which nearly fit him now. But it did not look much as it did when our boy wore it through the iron gates for the first time. By begging and pleading and offering every chore he could think of, Thomas had wheedled dozens of old necklaces and bracelets and earrings out of his mother, old, tarnished, broken things she did want any longer, broken clasps, broken pendants, broken chains. And with his book of trolls open before him, now split and torn and barely keeping spine and page together, he sewed them onto the shoulders of the beaten leather jacket until the golden chains and jewels and cameos and hoops and empty settings like little sharp crowns hung down his arms and back like a real, proper troll, like Carbuncle and Tufa and Jargoon and Porphyra and all the other legendary troll-lords in his books.

When he walked down the halls of the Kingdom of School, Thomas did not walk alone. There were no more Other Children, only Max and Frieda and Olive and Ronald and Polly and William and Franco and Susan.

And Tamburlaine.

Mostly Tamburlaine.

When he was eight, they'd crowned him Thomas, King of the Jungle Gym, and put a tiara made out of a jump rope on his head. The Rule he read to them upon the occasion of his coronation was: *The Kingdom of School is like Sherwood Forest and in Sherwood Forest it is better to be a bandit than an unjust substitute-king like Mr. Wolcott, who stole the throne from Mrs. McDermott when she went on Crusade and rules wickedly while she languishes in the Maternity Ward. Prince Wolcott takes everything good and makes it horrid or boring! We must sneak and pounce and win every scrap of wonderful poetry or tidy geometry proofs or volcanoes made of baking soda and vinegar!*

How they cheered! How they pretended to struggle through *Peter Rabbit* when Bad Prince Wolcott was looking on, and how they gloried in *A Midsummer Night's Dream* in the woods behind the school! The Big Kids smoked cigarettes behind the gym—Thomas's kids called each other Mustardseed and Cobweb and snuck glances at *The Faerie Queene*, which Tamburlaine had smuggled to them from her house. She revealed it the way an older girl might open her satchel to show a stolen bottle of gin out of her father's cabinet. Sighs of longing sang up among the children at the sight of its gilt cover. Tamburlaine let them all touch it, one by one, cradling the book like a kitten they could all play with, if only they were very careful not to spook the poor thing.

Thomas had once tried to call her Tammy. It was the only time since that first day with Max that Thomas thought he might be in for a punch in the chin.

"Tam, then," he tried again.

A strange and shadowed look came over her face. She shook her head harshly.

"Not Tam, either. And certainly not Tammy. My name is not Tammy. It's Tamburlaine. Use the whole thing or don't use it at all. Shortening things just makes them less interesting."

But until the day of the baseball, which ought to be called fateful, not because it was fated to happen, for it was not, but because it caused a number of things to fall into fate's filing system that otherwise would have remained stuck under a cup of old coffee, Tamburlaine never said a word to Thomas that did not concern their Teachers, Oberon, or Mr. Spenser.

Thomas always played outfield, because that was the best place to be if you didn't really want to play at all. He stood far, far left field while the rest of his class went up at bat and pitched and stole third. He liked to see how long he could look at the sun, or how many fairy Kings he could list in his head, or practice his Stances. This last he went through in the field-grass like calisthenics: A Bold Stance, a Fighting Stance, a Heroic Stance, a Pleading Stance, a Humble Stance, a Dueling Stance, a Fearful Stance, a Lover's Stance, every one he had read about and a few he had made up on his own. Tamburlaine also preferred outfield, experimenting with how far "out" she could field until Mr. Granberry hollered at her. *Quit inching, Miss Wheel! None of you could hit that far if you were batting bluebirds! And you, too, Rood! Stop flailing around out there like a showgirl!* And they would wink at each other and take a couple of sullen steps infield before starting up their private games of avoiding sports again.

It was Spring that day, one of the very first warm days, when the sun seems to be trying on Summer for size, turning this way and that, blushing and hemming and hawing and opening its top button, just to be daring. The grass shone with dew and damp. The trees all round had just let a few green buds out to survey the situation before any real leaves risked their necks. It was fine, and Thomas felt fine, his bones remembering heat and life and the fun of moving, all those things they had found too depressing to think about while the snow was throwing its weight around and feeling big in the chest.

Now, though the class had a perfectly good baseball to beat about during physical education, Thomas was carrying his own in his pocket. He often did. He didn't know why. He just liked having it near him, knowing it was there. He felt better with its sure weight resting in his coat or his pants' pocket. He liked to run his fingers over the thick red stitching in class, or walking home, or before he fell asleep at night. He would count the stitches over and over, for no particular reason at all, one through one hundred and thirty-six, and by the time he got to one hundred and thirty-six, he always felt quite calm and pleased with himself.

If Thomas had ever done his counting with the school ball, the one just now being cocked back in Max Barrie's hand, ready to fly over home base, he would have noticed that it had only one hundred and eight stitches. But he had not, and so he did not. Such little, unimportant things are so easy to miss, you know.

Max threw his pitch, the best pitch he would ever throw in his life. It was, in fact, the best pitch anyone would throw on any field until the end of time and outdoor sports. His form turned suddenly, wonderfully, completely perfect, his follow-through as graceful as a ballerina, the speed of the ball shattering records that had not yet been set. A certain portly gentleman taking the field in Boston at just that moment shuddered from head to toe, for some tiny part of him knew that he had just been bested by a twelve-year-old boy in Chicago who hadn't done so well on his last math quiz.

The ball left Max's grip like a shout, hurtling toward an alarmed Franco Moretti, who had no idea what was happening to him. He shut his eyes in a panic and swung wild, hoping only to avoid taking that perfect throw between the eyes. Max sagged—he didn't know where that pitch had come from, how it had found him, or what he'd done to make friends with it.

Sometimes, magic is like that. It lands on your head like a piano, a stupid, ancient, unfunny joke, and you spend the rest of your life picking sharps and flats out of your hair.

Franco's pinwheeling swing connected with the fantastically satisfying sound that happens when a piece of wood and a piece of leather conspire to make a lump of cork fly. The ball soared high, higher, into the startled sun, invisible for a moment, and then plummeting down, down, down toward Tamburlaine, who raised her glove hesitantly and rather hopelessly. Arm outstretched, she stepped backward, stumbled backward, careened backward, trying to get underneath Max's juggernaut.

Just then, the baseball in Thomas's pocket tumbled out onto the grass as though it had had quite enough of being left out of the game for which it had been made. It rolled toward Tamburlaine with a deliberate gait, if a ball can be said to have a gait. The new, wet grass striped its white leather with green as it trundled on, as determined as a dog in sight of its mistress. The baseball came to rest just behind her, very self-satisfied indeed. Tamburlaine stepped backward once more as Franco's home run finished its daredevil act—and her heel landed crunchingly on Thomas's ball. She fell over her suddenly tangled, cartwheeling legs, hitting the earth heavily, awkwardly, and with a hideous thick *snap*.

"Tamburlaine!" Thomas screamed, and ran for her, his legs moving before her silly long name had even gotten all the way out of his mouth.

The infielders had seen her fall, though all *they* wanted to know was whether she'd fallen with the ball in hand or not. Thomas fell to his knees beside her. Tamburlaine's wide brown eyes shone with fear. She breathed hard, staring up at him in what was plainly, obviously, a Pleading Stance.

Mr. Granberry was already striding across the field toward them. "Rood! She okay? She need the nurse? Tammy, honey, walk it off, there's a girl."

"Tom," she whispered, "*Tom*. I'm fine. Say I'm fine. Tell him I'm fine. Don't look. Just tell him I'm fine."

But he did look. He couldn't help it. Once a body tells you not to look, you just have to.

Tamburlaine's leg was broken. It was broken almost in half. But there was no blood, no bone peeking through, no horrible mash of ruined girl. There wasn't even a leg, not really. Under her skin there was sap, running freely, like awful water. There was bark, sheared and torn up. There was a straight, long branch, with only one or two knots and a little green moss on it, cracked nearly in two.

Under her skin, Tamburlaine was nothing but wood.

"You are *not* fine!" Thomas hissed. "What is that? What's wrong with you? What? What?" Thomas's head refused to speak to what it saw. *That, that makes no sense and it can not come in,* his head insisted. *It'll track bunkum all over the carpet.* But his heart began to beat very fast, and with a terrible bright joy.

"Shut up, shut up, shut *up!*" Tamburlaine had never snarled at him before. Her gentle mouth was twisted up into a grimace. "It's nothing, it's nothing."

The girl who had once given him back his Golden Galosh put her hands over her wounded shin. Amber sap oozed between her fingers. She tugged on the ragged wooden ends of her bones until they matched up again, like puzzle pieces. She drew up the frayed edge of her skin like a blanket in the wintertime and tucked it in under her kneecap. She did it as fast as slapping a mosquito, but when her fingers came away her leg was utterly whole once more, with only a new little thin line, like all the many others Thomas had noticed on her body the first time he saw her, across her knee.

She fixed him with a stare like iron chains. "I *am* fine. See? I am. I'm just fragile. That's all. Come on, Thomas. You're my friend. Friends keep secrets for each other. I've kept yours. So you owe me. Holler at Mr. Granberry so he goes back to the dugout. Don't let him *see*. Please, Thomas. Please don't let him see me."

Thomas found his voice.

"It's . . . uh . . . it's okay!" he yelled downfield. His eyes did not move from the shattered wood of her leg. "She's fine! She caught it!" He grabbed the ball, which had landed in the grass near them, and hoisted the victorious catch in the air. Their teammates cheered. Tamburlaine popped up on both legs, grinning and jumping up and down as though nothing could be the matter. *What did she mean she'd kept his secret?*

While Thomas sat on the grass, stunned, his heart giggled madly and turned somersaults over and over in his chest, for no reason he could tell. His baseball rolled quietly back into his pocket with the warm sense of a job well done in its secret guts.

CHAPTER VII

THE MONSTER ON TOP OF THE BED

In Which Thomas Finds Himself Alone with a Girl, Sees Her Without Her Clothes on, Obeys Vampire Law, Comes Face-to-Face with a Gramophone, and Says a Very Important Word

Tamburlaine's house stood dark and quiet. Thomas raised his hand to knock. He hesitated. It looked as though no one was home. He clutched her note in his hand like a gentleman's calling card, though that seemed silly now that he was here. It's not like she would demand proof before she let him in. She'd written: *Meet me at my house After School. 5 Ginger Road.* She wanted him to come. She wasn't angry, or she wouldn't have used capitals: *After School.* They always did that, all of them, when they wrote notes in class, to show that they were part of the secret elite who knew the truth about the world. All Countries are proper nouns; they get to wear the big letters like medals on their chests.

Tamburlaine asked him to come. He was supposed to be here. But the house was tall and thin and it seemed to be holding its breath, one birch tree in a long row of other birch trees just like it, only this one had a squirrel in it he desperately needed to talk to.

Thomas Rood held his breath, too. Something Awfully Big was about to happen. He felt it like an old fisherman feels tomorrow's storm in his knee. He knocked.

The door creaked open and Tamburlaine was there. Her big eyes, her long hair, her nervous way of standing—the Fleeing Stance. He could hear music far within the house. He knew the record; his parents had it, too. It had a lady in a lime-green dress and lime-green diamonds on the cover, singing to a bluebird she held in her hand. That lime-green lady sure loved her old ragtime-y songs. Just then, in the snuggling depths of warm, brown-gold house-shadows, she was singing about apple blossoms.

"Hi," Thomas said.

"Hi," she answered.

She reached out her hand and drew him inside, quick as a hiccup. Was she afraid someone might see him there? Would her parents be mad if they caught her alone with a boy?

The shadows of the house closed on them. Tamburlaine had all the lights shut off, but the late-afternoon sun danced with the dust below the windows. It smelled nice in her house. Like paper and new milk and trees growing close together. As his irises opened up to let all that dusky softness in, Thomas saw that Tamburlaine's house was a house of books.

It was not the house of someone who *liked books*. It did not have a *well-stocked library*. It was not even *stuffed with books*. Thomas could not see any part of the house that was not mostly *book*. Books rose from the floor to the ceiling in unruly, tottering towers. Books held up tables and chairs—and sat in the chairs, at the tables, as though quite ready for supper to be served, so long as supper was more books. They sprawled over the dining table like a feast of many colors. Books climbed the stairs, ran up and down the hallways, curled up before the fireplace, were wedged into the cabinets beside cups and saucers, held open doors and locked them shut. They left no room on the sofa to sit, nor in the kitchen to stand, nor on the floor to lie down. Books had already taken every territory and occupied it. Where the books were content to rest on shelves, like other, less ambitious of their cousins, they had been squashed in so tight their spines bulged, and then bowed under the weight of the books stacked up on top of their sagging rows. Brick and wood only peeked through in a few places, and where they did they looked positively embarrassed, apologetic. *It's only that someone is borrowing* The Picture of Dorian Gray *at the moment, you see.* The Thousand and One Nights *has had an accident involving grape juice and has gone on a little trip to the binder's; please don't think anyone left this space empty on purpose, goodness no!*

"Is your mom home?" Thomas asked, dumbfounded. His voice sounded too loud in his own ears. He had books, of course, and so did his parents. But their books . . . their books *behaved.* They didn't grow and sprawl and soar. They didn't gobble up a house like they were hungry.

"She's at a Ladies Auxiliary meeting," Tamburlaine murmured. "We have a couple of hours. Maybe you can stay for dinner."

For some reason, this struck her as unreasonably funny, and Tamburlaine laughed shakily, her laugh bursting free of her like bubbles from a soda bottle. She laughed too long, holding her stomach. Thomas waited. He thought maybe she was laughing so that she could put off whatever came next just a little longer. But laughs, even the best and most dearly needed of laughs, have a natural life span, and hers finally died on the battlefield of her nerves. She had nothing else to stand between her and having to explain what had happened on the baseball field that day. So she just sighed, walked straight up to her trouble, and asked it in for cake.

"When you were little," Tamburlaine said carefully, "were you ever afraid of the monster under the bed?"

"Sure," Thomas said. "Everyone is. It's Normal."

Tamburlaine narrowed her eyes. "Yes, thank you. But . . . were you *really* afraid? Did you really think it could get you and eat you up in the dark?"

Thomas felt sweat bead up behind his ears. There was no breeze in the house of books. Not enough air. That lime-green lady on the gramophone wouldn't shut up about her apple blossoms, either. He remembered Gwendolyn lifting her pretty hand to turn out the light before bed. Begging her not to. *Please, Mom! Leave the light!*

"No," he whispered. "Not really."

"Why not?"

Thomas remembered his mother laughing in a warm, thick, encouraging way, in the back of her throat. She saved that laugh for the rare occasion when he said something a Normal child might say. *Oh, darling, are you afraid of the dark? Shall I check for monsters under the bed? Will that make you feel better?* And the look on her face when he answered, like he'd just unzipped his skin in front of her. He couldn't bear the thought of Tamburlaine's face twisting into that same expression.

"Thomas, why weren't you afraid? Did you not believe in monsters?"

"No, I believed in monsters."

Tamburlaine had wooden bones. He'd *seen* it. He'd seen her blood oozing sticky sap.

"Then why not? Like you said, everyone's afraid of them. It's normal."

He could tell her the truth. She wanted him to tell her. That he'd never been afraid. That he only wanted his mother to leave the light on so he could read.

Monsters don't live under the bed, Mom. Don't be silly. It's dirty down there.

He took a deep breath.

My clever son. Where do they live, then?

Thomas lifted his eyes to Tamburlaine's, searching. What did she *want*? He'd seen her wounded—did she want to see what he looked like on the inside? It seemed suddenly that standing in this hallway talking about what lived under the bed was quite the strangest thing to happen to him today. A girl with sap for blood didn't compete. He would tell her. He would.

"I wasn't afraid of monsters under the bed because I was the monster on top of the bed," Thomas confessed. His face burned in the half-light of the house.

Tamburlaine breathed relief. Her soapbox smile raced across her face. She nodded twice. "Okay. Okay. Do you want to see my room?"

Now, in the Kingdom of School, to be asked into another child's room is like being asked inside their heart. Thomas knew that. It was Inspector Balloon's Rule #309. Your room is where you keep yourself, or at least all the parts of yourself that live on the outside. It's a shadowy lair, a thief's den of favorite objects and pictures and books, toys you're meant to have outgrown, as if you could ever outgrow a creature made only to love you and be loved by you. Your secret possessions—diaries and notes passed under desks and treasures hoarded from summer trips to the seashore, some few things your parents don't know you have, a novel you're too young to read, a pack of gum you swiped from the corner store last Autumn, too exciting to throw away, too shameful to chew. A child's room is no different from a Wyvern's nest—it is full of cloth and bone-trophies left over when the meat of music and reading and dreaming has been devoured, and all of it warms the egg of passions and pleasures and secrets waiting to become a Grown-Up Beast.

Thomas had never asked anyone into his room. He had played in Max's and Franco's and William's, though they had too many toy soldiers and not enough of anything else. Would a girl's room be different? Was it somehow more serious to play in a girl's room? At least he was pretty confident she would have more books than soldiers.

Tamburlaine led him down a hall so swaddled in books he had to turn sideways to squeeze through. He almost apologized to the books for disturbing them, but caught himself in time. Tamburlaine's house seemed more a place where books kept their people than where people kept their books.

The neat, dark door at the end of the hall stood shut. Thomas knew without being told that Vampire Law held sway here—he could enter only if invited. She'd said he could *see* it, she hadn't asked him *in*. Suddenly Thomas's heart beat very fast. He had no reason to feel nervous—this wasn't a stranger's room! He had known Tamburlaine since they were tiny children. But he had never been alone with her, not really alone. Grown-Ups talked about not leaving boys and girls Alone Together in quiet, concerned voices. As if something terrible might happen if a boy and a girl were brought too near each other without shields and swords. As if they were baking soda and vinegar and only the presence of other people kept them from becoming a volcano.

They were Alone Together now. Nothing had happened. The book-sodden air in the hall felt thick and hot. Thomas had the alarming thought that the books were *breathing* on him, blowing their thousands of words onto the back of his neck.

Tamburlaine laughed and shook her head—and the thick hotness broke, like a Summer storm.

"Come on, Thomas. It won't bite you."

But it did.

She had a bed and a desk and a lamp and a chest of drawers and all the usual things that make a bedroom a bedroom and not a kitchen. Her bed and her desk didn't trouble him—it was everything else. Tamburlaine's room had no books in it. She had made some sort of treaty with the rest of the house. The marauding books left this one place uncolonized. But really, *really,* Thomas thought, there was no room for books in here. They would only get in the way. Thomas felt thick and hot again—and thirsty and unsteady. He wanted to sit down, but where could he sit?

All over the walls, all over the floor, all over the ceiling and the window frames and the wardrobe door, Tamburlaine had painted a forest.

He knew she'd done it. The forest started on the back of the bed-room door, and the forest on the back of the bedroom door was not very good. It was a little kid's idea of a forest: Stick-figure trees with big squiggly leaves splashed in splotches of screamingly bright green, a not-quite-round yellow sun, handprint flowers made by dipping little fingers in pink and blue and purple paint. But as the woods wound on around the room and over the floorboards, they grew deeper and wilder and thicker as the painter learned, the colors and shapes smoothing out, becoming more graceful, more deft, until the thicket around Tambur-laine's bed looked so real you could fall into it.

But it wasn't any forest Thomas had heard of. It wasn't Sherwood or the Forest of Arden or the Shawnee National Forest. All Thomas could think was: *It looks like Hansel and Gretel's forest. Or Snow White's. If they were real. Better than if they were real.* Some of the trees had deep sapphire-colored leaves, with glowing fruit hanging from them like pale-blue lanterns. Some were startlingly white from root to leaf-tip, but swarmed with bloodred and blood-purple butterflies. Wide, curious green eyes stared from the backs of their wings, reflected in still pools and streams. Some of the trees burned with a beautiful scarlet fire, and from the flaming trees flaming birds burst up like peacocks startled into fireworks. One pine bristled with delicate, decorated daggers, the kind Italian nobles hid in their coats when they had wicked business to do. Even the trees that looked like trees seemed to be hiding creatures in their green depths. Red tails snaked around dark trunks, bright, wicked eyes sparkled from shadows, spangled hooves danced just out of sight. Delicate wisps of smoke rose from invisible chimneys, drifting and coiling up to the ceiling, which glowed indigo and white, blazing with stars, with constellations Thomas did not recognize—and he was on social terms with Orion and Auriga and Taurus and Cassiopeia and both Ursas. The forest floor, the floor of the bedroom, clotted and boiled over with wildflowers. When Thomas looked down at the peonies and lobelias and snapdragons, he could see impossibly tiny little cities in their petals, all full of towers and alleys the color of Spring blossoms.

It was no place he had ever seen.

But how horribly, achingly, quiveringly familiar it shone! Looking into Tamburlaine's wood was like looking at a photograph of your parents when they were young. Who are those strange people? Could they ever have been real?

Thomas wanted to look at his friend. He wanted to tell her she was awfully good at painting. He wanted to say it was the most wonderful room in the whole world. But he couldn't stop staring into the wild, wandering paths of the wood, trying to peer in toward whatever they led to. The lime-green lady's voice seemed louder, more insistent, closer. She'd finished her apple blossoms now and was on to green and yellow baskets.

"You did this," he said at last. His voice was raspy and soft, like snagged wool. It was not a question.

"Yes," Tamburlaine whispered. Anything but a whisper seemed wrong just now.

"By yourself."

"Yes."

"How?"

"Do you mean how do you draw something so it looks like it has depth and shadow, or how do you paint something this big? Daddy bought me the paint and the brushes. On Easter I get baskets of paint tubes. The brightest and darkest colors. I haven't asked for anything for Christmas and birthdays since I was four other than painting lessons. I still need to learn how to do people. I can't get it right. Mom says I can have the garden shed when she gets around to clearing it out. Because I'm almost out of room here. There's just the inside of the wardrobe left. I never paint over mistakes—you can see the parts where I hadn't got good yet. Okay, once I made a mountain just there, there—" She pointed at the wall around a tall window, which now showed a maple tree with leaves of delicate ice. A hundred little doors opened in the wood of its trunk. Out of some of the doors, elegant gloved hands stretched out, presenting porcelain pots of syrup on their palms. "A mountain with a big church window in it. But it wasn't right, I knew it wasn't right. It hurt me how much it wasn't right. I couldn't sleep. So I rolled Eggshell White over it and crawled back into bed and didn't wake up for two whole days. I was more careful after that. To get it right."

"How do you know what's right?"

Tamburlaine looked down at her floor of incandescent flowers. She twisted her long hair in her fingers.

"Thomas . . ."

Thomas couldn't breathe. He felt like his head was going to come off and fly up to the sun like a lost balloon. He knew, he *knew* what she was going to say, even though she hadn't decided yet whether to say it. It was going to be Something Awfully Big.

"How do you know?" he said again. Thomas looked away from the painted forest, into her fretful hickory-hazel eyes. *It's a secret,* her eyes pleaded. *It's a secret and if you tell a secret the secret comes alive and can never be kept safe at home again.* Tears gleamed on her cheeks. Her face grew red and warm. She clenched her fists at her sides and looked up help-lessly at her private night sky.

"I *remember* it," Tamburlaine said, and she did not say it quietly. She said it clear and loud, daring him to laugh at her or call her crazy or any of the thousand cruel things Other Children might do. But then she lowered her voice to a library hush. "Thomas, I know a place where everything is alive."

The troll that had slept in Thomas's heart for so many years jolted up, wide awake. It jumped and leapt and tugged its hair and turned back-ward somersaults. It laughed and sang along with the lime-green lady and beat its chest. It tried to climb up out of his heart and into his throat, into his mouth, into his head. But it was not strong enough. Thomas had been human so long that the pounding and hollering and galumphing of his troll-self just felt awful, like starving for food while sick to his stomach. His human body wanted to stay human, and it punished his troll-self whenever it tried to wake.

"I don't *exactly* remember it," Tamburlaine said slowly, searching his eyes for understanding, for panic, for how much it was safe to say. "Or I don't remember it *exactly*. It's like . . . it's like a dream I had while I was dreaming. Or like trying to remember a book I read when I had a fever, only the book had a fever, too. I remember it in scraps and handfuls. I chase it through my head, and it's always faster than me. Sometimes I'm eating eggs at breakfast and I just can't taste them anymore because I'm tasting something like sarsaparilla and coffee and molten gold and hot sugared limes mixed all up and my mouth is so full of that taste I feel like it must be dribbling out all over my chin, but it isn't, because it's only eggs. It's only eggs and I'm remembering something from *There,* something that tastes like sarsaparilla and coffee and molten gold and hot sugared limes and rolls down my throat like cream-velvet. And eggs get ruined, ruined forever, because they'll only taste like disappointment now. I can barely eat anything. I'm down to oatmeal and fried bread and cinnamon candy and persimmons and trout. Everything else tastes like it's making fun of me. Teasing me because it knows it *could* taste like moonlight and whipped cream and watercress and teardrops, but it *won't,* just to spite me. And sometimes I wake up and I know that some trees have clocks for fruit and if you eat one you'll age sideways, even if I haven't the faintest idea what that even means. But not *here.* Trees here have fruit for fruit. *There. There* is a real place. I came from *There.* Somehow I started *There.* And I think—I *think*— I could be really, *really* wrong—but I think you did, too."

The troll inside Thomas pranced and whirled. He felt dizzy. The gramophone music pounded on his head now, so awfully loud and close.

"I . . . I don't understand," he stuttered. "I'm not like you. I broke my arm trying to climb up to the chandelier when I was four, so I know. When I'm hurt it's nothing interesting. Red blood and crying. I'm just a boy. I'm Normal."

"Everyone's interesting when they're hurt," Tamburlaine said in a curious voice. She scratched the back of her neck. "Stay here. I want to show you something."

Tamburlaine sprang up and out of her painted, wondrous forest. He could hear her rummaging, knocking things over, stacking them back up again. She returned, out of breath, her arms full of books—big, wide, illustrated ones with ribbonmarks and colored edges. She laid them down in front of him one by one like gifts. *Thomas the Rhymer. The King of Elfland's Daughter. The Compleat Childe Ballads. Tam Lin.*

"This is us," she said softly, touching the books with her long fingers. "Heaven knows why they allow books like this in the world. Lying about without locks, where anyone, anywhere might just pick them up! It's like leaving instructions for making tornados at the bus station!"

Thomas shook his head. He had read those books. (Well, not all of them. There were just so *many* of those ballads.) Maybe they were about her. Girls who were wooden on the inside, like Pinocchio, sure. But they weren't about him. Even as he shook his head, Thomas started to cry. He *wanted* her to be right. He *wanted* to be Thomas the Rhymer instead of just Thomas the Un-Normal, Thomas the Patient of Dr. Malory, Thomas the Interviewed by Three Separate Schools for the Disturbed This Week. He wanted to be Tam Lin, he wanted to be special, but he wasn't, he *wasn't*. It was her, Tamburlaine—Tam! It was even in her name!

The troll in him cried out to be heard: *It is us, it is! Listen!*

"Look at me, Thomas. I'm going to show you something. I know you won't tell." She ducked her head to catch his eye and lifted up his chin with a soft fingertip. "Look. It's not scary, I promise."

Tamburlaine reached up behind her ear and grabbed something there. She screwed up her nose and pulled out a hairpin. One, two, three more clattered to the floor. And all that beautiful hair, that long, dark, thick hair he'd stared at in class for six years, came away in her fist. She folded her wig very carefully in her lap, tucking in the ends so they didn't get dusty.

Flowers tumbled down from Tamburlaine's head. Long, thick, bright purple garlands like braids burst free and stretched, able to breathe at last. The sunlight streaming through the window pooled and played in the branches of Tamburlaine, turning her violet, indigo, fuchsia, rose. Thomas thought they were plum blossoms. She began to rub her arms as though she'd caught a chill, rough and hard. She scrubbed her cheeks with her palms—and her cheeks washed away like soap. All those little lines, the thin, strange scars she'd always had, were not scars at all but woodgrain. She was a girl made of fine, polished wood, the deep, dark, expensive kind, jointed and bolted at the elbows and neck like a doll. Tamburlaine breathed in little quick gasps, full of thrill and fearing, smiling all the while so that the green buds of her teeth showed.

Tamburlaine was the part of the forest she had painted all around her in colors as bright as her own.

"It's not always like this," she laughed nervously. "It's only that it's springtime. Oh, Thomas! I've kept quiet so *long*! I knew you were like me that very first day. When you talked to your desk. I was sure when you enchanted the whole class under the jungle gym. Just talked to them, just a few words, and they'd follow you to Hamlin if you had a pipe. You came to school in your coat with all that treasure sewn onto the shoulders—and now even the high school kids are wearing their grandmother's brooches on their coats. Thomas, Thomas, don't you know? Haven't you always, just always felt you didn't belong to your family, not really? Haven't you always known there was something different about you, something off? That's why you keep your little book of rules, because this world is so *hard*, isn't it? It makes no sense; everything's always upside down and sideways. Haven't you always felt like the strangest boy in the world? Like nothing inside you matched the outside?"

Thomas Rood's vision swam. Sweat wriggled through his hair. *Maybe this is what dying feels like,* he thought wildly. But before he could stop himself he was talking, talking like his tongue could outrace the dying.

"When I was little, they took me to the optometrist and I sat in the chair while the doctor put a black mask over my face and slid lenses in and out of it. And every time he asked if I could see better out of one or the other. One or the other. But I couldn't see at all. I couldn't see the room or my parents or the doctor. I looked through one lens and I saw a beach covered in gold and jewels and coins. 'How about now?' he said, and I screamed. So he changed the lens. 'How about now?' And I saw a city made all of wool and yarn and silk with a river of tea flowing round it. I started to cry. 'How about now?' And I saw a herd of giant bicycles barreling over a meadow toward me. 'How about now?' But all I could see was a great lavender eel speeding along under a million stars with people riding on it like a train. I screamed and screamed and clawed at the mask. They thought I was trying to get it off but really, really I was trying to get *in*, to that place where those things lived." Thomas was out of breath, his hair sopping sweat. "I never told anyone, never ever. I never wore my glasses even once, even though I can really only see things close up—I'm useless at anything far away."

Tamburlaine nodded eagerly. She held out her hands to the forest on her walls, throbbing with color. "You see it too. *There*. We're the same, you and me. Tom and Tam. And there's a word for us." She ran her finger along the edge of *Tam Lin*. "You know what one. Say it. Come on. Say it once."

"No, I don't want to. I'm Normal," he begged her. He could see his father's face before him, rubbing the bridge of his nose under his own glasses and saying the names of medicines he did not want to send for like a magic spell. "I can be Normal."

The lime-green lady's voice trumpeted in his ears, deafening. He whirled around, expecting to see her crouching right next to him, singing into his skull. But there was no lady. Thomas stared down into the wide, flaring brass mouth of a gramophone. He screamed, but it couldn't quite get out, and turned into a squeak instead.

The gramophone stopped short. It lifted its own needle. The music crackled down to nothing. And as Thomas stared, his heart coming utterly apart and rearranging itself around what it was seeing, the gramophone unfolded four long, curved brass legs from its wooden table. Each of them ended in a curly lion's paw like Thomas's bathtub. It had been very beautiful once. Bold green and blue filigree patterns still gleamed on its bell, though the paint peeled and cracked. The gramophone tottered up and backward like a baby bird, and though it had no face to flush or furrow or cry, Thomas knew he had hurt its feelings by shrieking.

The gramophone was *embarrassed*.

It clattered over to the corner of the painted room and stood with its bell facing the wall, punishing itself for scaring him. After a moment it put its needle down again. Its crank wound slowly. The lime-green lady sang out—and though he had heard her sing many times, somehow, now, it sounded almost apologetic:

> *In the mornin', in the evenin'*
> *Ain't we got fun?*

Then it lifted its needle again and went quiet.

Tamburlaine got up and went to the gramophone, stroking it like a German shepherd scolded for barking too loud. It turned its bell up to her lovingly. She looked back over her shoulder at him, plum blossoms falling down her back, her face framed by the spires of a distant city beyond the forest she'd drawn, a city of many colors, a city that looked as though it might just be made all of cloth.

"Say it, Thomas. It's not a bad word, it's not. Say what we are."

The troll in Thomas Rood laughed and wept and wrote the word over and over on the walls of his heart, on his ribs, on the insides of his eyelids.

"Please?" Tamburlaine begged. "Tell me I'm not wrong." Green tears welled in her eyes. "Tell me I'm not alone."

Thomas put his hands over his face. From beneath them, he whispered:

"Changelings."

"Changelings," she answered, and the gramophone shuffled its brass feet, singing over and over:

> *Ain't we got fun?*

CHAPTER VIII
Please Be Wild and Wonderful

*In Which Thomas Summons a Guest (and Her Dog), Learns
How a Piece of Wood Became a Daughter, Writes Out a Recipe
for Wombat, and Becomes the Legal Property of a Marsupial*

Time ran differently in the Empire of After School. If you didn't go
home, it could almost stretch on forever. It wasn't like the Kingdom of School. It wasn't a particular place. The great clanging bell could
ring at three o'clock and you could play on the swingset and throw a
ball against the brick wall of the schoolhouse and still, somehow, not
find your way to the Land of After School. But you could drag your
feet walking home, spend a precious dime on a strawberry pop, cut
through the park, kicking a pinecone down the grass while thinking
about what it would feel like to be a hippopotamus and take your
baths in the Nile and suddenly find yourself there, in the long orange

hours before supper, where a hundred games and a thousand jokes can squeeze in.

The trick to making it last, as Thomas faithfully reported to Inspector Balloon, whose cheerful cover had grown a bald spot and many wrinkles, as befits an old scholar, was to avoid the Enemies of the Empire, which is to say, anyone bigger than you. Teachers would tell you to get on home and remind you to read the longest book they could think of just at that moment for a surprise quiz tomorrow. Big Kids, if they had suffered one of the strange and mystic sorrows that plagued their kind and had a mood on, would probably wallop you one or trip you flat. Parents would flex their magic and you would find yourself boiling spaghetti or sweeping the porch or doing math problems at the kitchen table no matter how much you struggled and strove.

But the best part of the Empire of After School was coming home to an empty house all to yourself, knowing your parents have got to be away visiting their own exotic countries: the Duchy of Dinner Parties, the Commonwealth of Overtime, Dance-Hall County, the misty and mysterious nations where Grown-Ups venture alone, like the dancing princesses disappearing at night.

On this particular evening, Nicholas and Gwendolyn Rood had mounted an expedition to the Marshes of Politics, attending a rally to benefit men like Nicholas, who had gone away to war and felt that things ought to have been better when they got back. The Country of War was so distant and dreadful that Thomas could hardly think about it, could not begin to make a section for it in Inspector Balloon. His father had been there, had lived there, but he would not talk about it. Thomas understood that the Country of War casts a spell of silence when you leave it, so that it can keep its awful secrets forever. Thomas never wanted to go to the rallies—and today would not be the day he changed his mind. Tamburlaine was coming, and thus a herd of Egyptian hippos could not drag him out of his house before she arrived.

It was his turn to let her into his house, his room, his little Nation of the Learmont Arms Apartments, #7. He raced home and tried to think of the rituals his mother used to summon a visitor: sweep the floor, put flowers in the vase on the dining table, turn up the lights, put the kettle on, make little miniature sandwiches. Thomas always vanished into his room when his mother's friends arrived, so he did not know that the kettle meant tea. It only seemed important to fill it with water and make it whistle. Nor did he see why the sandwiches had to be so tiny and thin when people were always hungry in the afternoon and those wouldn't feed a doll, but he did it anyway, slicing cheese and radishes carefully with the big knife. He made his bed, which he never did, preferring to keep it as more of a nest or a cave than a bed. He brushed out all the cobwebs in his room and shoved his clothes into his chest of drawers till it was packed so tight it groaned. He made sure all his troll and fairy-story books were lined up neatly on his bookshelf where Tamburlaine would see them straightaway. And he waited. The kettle screamed— and the summoning seemed to work, for a knock rapped at the door.

Tamburlaine was wearing her wig and her skin again. Behind her she pulled a huge red Irish setter with chocolatey, warm eyes. Thomas hadn't heard a dog when he'd visited her house! Perhaps he lived out-side. Tamburlaine seemed strange to him, now he knew what she really looked like. Like somebody wearing clothes she had outgrown years ago. But she didn't take them off or shake out her plummy hair as she had before. She looked around politely, thanked him for the sandwiches, and munched on one with a thoughtful expression. The Irish setter sat on his rear and yawned. Out of her own house, Tamburlaine seemed much less sure of everything in the world.

"I didn't know you had a dog," Thomas ventured.

"A dog? Oh! Silly me."

Tamburlaine reached up a hand and smacked him hard on the side of his head. It made a loud *thwack* in the quiet. And it hurt like fire.

"Ow! Hey!"

Thomas's eyes crossed a little—and when they came uncrossed, the Irish setter had vanished. The gramophone stood hesitantly behind Tamburlaine, shifting bashfully on its long brass legs, tilting its bell this way and that.

"He wanted to come," Tamburlaine explained. "He likes you. Thomas, this is Scratch. I made him, and he's just the most marvelous thing there is. Do you have anything for him to eat? He likes ragtime and jazz and torch songs . . . but it has to have lyrics. He doesn't have a mouth, you know. He can only say what's on his turntable."

Scratch arched the neck of his bell in pleasure. He wound up his crank and dropped his needle. The lime-green lady's voice poured out:

> *Now the curtain is going up*
> *the Entertainer is taking a bow!*

Thomas thought he might cry again. But his face decided to grin instead. Scratch was an alive thing. A talking thing. Alive and talking the way he'd always wanted everything, just everything, to be. Thomas went over to his parents' gramophone, which seemed rather shabby and dull just now, and pulled a record out of the cabinet where his parents kept them. It had a great handsome fat man in a sky-blue suit on the cover, his mouth wide open to let the music out.

"And . . . and sometimes he's a dog?" Thomas handed it over and tried to sound casual, as if he already knew that sometime gramophones could be dogs.

Scratch shook his bell and moved his needle to a different groove on the spinning black record. He sang again:

> *No, sir, don't mean maybe . . .*

"No, no," Tamburlaine laughed, petting Scratch's bell. She took the record from him and changed out the lime-green lady for the sky-blue man.

Scratch lowered his needle gingerly.

> *Tell me, tell me, what did you do to me*
> *I just got a thrill that was new to me . . .*

Scratch bounced his bell joyfully. He liked the record. It would let him say new things, exciting things. Tamburlaine gave him such a tender, happy smile—a new smile Thomas had never seen her make before, and he wished it had been made for him.

"It's a glamour," she said. "So that we can walk down the street together without people staring. A glamour is like . . . if there's a hole in your wall because somebody opened a door too fast or wasn't careful enough moving a bookshelf, you could hang a picture over it, so nobody sees. The hole's still there, it's just hidden." She seemed to grow suddenly shy. "I could show you . . . if you want."

Thomas did want, more than anything. "Tam . . . can I call you Tam now? I know you said not to but I understand now why you didn't like it. It can be just our secret, I'll only say it when we're alone. Tam . . . I know you think we're the same, but you must see we're not. I can't make a Scratch. Believe me. I've been trying to since I was little. Nothing comes alive just because I want it to be alive. I don't have any flowers on the inside. You . . . you *are* marvelous, and your gramophone is, and your painting . . . but I can't do any of that. I wish I could. You have no idea. I know what I said the other day but . . . but I'm still just Thomas. Just a boy." Tell me I'm wrong, his heart begged. I want to be wrong.

Tamburlaine nodded. She put down her plate and wiped her mouth. "I can prove you're not. I guess . . . I guess I thought it would be nice if you believed me. Because I'm technically your oldest friend and all. I guess I thought it would feel nice if you just looked at me and *knew,* down deep in your gut. The way you knew the word *Changeling.* But that's okay. This will be fun, too. It'll be like when we made those clay mugs in Mrs. Miller's class."

Thomas licked his dry lips. He'd made a beautiful mug—shaped like an elephant, with a little clay palanquin and a little clay prince for a lid. His father had dropped it a week after he brought it home and shattered the poor prince all over the floor.

"First: materials. Do you have anything you can use like a wand? Something that's yours, not like a rolled-up sheet of math problems. Something you like."

Thomas shook his head, trying to shake it into sense again. A wand? He was having a conversation with a girl in which wands had a starring role.

"Um . . . yeah. Sure."

He knew what it had to be. Without even thinking about it, it popped into his head like the answer to a riddle. Thomas darted down the hall to his room and yanked open his desk drawer. He pulled out a long, yellow No. 2 pencil. The Magic Pencil. When he turned around, Tamburlaine was standing in the doorway to his room. Scratch peered curiously over her shoulder. She knew Vampire Law, too: You have to wait to be invited. Thomas held out his pencil toward her.

"I've had it since forever. My mom gave it to me. When I was a baby. She pulled it out of her hair and gave it to me and I've been really careful, I haven't used it up yet, because . . ." He was aware he was babbling, and clammed up before the rest could come hurrying out. *Because I'm on a quest. She gave me a quest. She pulled this pencil out of her head like a sword out of a scabbard and I knew it was a sacred quest, the kind Galahad got. She charged me to go to the Kingdom of University and meet a Girl Called Lovely and Practice Psychology like my Father before me. And I want to, I want to, but it's taking so* long. ". . . Well, I guess for no good reason. It's . . . it's okay, you can come in."

Tamburlaine stepped in lightly and sat on his bed. He wished his quilt weren't so plain, that he had something extraordinary to show her besides cheese sandwiches and a pencil. She squinted and eyeballed his pencil, turned it over in her hands, poked her fingernail into the eraser.

"Okay," she said, nodding satisfaction. "Now, pick something you like." Tamburlaine grinned up at him, eager, enjoying being mysterious, stretching out the game like a stage magician.

"What do you mean?"

"In the house. Pick something you like. Anything you think is pretty or interesting or nice?"

"Why does that matter?"

"Just pick something, silly. We don't have all night. It has to be something you like or it won't work. Don't ask me why. I don't have any whys. I only know a couple of things and they're only the things I know. And the only reason I know things you don't is that I couldn't help knowing. It's hard to go along thinking everything is fine and someday you'll go to nursing school when you have plums growing out of your palms."

Thomas looked around. He didn't have much in his room—he'd broken most of his toys ages back. His baseball sat quietly on his desk, his books in their shelf, his alarm clock, his bedside lamp . . . and his wombat. Thomas's eyes fell on the scrap-yarn wombat his mother had made him so long ago, her patchwork colors mismatched, her stuffing showing near her tail, her lopsided button eyes dull and scratched. Tamburlaine followed his gaze.

"Perfect," she said. She picked the scrap-yarn wombat up off his pillow with both hands—she was really rather enormous for a toy—and handed her to him. "I like wombats. What's its name?"

Thomas hesitated, scratching the back of his neck. He had never told anyone the names of his belongings before. "Her. Her name's Blunderbuss. I like to name things; I know it's dumb."

"Of course you like to name things," Tamburlaine said with a little smile. "We all do."

"Tam, what if I can't do . . . whatever it is you think I can do? You keep saying we're the same but I'm not . . . I'm not a tree."

The troll inside Thomas clapped its hands. Not a tree, it giggled, a rock.

Tamburlaine looked startled for a moment. Then she laughed, and under all her strangeness was a twelve-year-old girl again.

"Well, I'm not either!"

He looked doubtfully at her wig, hiding its secret flowers.

She waved her hand. "I'm not. Honest. Thomas, we're only different to look at. It's like how you're a boy and I'm a girl, but it doesn't make any difference. We're both people." Tamburlaine clapped a hand over her mouth, as though she'd just accidentally let a curse word slip. A wicked excitement flooded her eyes. "Only we're not. I'm not. You're not. I'm a . . ." She trailed off just as he had done, and he realized all at once that she had never told anyone about herself before, either.

Be kind, Thomas. The first time is always hard.

"I'm a Fetch," Tam finished. The word sounded like a light switched on in Thomas's head. "At least I think I am. I don't know what else I could be, really." She picked at her fingernails. "My mother is a gardener and my father is a librarian. That's nice, don't you think? She minds trees while they're young and he minds them when they're old. There's a logic to the two of them. It's almost like magic. Sometimes they joke that they should have known something like me would come along. Altogether too much time in the woods. Well, they fell in love and my father built a house made of books and roses and radishes in tidy beds beside the Postbox. They had a baby girl and when she came along they compromised. They named her after a play and a flower—my middle name is Violet. When the baby was a year old, she got very sick, so sick her ears were red and her face was red and her belly was red. She burned up with fever and redness, day and night. And then one morning, they woke and the fever was gone—and so was their daughter. In the crib lay a little poppet made out of wood and branches and green leaves, screeching like a barn owl. Not all Changelings are meant as a fair bargain, a child for a child. Some are just dumb dolls meant to scream and turn the teakettle into a rattlesnake and burn the house down, not necessarily in that order, but as quickly as possible."

"Did you burn your house down?"

"No," said Tamburlaine slowly. "But I want to. All the time. I was built to wreck things. I *like* to wreck things. Nothing feels as good as the moment right before you break something. Every day I try like the devil not to wreck anything. It's so hard. I got to painting because paint wrecks a white wall, so I like it, but it wrecks it into something better, so my parents like it. The thing about Fetches is we aren't meant to last. We're meant to go off like a little stick of dynamite after a few months and that's it. Do you understand? We're a kind of joke *There* plays on *here*. Like a buzzer that zings when the worlds shake hands. But my parents are strange people." She laughed. "If I'm a joke, they have a *really* good sense of humor. That's what comes of loving books and plants— things alive but not alive. My father was pretty certain he knew what had happened. He's read just everything in the world. They mourned for her. The other girl. Their real daughter. In the quiet and the dark where they thought I couldn't hear. But Mum knew how to take care of a tree and Dad knew how to take care of a chapter from a fairy book. When I wouldn't stop screaming she took me out in the rain until my leaves unfurled and drank up the sky. When I tried to eat the wood-stove, he gave me a rapier and a straw griffin to fight. And when I broke . . . because Fetches always break . . . she grafted me and wound me up with twine and put me in the sun till I got well. I'm fragile. Like a motorcar that breaks down after ten years, not because it couldn't be built to go for fifty, but because Mr. Ford likes people to buy new cars. Planned obsolescence, that's called, and that's me. I bet your parents don't even know you're not their son. I think that would be nice. Easier. To grow up thinking you had the whole world in front of you."

"It's not," Thomas said, too loud and too fast. "It just means there's something wrong with you and you don't know what and they don't know what but if you were a better son, a better *man,* you would be able to fix it. It's funny, you know, they're always telling me to *be a man, take it like a man, act like a man,* like they're afraid if they don't keep reminding me I'll grow up to be a centaur or a dining room table, like they *know*, somehow, that I'm not a man, like it's a spell they can cast, if they say it enough I'll be tricked into being a man forever." And that was the first time he had let himself say he wasn't a man, say it, and know that it was true. He wasn't like Tamburlaine, but he wasn't like his parents, either.

"Yes." Tamburlaine nodded. "They always say: *be a lady, speak like a lady, behave like a little lady, that's not very ladylike, is it, dear?*"

"Well, I won't be a man, or take anything like one or act like one!" The troll inside him rubbed his hands gleefully, crackling with anticipation.

"Come on, then," Tam urged. She grabbed Inspector Balloon off his desk, opened the cracked red cover to a blank page, and pressed it and his pencil into Thomas's hands. "Don't let's be men, or ladies either. Don't let's act like them or behave like them or speak like them."

"But what else, then? If you're a Fetch, what am I?"

Tamburlaine shook her head. "I don't know exactly. I'm not an encyclopedia. Maybe you're a Fairy. Or a Minotaur. Or a spriggan or a Glashtyn. It's like a Christmas present you can't open till the twenty-fifth. And that might bite. We'll find out together. But now, right now, be a Fairy. A *bad* Fairy." Her eyes glittered like rain on new leaves. "Write out what you want. Like a letter. Use your good handwriting—your real handwriting. Make it short and really specific—magic sort of squirms into the cracks in what you want and fills them up with trouble."

"No eye of newt or frog's heart or belladonna?"

"If you'd picked a ladle or a gravy boat or a wooden spoon, maybe. You have to use a wand the way it's supposed to be used. Magic has a logic, like algebra. Once you get to know it, it's easy. If this, then that. You write with a pencil, you don't make frog soup with it."

"But I've written loads of things and nothing's ever happened."

"Well, you have to sort of . . . get it ready first. With a pencil, I suppose you'd have to . . . um . . . sharpen it? That sounds right."

"What's yours? Your wand."

Tamburlaine reached into her satchel and produced a beautiful wooden paintbrush with thick badger bristles and a copper band around the neck. Of course. That room, those walls all bright with the colors of *There*.

"I don't suppose you mean to use a sharpener," Thomas said.

"No. Magic is something you do with your body." Scratch tucked his bell under Tamburlaine's arm like he really was an Irish setter who just wanted a good petting. Tam laughed softly and hugged her gramophone to her side. "Like if you open a music box and a little ballerina dances. You opened the box. You made her dance. You made a dance where there wasn't any before, but that doesn't mean *you're* dancing. It's always something to do with your own body. And . . . well, it's usually something a little disgusting. I figured I had to get mine wet, like you do when you're painting watercolors. So I cut open my arm and rolled it in sap."

Of course, Tamburlaine could not know that only Wet Magic works this way. There are many other sorts that turn up their noses at such unsanitary conditions as spilling blood of any sort, such as Dry Magic, which mainly confines itself to books and sandstorms, as well as Fan Magic, which can't do a thing without lace.

But Thomas was impressed. He could imagine her running a paint knife across her biceps, wincing, believing hard. He considered it, trying to think like magic might think, if magic was a funny little person who lived next door and stayed up all hours playing the radio too loud and throwing books across the room. Experimentally, he stuck the tip of his pencil between his teeth. It tasted metallic and dirty and woody and awful. For a moment that was all it did—and then a rolling, tumbling, swollen feeling surged up in his chest. His troll-self stretched and reached up from his belly, popping its aching joints, pushing aside all the bits of him which were not-troll, straining toward the pencil with jaws open. The troll was ready. Finally, it was his turn. The troll in Thomas seized the end of the pencil in his own sharp teeth and chewed it into a fine point, delirious with the happiness of having something to do. It felt like biting into a quarter and spitting out pennies. Thomas coughed, then gagged, then tried to wipe the pencil out of his mouth with his finger, which only made him gag harder. Had he done it? Was his Magic Pencil really magic now?

On the blue lines of Inspector Balloon's paper, Thomas and the troll within him wrote together in glorious big looping, leaping letters:

Dear Blunderbuss:

Please wake up right now this moment and be alive like Scratch and be a real wombat and be able to talk and walk and bite and do marvelous things like firing passionfruits and horseshoes and whiskey bottles out of your mouth at our enemies and singing the ancient songs of the Land of Wom, which we both know is the most beautiful Land that ever was a Land. Please like me (and also Tamburlaine; she is very nice and even though she is made of wood so you oughtn't gnash her or play catch with her or bury her in the yard but instead be very careful as she is splinterable. But you can gnash me a bit if you like). Please be as real as I am and not a doll or a robot *or a puppet who can only do things because I say so. You can be cantankerous, I don't mind. If you don't like waking up in the morning I shall make you a bucket of coffee. Please be wild and wonderful. Please be fierce and stubborn because I am also those things, and if we are both fierce and stubborn neither of us shall mind when the other is especially one or the other.*

Thank you,
Thomas Michael Rood

Thomas breathed in great awful gulps. Would it work? It wouldn't work. Would it? It couldn't. It could. Never. Never. Perhaps?

Tamburlaine showed him how to rip out the page so that it was all one piece, with a very straight edge and no tears through any of the words. She showed him how to fold it as small as it would go and put it in the scrap-yarn wombat's mouth. He could feel the paper poke through the loops in the yarn and press into Blunderbuss's stuffing. Down, down it went, into her fuzzy heart. It wouldn't work. He would feel something if it were working. But maybe the magic was only in the writing. Maybe it was already outside of him, whispering its work where he could not hear. *Please, please, please.*

The troll inside Thomas peered up through his eyes like a child pressing his face to a shop window. Tom and Tam held their breaths.

Blunderbuss's left eye was a pearly magenta diamond-shaped button with a thistle carved on it (which had belonged to one of Gwendolyn's spring dresses) and her right was a thick round brass button with a sailing ship stamped on it (which had come from one of Thomas's peacoats). This meant that she always looked as though she was winking at something secret and funny. She looked that way now, and Thomas couldn't help it—he winked back, as he so often did when the world was baffling and only something big and soft and grabbable could make him feel better.

And Blunderbuss winked back.

The chocolate-colored yarn over her magenta eye bunched up like a real eyebrow and shut. Then it sprang open again. Next, the bold blue yarn over her brass right eye tried it. Finally, the scrap-yarn wombat waggled her pea-green and tangerine ears. She waggled her maroon muzzle. She waggled her lilac tail. She pounded her gold and turquoise front feet on the bed, then her white and black back feet. She dropped her front half down and wiggled her motley, patchwork rump in the air. At last, Blunderbuss the wild and wonderful wombat opened up her cherry-red mouth, showing two long, powerful cloak-clasp teeth, and gave a chittering cry, like a pig and a songbird snorting and singing at the same time.

Blunderbuss gave a great leap, which was slightly less great than she expected it to be as wombats have quite short legs, but can never seem to remember the fact, and pounced onto Thomas, knocking him to the floor. She landed on his chest with a weight like a heap of cannonballs, her dense, muscley chest crushing him, her breath smelling like wet wool and a little, just a little, like bush grasses and a blazing hot sun beating down on dry dust.

"Troll! Troll Troll!" the scrap-yarn wombat chortled. Her voice was just perfectly rumbly and throaty and grumbly, like wool all frayed and felted together. "Yes! No! Yes. Yes. No. No. Maybe! Green. Pineapples. Gin." Blunderbuss banged her front paws on Thomas's chest, making him cough all over again. She beamed. "TA-DA!" the wombat cried, and, quick as a pub-dart, dove in and bit him on the neck. Thomas squealed.

"You said I could!" Blunderbuss grumbled. "You said I could gnash you. If you get mad now that's like breaking a promise. Besides, in the Land of Wom, we bite to show we like a thing. And that we don't like a thing. And that we think a thing is delicious. And that we think it is ours! Because anything you bite is yours, that's just obvious! We bite when we are angry and hungry and joyful and excited to go to the cinema and frightened of wild dogs and because it is Tuesday but also because it is Sunday and especially when we are DELIGHTED but NERVOUS. Nothing says I AM HAVING FEELINGS like a bite! And I bit you so you are mine, Tom Rood. I own you. Wombat Rules. I own a troll!"

Blunderbuss sprang off of him like a firecracker, circled the room twice, snagging her worsted claws on the floorboard nails. She jumped with all her might, forgetting once again that she was not, in fact, a kangaroo, and thus missing the desk, whacking into it mid-belly and pumping her hindpaws in the air till she could clamber up and collapse on top of the red notebook with balloons on the cover, panting, her eyes shining and wet and alive.

"I'm a troll?" gasped Thomas.

CHAPTER IX

The Emerald Thermodynamical Hyper-Jungle Law

*In Which Tom and Tam Host a Very Boisterous Party
in Apartment #7, Play a Game of Red Light, Green Light,
and Are Kidnapped by a Baseball*

Thomas and Tamburlaine played for seven hours, which is the proper number for this sort of thing. It takes a span of seven, at a minimum, to make a new world.

Seven days, seven hours, even seven minutes, if one has had a very good breakfast. Less won't do; you spend the first bit just measuring fabric and trying to find the hammer you had in your hand just a moment ago. And if you go on and on and procrastinate and sleep in weekends, before you know it you've spent a year on one little curlicue on one tiny blue fjord and the whole thing starts to seem less interesting than starting over with a shiny new gas giant.

Don't look at me so suspiciously —you and I make new worlds, too. It is only that our hands are too small to manage seventeen moons at once, or a great red storm that goes on blustering for centuries. We make our worlds of stranger stuff: We choose people who do not annoy us, places of green or glass and steel that feel as alive and necessary as our brothers and sisters, houses in which everything has a place, rules such as *Do Not Take Things That Aren't Yours Unless No One Is Looking* and *Good Things Happen to Good People* and *A Year Is 365 Days* are agreed upon, even when they aren't true, perhaps especially so.

You and I have made a little world here together, a world only we know, with a lovely red door and glinting eyes peeking out from under the geraniums. A secret world all our own inside the one everyone knows about, and a very fine one, at that. A new world is always made when one creature speaks and another listens. There is no gravity in here, but oh, how everything flies!

Thomas Rood managed two worlds in seven hours. We should, frankly, congratulate him on a new land-speed record. The first one was a matter of survival. He didn't mean to do it. No one does, really. It's only that when nothing is as you thought it was, a body has to cobble together a new universe out of the rubbish left over when the old one burst and turned into a wombat. Nothing could be certain anymore. New gravities were necessary, new boiling points, new E's and mc's and squares. Why settle for the second law of thermodynamics? That's the old world's tune. When gramophones dance and girls grow plums like earrings, the reign of the Emerald Thermodynamical Hyper-Jungle Law has come: Everything lives and grows and thickens, nothing decays, nothing fades, nothing ends.

He didn't make his worlds alone, of course. No one does. Moving alone upon the face of the deep is awfully boring.

And lo, in the first hour, Thomas and Tamburlaine went a bit mad with giggling and chocolates liberated from the high cabinet and egging each other on and committed a number of crimes against Apartment #7. Thomas excavated the ancient archaeological site of his closet and unearthed several half-used tubes of oil paint rolled up at the ends like toothpaste. Tam showed him how to use a bit of egg to freshen up the colors. Together, they pushed his tall bookshelf to one side, revealing a fresh, blank patch of easily hideable wall. Tamburlaine rubbed her arm from wrist to shoulder until the dark, polished wood of her real body came up. She squirted out lines of cobalt and vermilion and custard and olive onto her forearm and began to paint, while Thomas scribbled his notes to the furniture with the fervor of a grandfather writing letters to the newspaper editor.

Dear Gertrude (my bedside reading lamp with the green shade and missing pane of glass through which you can see wires):

Please wake up right now this moment and be alive like Blunderbuss and be able to walk and talk and remember all the books you read over my shoulder from the time I was tiny and you seemed as big and bright as the sun. Please like Tamburlaine and I and never pop your bulb again and forgive me for not ever dusting you even though every night when I went to bed I thought you really needed it.

Thank you,
Thomas Michael Rood

P.S. Please do not be malevolent.

Tamburlaine drew her brush upward in a long, graceful, custard-colored stroke, a stroke that if you or I or Thomas had made it, might only have been a stripe on a wall for which we'd have been rightly scolded, but when Tam did it, clearly belonged to a tree whose leaves and trunk would soon catch up with the rest. While she did it, Blunderbuss snuffled around the kitchen until she found the bread-box, whereupon she dove into the dinner rolls headfirst, her woolly feet waggling in joy. "Wombats have to fill their bellies! Priority one! An empty belly is an angry belly. You are my very first dinner rolls! I will remember you always and sing songs of your courage!" she cried.

Scratch kicked his long brass legs like a dance-hall girl as Gertrude the Green Lamp clicked on, then off, then on again, rocking from side to side on her squat, round base, then leapt to the floor and bounced madcap round the bedroom, her light flashing on and off, faster and faster, while the gramophone sang:

> How 'ya gonna keep 'em, down on farm,
> After they've seen Paree?

Thomas ran through the house, writing with his paper propped on the wall, on the dining table, on the floor, on his knee. *Dear Hephaestus, Who Is a Woodstove with One Dented Burner; Dear Ophelia, Who Is a Vase of Five Sort of Wilted Irises; Dear Grandfather Horatio, Who Is a Grandfather Clock!* And Hephaestus roared in patterns of flame and dark, and Ophelia opened and closed her blossoms and bounced along with Gertrude in a foxtrot, and Grandfather Horatio bonged out seventeen o'clock. Tamburlaine looked up from her painting and tilted her head to one side. The apartment quaked with stomping and crowing.

"You only asked them to talk. You didn't give them mouths. They're like Scratch; they talk with the parts they have. Though Gertrude seems to know Morse code."

The green glass lamp flashed gleefully: long, short, long, long.

Under her hands a chartreuse tree was growing. Its leaves unfurled in ultramarine, boiling hot colors dripping with light.

Thomas looked up at the chandelier in the parlor.

"Will-o'-the-wisp, if you come out today I shall love you until I am dead."

Thomas wrote to the chandelier. He called her Citrine as he always had. I shall not tell you what he wrote, for some things that pass between a boy and a lighting fixture are secret and strange. He got up onto a ladder and coiled the note around one of the silver flourishes hung with crystal. He waited. His heart felt as though it were bursting and collapsing back and bursting again.

Nothing happened. No will-o'-the-wisp soared up out of the lights and settled on his shoulder. Thomas shook his head. It was the first disappointment of his new world. He tried to reason it out. To invent a rule, for rules give one a little kingship over disappointments. It was not, after all, Thomas's fault if he had run afoul of a Law of the Universe. They weren't posted; he hadn't known.

"I think maybe I can't make new things," he called out to Tamburlaine, who was shading a stained-glass pinecone in maroon. "Just wake things up. Have you ever made anything new, something that wasn't there before?" And in his heart he thought: *Is this what a troll does? Is this troll magic?*

But Tamburlaine did not answer. She was too full of her new trees.

Dear Arabesque, Who Is a Girl Dancing with Orchids in the Hallway Painting . . . Thomas began to write. He concentrated so fiercely that he did not see a pair of crystal legs bathed in daffodil-colored light unfold from the ceiling and pirouette down. He did not see the slender, gentle body of teardrop-shaped crystals, nor the hair of silver curling chandelier arms, nor the glowing eyes of round glass bulbs until he turned round to take his new note to the girl in the hallway painting. Thomas stared at Citrine. She stared back. Not a will-o'-the-wisp—alive all the same. She smiled with her glittering glass mouth and swept up Thomas into her arms, spinning him in a crystalline polka round the apartment, grabbing Tamburlaine as they passed the bedroom, clutching her with jeweled fingers, making a clumsy, hopping, lovely three-person step from corner to corner to corner. Scratch leapt along behind them, singing, moving his needle double-quick, back and forth across the record:

> How ya gonna keep 'em down on the farm,
> After they've seen Paree?

But then, in the second hour, Thomas was compelled to teach the citizens of his new world a game, for Nicholas and Gwendolyn would not stay away forever. The wild objects of Apartment #7 gathered close round: the green glass lamp and the vase of irises leaned in, the woodstove strained to hear from the kitchen, the draperies swirled open and shut, the grandfather clock put his hands into his best attentive position. The girl in the painting put down her orchids and stood on tiptoe. The chandelier sat cross-legged on the parlor rug. Blunderbuss snoozed, uninterested, her yarn nose twitching.

"Everybody, please, listen, this is very important!" Thomas cried. "We must learn a game, all together. It's a very easy game. It's called Red Light, Green Light."

The green lamp flashed delightedly.

"Yes, I expect you'll be very good at it, Gertrude! Now, when I say Green Light, we can all do as we like and roll about and pounce and howl. But when I say Red Light, you must freeze, back in your old places, and hold your breath, and not move even a little. Red Light means someone is coming who wouldn't understand why you are all suddenly interested in pouncing, and might take us all to the dump if they found out. Let's try? Red Light!"

The house eagerly leapt to order. They practiced all afternoon, except Blunderbuss, who slept the hours away below Tamburlaine's chartreuse pine, snoring up into the blue needles, each one a tiny rapier glinting under the stars of a faraway place.

In the third hour, Blunderbuss begged Thomas to take her to school.

"In the Land of Wom, we learn by fighting! If you spy a wombat who looks like he might know something you don't, you sneak along behind him while he's looking for grasses to eat and when he thinks he is very safe, you LEAP out and POUNCE on him! You bite his NECK and dig your claws into his RUMP! You hold him down till the things he knows start trying to wiggle out so that at least they can escape your wrath alive. Out of his furry wombat muzzle might shoot snowballs with the formula to convert Fahrenheit to Celsius written in the ice! Papayas with seeds who bear the faces of all the Prime Ministers of Wom, in chronological order! Painted eggs you can crack open and suck out the Code of Hammurabi! Did you know Hammurabi was part wombat? Well, children are ignorant these days. I want to go to this Kingdom of School and fight humans for their know-how! Who knows what I can pummel out of *them*?"

"Nothing," Thomas begged her. "That's not how it works here. You can't pummel them at all. If I take you tomorrow, *if* I take you, you must stay completely silent. The Reddest of Red Lights! You must stay in my satchel and not come out until it is all over. Promise, Blunderbuss. Or you stay home with Gertrude and her flashing will give you a nasty headache."

Blunderbuss reared up on her squat black-and-white hind legs. She held up one turquoise paw. "I solemnly swear on the soul of Wattle, the great wombat empress who stood up to the kangaroos and told them what's what. I will stay in your satchel and not make so much as a snort."

In the fourth hour, Tamburlaine began a new tree to the left of the stained-glass pine, a violently violet willow whose drooping branches sprouted all over with pocket watches. And Thomas got very close to Blunderbuss's woolen ear and said: "You called me a troll."

"What I see I say, and what I says I seen, I sawed," nodded the scrap-yarn wombat.

"But I don't look like a troll. I've looked at heaps of pictures of trolls, and they're . . . they're so-so much prettier than me."

"A wombat also sees with her nose. And her teeth. You *reek* like a troll and you *taste* like a troll. Don't worry, it's a nice reek. Mossy and muddy and a little like a diamond. In the Land of Wom, we collect reeks like stamps. When I was a bub I had a book with twelve kinds of cockatrice reek in it. Would have knocked you down dead just to turn the page."

Thomas tried to smell himself, but he only smelled like Thomas to his own nose. Is it true? Would a wombat lie to him? What if she was right?

In the fifth hour, Tamburlaine's third tree sprang up, an applejack tree whose fruit were glassy green flasks sloshing with powerful cider. She worked so fast it made her pant and sweat. The way she stared at the forest on his wall made Thomas shiver. A gaze like that could set a poor unsuspecting wall on fire. He sat back while the apartment thundered around him, creatures running up every which ceiling, laughing and chattering in their many peculiar tongues. The girl in the painting waved at him; he waved back. Though he did not know it, Apartment #7 now looked very like a house in Fairyland. It was nearly an outpost of Fairyland itself, so thickly did it swarm with magic.

In the sixth hour, Thomas Rood cast about for some new thing to enchant. The icebox was too big, really. An icebox come alive was too close to a Yeti to keep in an apartment. The jewelry on his beloved coat seemed like a good prospect, but then he should not have the coat any longer, once the necklaces on its shoulders had minds of their own.

In the depths of his satchel, having waited patiently for its moment, Thomas's baseball stirred.

It rolled forward, pushed open the flap of the satchel, and peeked out, its red stitches gleaming invitingly. *Look at me, Tom,* the ball seemed to whisper. *How much fun I am!* But Tom was considering the virtues of his Sunday suit coming to life and not paying attention where it ought to be paid, thank you very much. But the ball was quite proud. It would not be ignored. It nudged forward again, boldly tumbling out onto the floor where it could not be missed.

"My old ball!" cried Thomas. "Oh, yes! It's perfect! Just this last one, I think. It's getting late."

"It is," sighed Tamburlaine, rubbing her eyes. "But I don't want to go home yet, Tom! Just a little longer? There hasn't been room on my wall for three whole trees since I don't know when!"

Thomas ran to her and squeezed her tight, and this was the second world they made, though if we told them they'd done it, the Changelings wouldn't know a bit what we were on about. Tamburlaine, who hardly let anyone touch her besides her parents, lest they feel the hardness of her shoulders, her arms, her hands, stiffened with panic. And then smiled, where Thomas could not see.

"One more, then," he whispered in her ear, and using her back as a desk, dashed out his note. To be honest, he had begun to get a little sloppy with his requests, as everyone seemed to come out right no matter what he wrote. *Anyway,* he thought, *it's good to be brief and to the point. That's what Mr. Wolcott says.*

> Dear Baseball, Which I Have Had Since Forever and a Little Longer,
> Please come alive this very moment and be able to walk and talk and think and fly even farther than you could when you were just a baseball that couldn't walk and talk and think. And please forgive me for not playing with you very much. It is not your fault you are not a book and therefore not one of my favorite things. Please be one of my favorite things now! Thank you!
>
> Thomas Michael Rood

A baseball has nowhere convenient to put a note, which flummoxed Thomas for a moment. Tamburlaine left off her fourth tree, half finished, only the bare outlines of the rest sketched out. It just so happened to be a hawthorn, full of glittering, many-colored toads with runes on their ballooning throats, all singing together in its branches. She took the paper from him and wrapped it around the baseball good and tight. So we must admit that Thomas did not do it alone, and cannot be blamed completely. The two of them can share, like a very unpleasant lunch.

Tom put the ball down in the center of his room. Blunderbuss snuffled at it. Scratch leaned in, murmuring:

Ain't we got fun?

At first it seemed a dud—the ball sat stubbornly and did nothing. The paper did not even crinkle. But then, slowly, it rocked back and forth, back and forth, swelling with each *forth*. The notepaper shredded into snow. It grew to the size of a basketball, a beach ball, a mammoth prize pumpkin from some terrifying county fair. Thomas and Tamburlaine clutched each other's hands. Nothing else had grown huge and frightening. Gertrude had no awful ambition to light the whole of Chicago. But the baseball kept on growing. Finally, one by one, the hundred and thirty-six stitches popped with one hundred and thirty-six sounds like muskets firing.

And the baseball unfolded, unwrapped, unbaseballed into a great creature glaring at them with fiery magenta eyes. His clothes were white as the skin of the baseball, but now they were rough pale furs. Every kind of jewel that ever thought of shining clung to his cloaks. His nose bulged, barrel-thick, hanging down so far as to hide his mouth and mustache the tops of his golden lips—and those lips covered golden sharp teeth and a golden tongue. Furry green eyebrows concealed his gaze. His bald head had been tattooed with astrological gibberish, the graffiti of a hundred royal stargazers. He had scars all over his wrinkled skin, puncture wounds, as though long ago someone had sewn him up like a purse.

The creature panted. His eyes burned, actual flames flickering in his dark pink irises. His golden fangs showed wickedly. Tamburlaine bared hers, and reached out a slow, careful hand to pull Scratch closer.

I know what that is, thought Thomas. *I've seen one. In my books. If only he weren't blocking my shelf I could look him up. . . .*

But he did not get a chance. Blunderbuss leapt forward, dropping onto the floor between the children and the beast, growling, her own cloak-clasp teeth showing, her wool bristling in lavender, olive, burgundy, black.

And the beast roared. He put his head back, all its wild symbols crawling over his skull, and howled from the depths of his gold-plated soul. He swept his right arm round and seized Blunderbuss and Thomas in the crook of his enormous elbow, then swept his left arm and grabbed Tamburlaine and Scratch. Thomas's feet snagged on the strap of his satchel as they left the ground. Everyone screamed together, Scratch screeched as his record skipped, Tam beat at the creature's biceps. Blunderbuss cursed in Wom. Thomas reached back over that giant forearm at his wonderful new world of Apartment #7, 3 Racine Avenue. That brand-new dancing, all-alive world froze in horror as the jeweled baseball-monster took one savage leap—and disappeared into the painted forest on Thomas Rood's bedroom wall.

"Red Light," the girl in the hallway painting whispered, and dropped her orchids to the ground.

AN EQUATION IS A PROPHECY
THAT ALWAYS COMES TRUE

In Which Something Rumbles Most Dreadfully

The gears of Fairyland are trembling.

Deep beneath the bruisey-purple sea that washes the ruins of the Lonely Gaol, great stone cogs turn one against the other, biting, grinding, clunking, sending up strange bubbles to the surface. The teeth of the gears thunder into each other, the gears of our world slipping into the gears of Fairyland, which slip into the gears of other worlds entirely, worlds with names one can only pronounce with three tongues, penguin beaks, or flashes of pink and black light. The gears have turned forever, for as long as stars have known about combustion, as long as hydrogen and oxygen have known they were meant to love each other and make baby oceans. The gears of Fairyland have gone about their business for all that time, mostly uneventfully, only troubled by the occasional earthquake or wrestling match.

But now, they *wobble*. They *quiver,* like frightened kittens caught out of doors at suppertime. They tilt back and forth like tops' heads, churning the water to white foam. The sea above them is an upset stomach, heaving and rolling in sour distress. The bubbles that break on the waves have whispers trapped inside them now, whispers that sigh free when they pop:

Help, they cry.

And somewhere, a girl we know very well is trying. She keeps a very tidy desk, though her fingernails are black crescent moons of inkblots, freshened every day like polish. She keeps her hair braided up round her head so that it cannot get in the way. She has a mole on her left cheek and her feet are very large and ungainly. She can hear the gears rumbling, because she once bled on them, and spilled blood never quite forgets where it came from. She has ruined pages and pages with equations, scribbled, printed, crossed out, circled in nine different colors. The girl has learned that Fairy equations have only the vaguest acquaintance with numbers. They are more like pictures, like prophecies that always come true. They are more like stories. A child equals the mass of Fairyland times the speed of luck squared. She has become good at them, or they have become good at her. Her pages look more like comic books than mathematics. Every once in a while, the variables balance—but not often enough. The girl is trying, trying for her life, but she cannot make x equal everything back the way it was.

CHAPTER X
THE PAINTED FOREST

*In Which Thomas Finds Himself in a New Suit of Clothes,
Tamburlaine Meets Several Familiar Trees, a Baseball Throws
a Tantrum, and a Wombat Imitates a Gatling Gun*

It is a little-known fact that when one jumps through a bedroom wall, one does not so much *land* on the other side as *spill*. And when the five of them spilled into the bright, sunny day beyond the bedroom, they found themselves running, running already before they had any earth at all underneath them, not even knowing why it was so vital that they *must* run, their legs working in the air like fish gasping on a countertop. They spilled, running, into a forest so vivid and sore with color that the many little scratches and scrapes Thomas and Tamburlaine had got on the trip, dirty and stinging with bits of drywall and insulation, bled a little more freely and redly just to match. Trees stretched up in throbbing crimson, tangerine, aquamarine, glittering gold, opal-black. Their branches thatched a stained-glass roof over their heads, filtering the sun into prisms and silvery darts. They ran through mud like swirling paint, clingy and sticky and striped like candy.

A tree whizzed by on one side, a tree with a hundred white-gloved hands reaching out of it, offering little clay pots of syrup. Tamburlaine skidded to a stop. Blunderbuss ran headlong into her, knocking her flat into the mud. Thomas and Scratch wheeled round, suddenly unable to remember why they had been running so fiercely in the first place. The great *thing* Thomas's baseball had become stopped too, shaking his head like a bear troubled greatly by bees.

"It's my forest," Tamburlaine yelped.

But Thomas was not listening. The moment he stopped running, he looked down at himself, and even if a marching band made entirely of tubas and drums and brass bombs struck up next to his ear, he wouldn't have heard a single note.

Have you ever bundled up in a snowstorm? Piled on so many layers of scarf and sweater and parka and snow pants and mittens and great stomping boots that you could hardly move? Suddenly you are quite a lot bigger than before! You bang against bannisters and bounce off cabinets and tumble about in the icy drifts like a panda bear and not like a little human at all.

Then you may have some idea of how Thomas felt. He felt his old body padded up and stuffed and cushioned in a thick, heavy suit, so thick and heavy he couldn't feel anything the way he used to and would certainly go whanging and pranging into everything in sight if he wasn't careful.

But he was not wearing a snowsuit. Not even mittens. His hands were quite bare. And big. And strong. With knuckles the size of crabapples. Thomas squinted in the sunlight—a sunlight unlike any Chicago could boil up in her pots—warm, pumpkin-gold sunlight that *dripped*, that *poured*, that *fizzed*, that *tasted*, actually had a taste, and the taste was the taste of home. Thomas's eyes grew big to gobble up that sunshine. But the rest of him was big, too. So much bigger than he had been on the other side of his bedroom wall. His shoulders felt vast and bony and tough within his old jeweled jacket, which now squeezed uncomfortably tight. His legs wanted to run again, as though they had never run before—*Let us go fast,* they seemed to scream, bursting the seams of his trousers. *We're good for anything you can think of!* His chest gulped down champion breaths, so much air at once that it felt like drinking a whole pint of milk in one go. Thomas touched his hair. Thomas touched his nose. Thomas touched his jaw.

Only he knew, the minute he landed, feet squelching in churning rainbow mud, the moment his nose filled with sparkling, spiced air, that his name wasn't Thomas. It never had been. His name was Hawthorn. And he was a troll.

"It's my forest," Tamburlaine repeated. She was pointing at something in the distance. She tasted a dollop of mud from her thumb. Her wooden thumb—Tamburlaine's human skin and her wig were gone. She was a carved girl, her grain dark and rich and fine, her hair no longer flowers or even branches, but hard, chiseled waves cut deep into her wooden skull and wooden neck and wooden shoulders.

The monstrous baseball stared down at his four captives, sprawled out in the shimmering mud. He seemed suddenly not to know what to do with them. He panted, his fuchsia eyes blazing, his breath reeking of belladonna and mandrake and despair and other poisonous things. His truck-engine chest heaved; his shoulders arched. Thomas's stomach tried to hide behind his spine. No one moved. In the end, it was Scratch who was bravest. He wound his crank, set his needle down, and sang out in the big, boom-barrel voice of the man in the sky-blue suit on an album cover they might never see again:

> *Take me out to the ball game*
> *Take me out to the crowd . . .*

"Silence," the baseball-thing snarled. His voice sounded like a barrel of skulls and iron nails rattling all together. "How dare you speak to me, you blasted worms? How *dare* you?"

"Excuse me, sir," said Tamburlaine, her voice tight and thin as a toy aeroplane's rubber band, "but who are you? I should think we'd dare to speak to anyone unless we knew they were a principal or a president or a fellow in the movies."

"He's not any of that lot," grumbled Blunderbuss, shaking twigs out of her yarny ears. "Unless he's President of Being Left in the Backyard and Forgotten All the Time Because a Baseball's Only Good for One Thing and That Thing's Boring."

The creature blinked several times.

"Besides, this is my forest. If anything, he shouldn't be daring to speak to me!" Tamburlaine grinned a marvelously bossy grin. "Look, Tom—it's mine! My trees, the ones I painted. And look there!" She pointed into the distance again. The half-finished tree of frogs rose up on a little hill, its branches still only sketch lines, thin, wispy strokes where the leaves and burls remained unfinished. A wind kicked up and the gray outline of half a tree swayed. The baseball-beast opened his gold-plated mouth as though he wanted to bellow and call them worms again, but it couldn't quite come out. He shut it, and opened it, and shut it once more. When he spoke his fearsome voice shook a little, as though he were not quite sure of what he'd meant to holler.

"It's not your forest," the creature said. Wrinkles rolled from the nape of his rune-covered white neck around to his forehead. "You just got here."

"That's my butterfly tree there! And my eyeball tree up on that ridge, and my fireworks tree, and my dagger tree, and all of them! I thought I was remembering them but I wasn't, I wasn't! It's better than remembering! I made a forest! I'm its mum! Which is a flower, you know! I should have made more of those!" Tamburlaine fell over in the mud, laughing madly. "And you! Look at you, Tom! You look amazing! The handsomest warts I've ever seen on a troll! Your nose is spectacular! What can you do? Can you smell thoughts? Can you talk to the dirt? I feel dizzy." She lay down in the dirt and laughed again.

"Is it time for physical education?" the great pale beast said slowly, as though he'd been asleep all afternoon.

"Yes," chirped Blunderbuss. "Bend down and we'll whack you with a stick."

"What's your name?" Thomas said softly, holding up his hand to his old baseball. "I'm—" Half his heart wanted to holler out Hawthorn as loud as it could, to feel its own name again, and hear it, too. The other half had got quite used to being Thomas, and thus it was just the littlest bit faster. "Tomthorn," he stuttered. Tamburlaine stared. "Tom Thorn. That's fine for now. Tom Thorn. You were my baseball for a long time but now you're not. Isn't that nice? Not to be a baseball?"

The giant's magenta eyes kindled with some deep flame, beyond words and names and niceties.

"I'm hungry," he growled. "I'm starving."

"There's fruit everywhere," Tamburlaine said nervously. "I know I made a nice Sunday dinner tree when I was little. Roast pork pinecones, cornbread trunk, mushed pea sap, and plum pie blossoms. I'm sure I can find it."

"Sunday . . ." the giant whispered, spreading his massive, rune-scribbled hand across his chest.

"Is that your name?" barked Blunderbuss. "Who's named after a day of the week?"

Faster than falling, the giant grabbed Thomas in his fist again, hauling him up toward his glistening golden teeth. Slowly, horribly, he began to push his fingers into Tom's mouth like a cruel dentist. *What's he doing?* Tom thought wildly. *His fingers are too big, they'll never fit.* But they did. Tom felt a wretched stretching in his new, strong jaw, as though it were nothing but taffy. His lips and his teeth stretched, too, into a horrid, bone-cracking yawn. Those terrible huge fingers worked their way down his throat, searching for something, reaching for something, prodding, prying, and it hurt, it hurt so awfully much, he could feel himself coming apart, like a leg tearing off a roast turkey—

The giant screeched. He yanked his fingers away as though Tom had burned him. The stretching snapped back, the pain split in half, and Tom splashed down into the wet paint-mud of the forest floor as he was unceremoniously dropped on his back. Perhaps troll-flesh was poisonous to baseballs. Or giants.

But he was not so lucky—Tamburlaine crouched next to the creature's huge, scribbled-over leg, brandishing delicate, decorated daggers in each hand, plucked from the dagger-tree she had drawn herself so long ago. The wind rustled its boughs behind her and the clinking of knives, one against the other, filled the forest air. She had stabbed him, twice, in the hollow of his knee, and was quite ready to go again, her knees bent, knives raised, wooden teeth bared. The giant brandished his fist to knock her flat—and glass exploded against his face. Thomas whipped his head round to see Blunderbuss, rainbow mud staining her rainbow yarn, in the traditional Wom Fighting Stance, her bone-armored rump in the air, front legs splayed out before her, mouth gaping open in a tremendous snarl, spitting whiskey bottles, passionfruits, and horseshoes into the baseball's flabby cheeks.

"I'm not afraid of you!" the wombat yelled. "I saw you get stuck in the washing machine once. Round and round you went! Who's afraid of something that can't defeat a rinse cycle?"

The funniest thing happened. The tattooed giant blushed. They were all so shocked to see such a thing on his awful face that for a moment they hadn't the first idea what he was doing. Red spread over his sharp, starving cheekbones and his great bald head. He was embarrassed. It was gone in a second, but they'd all seen it. He looked so wretched, so confused, like a walrus suddenly deposited at the perfume counter of a department store.

"I used to be somebody else," he whispered.

"Me too," said Tom Thorn.

He could almost remember it now. A house with a well for a chimney. Bridges. Church bells. The ever-present danger of pirates. Something about a frog . . . or a toad. Something amphibian. "Me too. But if you try to eat any of us again, I still have my pencil and my notebook and I shall not hesitate at all to write you into a baseball quick as you can say *third strike*. Or worse! A golf ball. Or a little marble I promise to instantly lose down a storm drain."

He drew his pencil out of his satchel and held it before him like a sword. Its tip was broken, and he had no notion of whether or not such magic would work here, or whether he could turn alive things back into unalive things at all, but the main thing was to look as though he meant it. He did hope his new troll eyes were fierce and steely and all the things they ought to be. "Now, Mr. Sunday, which we'll call you until you come round to your senses again and can tell us it's Harold or whatever it is, you can come with us if you like—"

But it would seem the wild man did not like. He hissed at them, showing his golden fangs and the depths of his golden throat, and leapt away through the eyeball and firework trees, which boomed in his wake.

The Sunday dinner tree rose above them into the night sky, its porkcones glistening caramely brown, its cornbread branches oozing butter and honey and mushed peas, its plum pie blossoms dripping crust onto the little camp of four below. They had managed a fire of fallen firework branches. It blazed green, then blue, then purple, then green again, shooting up showers of sparks whenever it felt particularly festive. Tamburlaine sat a little farther back than her friends, so as not to scorch. They all lay back, very pleased with themselves indeed, as you might be if you frightened off a grizzly thing and followed that up with supper from a tree you'd invented yourself. The stars overhead glittered in birthday colors, unfamiliar and familiar all at once. Tam stroked Scratch's bell, which had got dented somewhere along the way. He sang softly, his crank turning:

> In the Big Rock Candy Mountains,
> There's a land that's fair and bright,
> Where the handouts grow on bushes
> And you sleep out every night . . .

"This is Fairyland, isn't it, Tam?"
"I think so, Tom."

"Well, it's not Sydney, you dimwits," yawned Blunderbuss. Bits of cornbread and peas made a mustache over her muzzle. "My favorite dimwits!" she corrected hurriedly. "Best dimwits in all the world."

Tamburlaine stared up into the Sunday dinner tree with the lazy, gentle thoughtfulness one straps on after a good meal. "It's my mother's recipe. Roast pork with mint and thyme. My mouth watered while I painted it. I think she'd laugh till she fell over to see her Sunday roast growing out of the ground. I wonder what it looks like in Autumn? It ought to have a Latin name. All plants have Latin names. Animals, too. It's the magic language of humans. Nothing's really official, really *real,* unless you can call it to lunch in Latin. *Porcinus delicia Ameliae,* I should think. That sounds mostly Latin."

Something moved in the long meadows outside the Painted Forest. Something vast and heavy and curious. None of our merry band could hear it yet. But it had scented them, and loped hungrily across the grass under the stars.

Tamburlaine rolled over onto her stomach and kicked her feet up, waggling them back and forth. Thomas looked up through the shadowy baked-apple leaves at the great dinner plate of the moon—dinner plate and bread saucer, for here in this place not one moon but two rolled through the sky, one enormous and one small.

"You look fantastic," Tamburlaine giggled, the firelight kicking up glints in her wooden eyes.

"Do I?" said Tom Thorn softly, suddenly shy. "I'm so big. I never thought I could be so big. I'm starting to remember things, too. I feel all over pins and needles, like my heart's been squashed asleep since I was born."

"Me too," nodded Tamburlaine excitedly. "I remember hands carving me out of a big slab of wood. One set of hands were red, and the other set were yellow. The fingers swelled up to do the long parts of me, like legs and arms, and shrunk up for the delicate bits. My hair, my eyes, my fingernails. Spriggans can do that, I think. Get bigger or smaller. Maybe I was made by spriggans!"

Tom Thorn picked at the soft napkin-grass below their wonderful tree. He still couldn't remember his parents—his real parents. His troll parents. When he thought of his mother and father, Nicholas and Gwendolyn's faces still rose in his head like balloons. Scratch's dented bell was turned toward them, listening intently. But now and again it began to droop, falling toward the strange dreams of gramophones, where no one needs cranks and all records are smooth and scratchless as skin. Blunderbuss, being nocturnal, was quite busily awake, snuffling about in the roots of the Sunday dinner tree for cornbread crumbs.

"Top grub," the wombat snorted. "We'll live here now. Yes. Much better. Much *best*."

And all the while, through the wild, unsown fields beyond the trees, something crept closer, closer, holding its breath so as not to startle its prey too soon.

Tom Thorn's body could hardly keep awake—but his heart was running circles round his bones. The troll in his heart was now free. The troll inside was the troll outside—and it hadn't the foggiest what to do with itself.

One question burned through him like a wish.

"Tam—oh, Tam! What are we going to do tomorrow? Everything's changed, everything in the whole world and the world, too. There's no school, no after school, no houses or bookshelves or apartments. Where will we go? What will we do?"

But Tamburlaine was already asleep, Scratch leaned up against her shoulders like an exhausted puppy. Tom poked the last of the fire into sizzling pieces with one of Tam's daggers. He settled back against a log shaped like a snare drum, fallen from a marching band tree growing healthy and full of green tubas next to the Sunday dinner tree. What a strange girl his friend was! Strange enough when he thought she'd only remembered this place, dimly, the way he now remembered Apartment #7. But she'd made it up, all of it, in her head, and painted it alive. Being in the forest was like walking and talking and sleeping and eating in her mind.

With his last scrap of wakefulness, Tom stroked Blunderbuss behind her fuzzy pea-green and tangerine-colored ear. He remembered that yarn. Gwendolyn had used it to make the pom of his polar-bear-and-kangaroo hat. His hat! He rummaged in his satchel, ever so grateful he'd managed to drag it along with them. There it was, bunched up at the bottom. Tom Thorn pulled out the long, wonderfully knit hat and pulled it onto his head. It stretched, thank goodness, big enough to hold a troll's thick skull. He felt better at once.

"Buss, when you first woke up," Tom slurred dreamily, "you said a whole lot of silly things. Yes and No and then two Yeses and two Nos and a Maybe. Green. Pineapples. Gin. Who were you talking to?"

Blunderbuss nuzzled up next to her troll. She bit his great, gnarled hand softly and looked up at him with her mismatched button eyes.

"You, dearest darling delirious dimwit," she growled gently. "When Gwennie first made me you asked me all sorts of things. I answered as soon as I could, for crying out loud. You were only little. You said: *Will you be my best friend? Do you want some of my ham sandwich? Do you miss the Excellent Land of Wom? Are you quite vicious? Will you gobble up Nicholas if he yells at me again? If I sleep with the window open, will you run away in the night? Will you stay with me forever and never leave? What is your favorite color? What is your favorite food? What's* really *in your little barrel?*"

By the time Blunderbuss finished, Tom Thorn was having his first snore as a troll—a deep, blossoming, bassoon of a snore that, should you listen long enough, would become its own odd melody, a secret song of sleeping each troll makes but never hears.

Toward dawn, the great something that hunted our little band arrived at the edge of the Painted Forest. It stood up on its tiptoes and peered through the branches at the sleeping children and their cold, ashen fire. Even the scrap-yarn wombat had burrowed into the dirt to dream of biting the moon. It had hunted them through the night and felt quite self-satisfied, having been such an excellent and stealthy stalker that the sweet little things just snoozed away like nothing at all was the matter. Colored lights poured over their faces, dancing, flitting, batting at their cheeks like hot butterflies. Long shadows dropped their black bars onto the forest floor. Rustling sounds filled the air—the great something could not keep quiet forever. Curtains opened in the morning air, coffee trickled into cups, ten thousand fair folk stretched till their shoulders popped delightfully. Newspapers opened, birds peeked out from under gargoyles at the new day, and a river flowed round and round in a circle. Spires of wool and silk and bombazine and corduroy and gingham sparkled in the clean, fresh sun. This huge, happy hunter gurgled along its morning rituals, waiting for Thomas and Tamburlaine and Blunderbuss and Scratch to wake up and notice that they'd been captured by a city.

Pandemonium had come for them.

An Audience with the King

*In Which Thomas and Tamburlaine Summon a City,
Are Forced to Share Their Breakfast with a Most Unpleasant
King, and Learn Some Important Facts About Changelings,
Eggs, Monarchies, and the Great Chicago Fire*

Tom Thorn counted again.

Tamburlaine, Blunderbuss, Scratch: three. Plus himself made four. Four at *most*. But through his bleary, thousand-ton sleep—for trolls sleep the sleep of stones, and cannot be roused quickly nor safely without serious technical equipment—he counted four lumpy, blurry, splotchy shapes round the cold fire, which adding himself made five, and that in turn made his head hurt and sleep seem deeply preferable to whatever nonsense that other lumpy splotch turned out to be. Scratch sang out in a jazzy, swinging, somehow worried voice:

Morning bells are ringin', morning bells are ringin'
Ding, ding, ding-a-ling dong . . .

Thomas rubbed his heavy fists against his eyes. If he pressed hard enough, perhaps he could punch through his eye sockets and scrub off the back of his brain till it decided to be useful. He felt stiff all over; he could hardly straighten his neck. When he sat up his spine gave several frightful cracks like pebbles rolling down a cobblestone street.

"Careful," Tam called to him. "You were a rock all night."

"What?"

"Malachite, I think. You were green. Pretty!" chuckled Blunderbuss. "Is it fun being a troll yet?"

Thomas opened his eyes and took in breakfast, sunshine, and the King of the Fairies all at once. He promptly shut them again.

"Is that a Fairy?" he whispered.

"Yep," the wombat barked.

"He has a crown on."

"Yep," sighed Tamburlaine.

"And he's eating our food."

"Strictly speaking," said the King of the Fairies between mouthfuls, "I'm leasing you this food on a limited, bite-by-bite basis and a generous payment-deferral plan. I'd have thought someone would have told you about Fairy food. You always pay, lad. I'm not running a charity delicatessen."

Thomas tried again. The Fairy was clearly ancient and venerable. He hunched over a delicate pink-and-yellow teacup with gold plating on the handle and gnawed at a neat, crustless mustard, watercress, and sliced crocodile sandwich. His gray hair was caught up in several wild pigtails around two barnacled goat-horns. He had rheumy eyes and glasses as thick as beer-mug bottoms and three gold hoops in one ear. He wore a thick ermine cloak with fiery pheasant's feathers on the shoulders and a soft, flowing silver shirt, belted with a string of sapphires, over old, stained, fraying sailcloth trousers. Two iridescent wings jutted out of the back of his cloak, rimmed in gold, glittering as the sunlight made spinning violet prisms inside them. On his head tottered a crown of golden crab's claws. Each of the claws clutched a blue pearl the size of a walnut. He had the kind of dejected look of those who make a profitable career out of being disappointed in the world. He seemed particularly dissatisfied with the contents of his teacup.

"You lot are in the presence of Charles Crunchcrab the First, King of Fairyland and all her nations. Lucky you. Amn't I enchanting? Doesn't my wrinkly left elbow just *sparkle* with an effervescence of magic?"

"You have mustard on your shoe," observed Blunderbuss.

"Magic mustard, obviously!" King Crunchcrab shouted. "Look, I ought to arrest you two whining little miseries and your sideshow! You've traipsed in here, put your feet up, tracked mud and grime and Pan-knows-what all over my nice, neat country without so much as a *mind if we leave our great big gauche forest here?* A forest *I'll* have to look after, by the way! Feed it and walk it and make sure it gets proper schooling and introduce it to society! What will the other enchanted woods say? An upstart thicket with no manners and old Charlie to blame again! And to top it all you've dragged my capital city out of bed in the middle of the night and led it on a merry chase to . . . good gobs of grief, where are we?" The King of the Fairies looked around with a grimace of distaste. "South Avalon, by the looks. Well, at least you have terrible taste in counties. The geographical equivalent of a pub with its windows shot out, ferrets on the card tables, and a lady at the bar insisting that a cup of dirt is whiskey."

Tom Thorn frowned. His head banged and throbbed, trying to shake loose of his bones. "Your city? Dragged out of . . . what? What could we possibly have done to a whole city?"

Tamburlaine jerked her wooden head up and back, smiling sheepishly. She looked a little proud, really. He followed her gesture and saw the great polka-dotted, striped, patchworked towers of Pandemonium looming over the wild branches of the Painted Forest, for all the world like a cat waiting to be let in for fish. Pink birds flapped from rooftop to rooftop.

"Pandemonium, may I present my latest irritations? Irritations, Pandemonium." King Crunchcrab bowed with a roll of his eyes and a clatter of his teacup. "I'm afraid she gets carried away and runs off at the first scent of a likely hooligan. Pandemonium, I hope you're happy with yourself. Can't stay put, my old girl. Moves according to the needs of narrative. It's *tremendously* annoying. Once she's got a bit of story up her nose there's no talking to her. And here we are! Here we find our rundown, secondhand selves, one with the other. You came pole-vaulting into my business, thanks much, so I decided to come out and sit on yours. So, out with it. Who are you, what do you want?" Charlie Crunchcrab's voice turned delighted and positively joyful. "What kind of vicious, nasty, repulsive little *story* have you got crawling around in your socks?"

Tom and Tam looked at each other nervously.

"We're Changelings," Tam said, and her voice thrilled to say the word aloud, and to a stranger!

"Ugh!" grimaced the King. His wings fluttered in alarm. "*Ugh*. Disgusting! Watch your language! What a filthy mouth you have!"

"But it's true," Tom Thorn protested, stricken. How they had held on to that word, passed it between one another like a warm ember in winter. It was a good word! "We were born here and taken away to live with humans but we've come home! We're home now! It's all okay, everything that's ever happened in our lives is okay, because we're home *now*. We belong here."

"You don't," scoffed the King. "Changelings don't come *back*! It's absurd! There's a *system*, you know—a jolly good one! We fed it all the very best cream and licorice and spreadsheets. You're meant to stay Over There and grow up to be terrible tricksters! Politicians and actors and bankers and writers and advertising executives! Mythical beasts with horns and cologne! And human children stay here. It's a fair swap—that's the whole point. They get something; we get something. I daresay the humans would be at a loss for what to do with themselves if all their politicians were honest gentle-hearts and their actors prudent puritans, if their bankers only traded money that really exists and their writers only wrote about things that could really happen and advertisements only said *Ours Is a Very Nice Razor Blade But So Are All the Others*! If Changelings start coming back, well, it's like any sort of rubbish you try to return to the shop. What are *we* meant to do with you? Put you out with the scraps come Friday?"

"I'm not rubbish!" Tamburlaine gasped, sap-tears filling up her dark eyes.

King Charlie peered at her through his thick glasses. "Nawp, you're a bit of kindling who thinks she's too good for the fire. I've never seen a Fetch as old as you! Shouldn't you have blown up and started the Second Great Chicago Fire by now? Now, *that* was a Fetch. We did up a holiday for her when we heard. Night of the Flaming Cow. You should of seen the little-uns, all lit up with tails on and pots of glue under the tree! You ought to be ashamed of yourself, young lady. We gave you a job to do and you *shirked*."

"You should be!" cried Tam. "You are, *you're* rubbish, you're a rubbish King with a rubbish crown and you're shameful, shameful! I gave you sandwiches and I made you a forest and you shouldn't talk to me like I'm trash. Like I'm nothing!" Her voice dropped to a whisper and great golden gobbets of sappy tears splashed onto her knees. "Like I'm still nothing. I hate you. I hate you!"

Scratch scrambled between them, pointing his bell angrily at Charlie Crunchcrab. He set down his needle and spun his crank so hard it skipped with fury and the loose, easy voice of the man in the sky-blue suit came hurtling out tight and thin and vicious:

> *Oh, there's none so rare as can compare*
> *With Old King Cole and his fiddlers three*

"Oh, stop it," sneered the King. "Can't shame me, you silly old crapheap contraption." Scratch recoiled, his brass bell burning with shame. No one had ever called him a harsh name before. Tam always spoke softly to him. Crunchcrab stuck out his tongue like a little child. "I knew King Cole, and you lot aren't fit to choke on his cigar smoke. Nor me neither, come to it. Now stop your scubbling and explain yourself. You've been abroad so perhaps you don't know what a King is, but in Fairyland you have to do as I say or I'm allowed to thump you, banish you, or turn you into an even-toed ungulate." He ticked these punishments off on his fingers. "I'm feeling generous today, so I'd let you pick between pig, deer, or pygmy hippopotamus. I could execute you, too, but Pandemonium wouldn't speak to me for a month. She came all this way, after all. So speak up, you naughty matchstick girl. How did you and your troll fella get here?"

"Stop yelling at her," Tom snapped. He didn't mean to snap. He knew, somewhere, dimly, underneath his hunger and the rock-heavy troll sleep still hanging off his mind like a snoring monkey, that he ought not to snap at a King. He'd met a congressman once when his father was given a commendation, which was like a little King as far as he could tell. Nicholas Rood had told him very firmly, so that he could understand it: *None of your nonsense, now. Mr. Collins is a political man, and a political man was born sour and spends his whole life pickling.* He'd held Tom's little hand so tight he couldn't have misbehaved if he wanted to. "We came through her painting. She painted this whole forest on her bedroom wall—and a little bit on my bedroom, too—and taught me magic and we sort of jumped through the painting and came out here." He didn't want to say they'd been kidnapped. It would only complicate things. They belonged here. They had a right. And besides, if they'd known where his baseball was going, they'd have run straight into that wall themselves.

Charlie Crunchcrab snatched Tom's fingers, filthy with dried mud-paint from his night as a rock on the forest floor. The Fairy held them up close to his milky eyes. "It's on account of the eggs," nodded the King, as if it were all a bit of nothing.

"Eggs?" Tam squirmed her hands away from him.

"You used eggs to thin your paint and make it all nice and glossy, yes?" Tamburlaine nodded. "Well, good on you, brat-brains! Top of the blighted class! Every country is full of hazardous materials—gunpowder, toadstools, ambition, that sort of thing. But some sorts of things are perfectly polite and sociable Over There, while Back Here they act like hooligans and wreck up the place. Iron's one. Eggs are another. Oh, you can fry one up in a pan or whip it into a meringue and it's all well and good—but Fairies know eggs are nothing but trouble. An egg is just packed full of *might be*—might be a chicken, might be a goose, might be a dodo, might be a Wyvern, might be anything! And so are

Changelings. Just crackling with the *might be* of what they'd have been if they hadn't got bundled off. Put Changelings and eggs together and you get a wet mess. Once some Cornish mum brewed up a thousand eggs while her Changeling daughter watched, and at the end of it the little wretch jumped right in the pot and the real daughter popped out, boiled pink and giggling. Of course *Mummy* was pleased. But it was frightful embarrassing for us. That girl didn't know her *place*. She didn't respect the system. She kicked the Unseelie off their thrones with nothing but an albatross, a piece of penny candy, and an old boot. Took centuries to clean up after her."

"Sounds like my kind of girl," Blunderbuss piped up. "Systems are for punching and biting and sitting on till they cry double uncle with ice cream on top."

Charlie Crunchcrab stared at the scrap-yarn wombat as though she'd only just then appeared. He opened his mouth to tell her what he thought of stuffed wombats having the gall to pipe anything at him. Blunderbuss burped scruffily and snatched his sandwich out of his hand, wolfing it down in a single smacking bite.

"Save it, King Snotty the Rude. You can't shame me, neither. I've had knitting needles in places you don't want to know about. I'd say that Cornish chickie had the right idea. I'm sure we can snuff up an old boot somewhere."

A thoughtful look crossed the King's face. Each of his wrinkles seemed to hatch their own individual notions, and argued one with the other. Finally, he scratched his riotous hair and beckoned Tom and Tam to lean in. His voice was suddenly quite different, rough and old and kind.

"I've been right rough with you poor pips, ha'nt I? Can't blame me, I only do's I'm told. Pandy came running the minute she heard you land, so you hafta be worth a thing or two. And I think I know that thing. I'll make you a shake-on-it: Help me and I'll see you're set up nice. Digs in the city, clothes on your back, a table that's never empty. Not even a whiff of a thought of going back to middle school in that ugly old world you hopped out of—so clever of you to leg it before you had to get a job! Wanna be a Baron? Easy as squatting. Wanna find your parents in whatever troll-hole they hang a mailbox on? Good lad—I've got me a goat who knows every name in Fairyland. When I'm done no one'll ever guess you spent a silly little summer overseas when you were young. Ain't good at much, old Chuck, but I'm a good friend."

Tom and Tam exchanged glances. It was hard enough to say no to Grown-Ups when they weren't Kings. Scratch hissed a blast of static at the Fairy, whom he had not forgiven.

"What do you want us to help you with?" Tom said, knowing very well that it would be something big, something awful, something too much for him or his wombat or his friend. And he knew he would do it.

"S'easy, kitten. I don't want to be King anymore, is all."

CHAPTER XII
The Crunching of the Crab

*In Which Tom Thorn Stuffs His Stomach Most Satisfactorily and
Hears a Great Deal Concerning Current Events in Fairyland*

"Can't you just . . . not be King anymore? Quit? Quitting's called abdicating when a King does it. Can't you abdicate?" Tamburlaine's tears were quite dry now that they were discussing things she'd read about in newspapers. She looked at the King of Fairyland and all his nations with sharp, pointed interest.

"Oh, well, I never thought of that, did I, girlie? Just holler out NOT KING NO MORE at breakfast and put my feet up? OLLY OLLY OXEN FREE? What a good job I have a scholar like you to advise me."

"You don't have to be rude."

"But I *like* to be rude," Crunchcrab pouted. "Don't you?"

"Do I!" crowed Blunderbuss. She scratched one ear with her back paw. Crunchcrab ignored her. "I suppose where you come from a man can just up and decide he's not in the mood for Kinging. Meet a nice girl and skive off to the tropics. It don't work that way here, my duck-hearts. Once they've got you, you can't get free without leaving your wings at the door, if you get me. Fairy countries mate for life. Once you've won her heart, Fairyland is the truest girl you'll ever know. She'll never leave you till she buries you, and that's the truth. See, when you're King of Fairyland, it's more like a marriage than a political system. Queens, too. She . . . she chooses you. A crown's a hungry beast. She chooses you and you hafta dance with the realm what brung you. And good gravy, the dancing's good—for a while! But it always ends cock-eyed. Revolution, assassination, accident, slow poisoning, take your pick. Elderly and abed is nice work if you can get it but it makes a dull story so the world won't have it. No, Fairyland loves me, Pan knows why. I've tried to let her down nice. Had a herald read out a writ in the square and everything. I, KING CC NUMBER ONE, AM HIGH-TAILING IT ON THE TOUTE-SUITE SO BYE BYE NOW. No one paid me any mind. And the little things of a marriage, the little daily things you don't think much on before you're married, they didn't stop either. I still had to put roses in the vase in the third washroom on the fourth floor of the Briary to make the Summer come. I still had to make sure the moonflowers outside my second bedroom opened every night, had to watch every one bloom with my own eyes, or else there'd be drought in Weepwallow. Do you know, if I don't have the milk of a dun cow, liegelime cordial, and a short stack of magnanimillet flapjacks every morning for breakfast, the Greatvole of Black Salt Cavern will wake from her thousand-year slumber? No one else can do what I do. Not even for a day. And *then* comes Parliament, which I wouldn't wish on a dishrag. I do not like my life, and that's the bald truth. Being a King is too peculiar for the likes of me, and I don't sleep half as well as I did on my ferry, under the open stars. I was happy as a ferryman, back and forth over the same patch of water, back and forth every day. Good and clean and simple. Predictable. No voles, Great or Average. I'm good at carrying folk, you know. I was good at that." King Crunchcrab the First sniffled miserably. "I don't want to be King anymore and I don't want to die, and I want you to sleuth out how to do the one without the other. Seems you're good at wiggling in between the rules."

"No," said Tom Thorn sharply. "No, no, no. Nope. Absolutely not. Breakfast. Not you. Not this. Breakfast. Yesterday I had a bedroom and a clean pair of pants and a geometry quiz and cold beef sandwiches in the icebox. Today it's Kings and walking cities and apparently I turn into a rock when I fall asleep but at least I'm a pretty rock, I guess? And you have to eat flapjacks to keep a vole asleep."

"A Greatvole," the King corrected. "She's got obsidian teeth and a pelt of knives and she breathes mossfire. So I eat me flapjacks, yes I do, thanks plenty."

"Nobody can take this sort of thing three minutes after waking up with nothing to hold down his belly! Not even flapjacks! Nobody! Where did you get your tea and sandwiches? Tell me! Then we can talk about how a city gets up and walks and a King mopes around like he's got too much homework and what in the whole wretched world mossfire is."

We ought not to judge him. It was Thomas's first day as the owner of a troll-stomach. They are not like our polite, well-mannered human stomachs. A troll-stomach is hungry the way you and I are awake. It would not be itself if it were not hankering after a leg of panther or a silo of strawberry ice cream. A troll-stomach cannot be ignored or put off or bargained with. It cannot have just a little of something. A troll-stomach must swallow everything whole—and a troll-heart is no different.

"You oughtn't talk to a King like that, I don't think. . . ." said Tamburlaine. Whatever Crunchcrab said, she had read a great many plays in which King thundered and walloped and roared when they were displeased. Kings, she had always thought, were like thunderstorms. They came and went with a lot of fuss but there wasn't much difference between one and another. And every once in a while they tore your roof off and electrocuted your cat.

"It's all right," King Crunchcrab shrugged. "Everybody does. The chief virtue of a King is how long he can stand being yelled at by several people at once. Leastwise the way I do it."

"There's a tea-tray tree." Tamburlaine pointed off down a little woodland path. Between a wombat, a troll, and a Fetch, they'd stripped all the reachable branches of the Sunday dinner tree bare. She smiled a little. She could not help being proud of having put so many useful things in their forest.

Tom Thorn roused himself—so much more self than there ever had been before—and went scouting for the tree. Blunderbuss trundled after him.

"In the Land of Wom," she offered cheerfully, "we don't bother with Kings and Queens."

"Then who makes the rules?"

"The Tobacconist, of course. We all write down rules we like. *Look Both Ways Before Crossing a Wombat Bigger Than You. If You Find Mangoes, Make a Whistle Through Your Teeth So We All Can Have Some, Too. All Wombats Are Created Equal, Except for Gregory. No Wombat Shall Be Enslaved, Left Behind, Abandoned, or Unloved. Not Even Gregory. Kangaroos Must Pay a Five-Percent Tax on All Goods and Services on Account of Being Kangaroos.* That sort of thing. We take them all to the Tobacconist (whose name is Tugboat). She sits on her porch and chews them up good. Then she spits them at the window of her shop and whatever sticks to the wall across the way is law. It's very fair, and no one has to wipe Parliament off their shoes at the end of the day. She wears a powdered wig when she's at her chewing, so it's all nice and official. Wom is the envy of the democratic universe!"

Tom could hardly hear over the stampede of his stomach. His hunger pounded on his head with a terrible anger. How *dare* he make it wait five whole minutes between waking and breakfast? His stomach began to send wild and dreadful thoughts to his brain. The tea-tray tree was so far! Why, there was a perfectly good wombat right there!

"Oh! Hey! You put that thought away, sweetheart," huffed Blunderbuss. "I'm hungry, too. Hungry all the time. I've pondered plenty what troll tastes like. And gramophone. And Fetch. Braise or bake, hm? Kabob? Souffle? I can't help it and I'm not ashamed! But I'm two-thirds wool. I'd stick in you like bubblegum. Also I still own you. You'll learn how to drive your belly soon enough. No snacking on innocent marsupials while you have your lessons."

"Aren't wombats herbivorous?" Tom frowned into the woods.

"I'll herbivore your left foot if we don't find that breakfast bush quick," Blunderbuss growled.

Finally, Tom saw the tea-tray tree. It jingled with tinkling coffee cups and teapots and jam jars and milk jugs and sugar bowls dangling from silverware branches. Clotted cream sparkled like dew on shining silver tea trays stretching to reach the sun. But it was only a tea-tray tree; it had no tea at all for him, no food, only china and silver and glass. The cups hung dry, the jam jars gleamed as clean as washing day. But there, there! All round the tablecloth-roots sprouted soft, thick mushrooms, mushrooms that looked quite a bit like mustard, watercress, and sliced crocodile sandwiches. He fell to, ripping them up with both hands, searching for more, his stomach quieting at last, but grumpily, and under protest.

"We've only been here a moment and we're in trouble, Buss," he said when, for that brief, wonderful time after he has just eaten, a troll is satisfied. "I'm afraid. A King is much worse than a teacher or a principal. He just wants to use us up like ballpoint ink. What should I know about un-Kinging somebody? And . . . and . . . it's no better here. What if I'm still the strange one, even when I'm home?" His throat got thick. "This is supposed to be my home."

"Everybody's strange," Blunderbuss said, pawing the sandwich-mushrooms with her paws. "Everybody's strange everywhere. Most of the trick of being a social animal is pretending you're not. But who do you fool? Nobody worth talking to."

When the wombat and her troll returned to the Sunday dinner camp, Crunchcrab was already partway through a long, hearty complaint. He groused like a grandpa, and the morning was filled with birdsong and the slurping of the King's tea. A long thread dangled from his cup. The tag read: *The Elephant's Fiery Heart.*

"Oh, it was fine at first! After the Marquess took her snooze, the Stoat of Arms came to see me down on the shores of the Barleybroom. Now, the Stoat of Arms is just about the most disagreeable creature ever born. I don't like to use words like varmint, but there it is. There's no talking to it. Them. That chatterbox zoo on eight legs. Imagine a unicorn and a little human girl juggling a mess of silver stars and black cockerels and sunflowers between them with a mean little Fairy on top like a cherry on a sundae, all riding on a palanquin drawn by two giant Stoats called Gloriana and Rex. They all talk at the same time and you can't pry one off the other with a crowbar because underneath? They're all the same animal! Even the sunflowers. Reasonably sure the royal robes are all ermined up because some poor sod couldn't stand the Stoat and skinned one a few eons back. Can't say I blame him. Fairyland wanted me, the Stoat bleated, and did itself a stupid little dance which I guess is a necessary part of coronating. And the unicorn was wearing *her* hat. All big and beautiful and black-like, it was. And when the hat saw me it shivered and swallowed itself up and turned into the claws you see clamped on my dumb skull here and now. There were only about five Fairies left back then. The others ran when they heard the Stoat of Arms coming for them. Guess I was too old to be fast. Won't tell you about the coronation. That's private. Between a man, or a lady, and his nation. So what did I get in exchange for my ferry? Rubbish with two helpings of ish, is what! A palace full of dresses and tiaras and angry, hurt people who had a beef with someone I didn't know to shout at. And the Stoat of Arms kept at me. Gloriana said: *You gotta learn to talk better! Talk nice like the lords and ladies in the pictures! Rex whacked me with his tail. A King's verbs agree in number with their nouns! A King doesn't end his sentences in prepositions! Those miserable black chickens clucked all over me like they were so high and fine. A King pronounces all his consonants CRISPLY and CLEANLY, not just the ones he likes best! And never says 'ain't'! The little girl in her ugly little dress would rap my finger with the silver stars: Now walk like you're in a play about being a King! Now, you don't bow to that man, even if he has a lovely coat on; he bows to you! And that rotten unicorn, who I hate more than hangovers, wouldn't hardly let me sneeze the way I liked: No more drinking whistle-gin, it's fine claret from the Infinite Cellar from now on!* And all the while doing stupid little stoat-dances every time it wanted to say something, because Stoats talk mostly by dancing because they are the worst. I did it all. Because Fairyland asked me to, and curse me but I do love her. But then, *then*, they came back. We came back. Everyone. The Fairies. I don't know what happened and I don't want to.

They came vomiting in like a rainbow that wouldn't shut up. Wings everywhere. And all of a sudden, I was Kinging wrong. Were there any wars? Any vanished counties? Anything left of the Marquess's meddling? No? No! But I, I had bungled it. The Seelies and Unseelies screeched at me day and night. It wasn't *Fairy*land anymore, they hollered. It was RiffRaffLand, RabbleLand, AnyOldSlobLand, EverybodyLand. Back to the Old Ways, they cried. Did I even *remember* the Old Ways? Well, I did, and they were trash. Nothing but stepping on necks and laughing while we did it, gobbling up the world and leaving nothing for anybody without wings. An empire! That's what they wanted. Just the way it was when they were in charge and no one could talk back. You'd think they'd remember what happened the last time, on account of what happened last time was they all got turned into rakes and shovels and typewriters and pitchforks for about a hundred years, but no, no, give them a Proper King and a Proper Kingdom or they'd hang me from Groangyre Tower. Well, I ain't brave. Never said I was. The Stoat of Arms did a stupid little dance of dread and defeat and I shuffled along, too. I did my best. I commanded that Criminal and Revolutionary be made Official Professions all over Fairyland. I thought somebody would come and knock it all down. But it keeps going on and I want to go back to being a man on a boat, please. I'm a bad Fairy. I thought I was a decent King. Middling, anyway. Average. But I'm a bad Fairy. They all say so. And every morning they send an assassin round at eight o'clock sharp in case I want to give it all up. His name is Simon. We get on quite well. Has a sense of humor, my Simon. He poisons my jam in alphabetical order. Arsenic on Monday, belladonna on Tuesday, cyanide on Wednesday. . . . I haven't had jam in five years."

"But your majesty," Tom Thorn said, trying to be gentle, as the old Fairy clearly needed to get a lot off his chest, "what can we possibly do to help? We've only just got here. We don't even know which way the sun comes up."

"Any way it likes, I expect," shrugged Crunchcrab. "But of course you don't know! You haven't got a crowbar for my crown in your back pocket. I know that. I'm not addled, boy. Nobody knows. Except the Spinster. And she won't tell. Mostly because we can't find her to ask. But you'll find her for me, won't you? There's a good boy. And girl. And gramophone. And whatever the yarn-pile is."

CHAPTER XIII
UNHAPPY FEET

*In Which Thomas and Tamburlaine Are Introduced
to Pandemonium, Fitted for New Shoes, and Meet a Gang
of Changelings, While a Walrus Gets a Nasty Cough*

Any city looks a bit like its mother and father. If you peer closely at New York, you will see that the old girl has Dutch ears and English eyes. London cannot hide her Roman nose—and Rome has a way of laughing that is awfully Greek. This is why you may see streets in one city with just the same name as the streets in another, and even cities with identical names, like two Joshuas or Amys in the same class. To be a city is to belong to a family, each taking after another, remembering fondly their old grandfathers and great-aunts, all the way back to the very first hut and fire and lonely cave with horses painted on it that had no name at all. In one city, if you are very clever and sneaky, you can spy out the whole world it belongs to, just as you can spy out a few thousand years of singing and dancing and making bread and putting babies to bed in any single person's face.

I tell you this so that, when I say Pandemonium looked just like Fairyland, you will know what I mean. (Traditionally, all cities are politely referred to as "she," though the actual situation is somewhat more complicated. As we should not like to look up a city's underskirts, we shall hew to tradition.) Pandemonium is the Capital of Fairyland, as a large Wyverary once informed us. But more than that, she is a miniature, moving, hyperactive copy of Fairyland itself, made and sewn and stitched and tied all of cloth, of wool and silk, of yarn and ribbon, of batting and bunting.

And she is rather prone to indigestion. You really cannot see it unless you are a roc or a pterodactyl or some other beast who does not need much air and can fly horribly high. Let us pretend we are pterodactyls! Look! There, in the northwest quarter, you can see all the crinoline apartments and customhouses and concert halls are orange and red and chocolatey brown, just as in the north and west of Fairyland the Autumn Provinces are forever colored in October's fire. In the southern part of the city, clusters of houses with bombazine chimneys make a stumpy, smoking forest that looks so very like Skaldtown. You must squint your eyes in the Seresong District, for nothing lives there that is not covered in organza origami flowers and birds and butterflies, in every shade of pink, of green, of violet, of gold, just as the Springtime Parish will scald your eyes with happy greens if you do not wear your glasses. (Only beware, the butterflies are quite vicious, being an ancient nation of warriors without mercy.)

From up here, we can see the Barleybroom River flowing in a circle around Pandemonium. Can you believe it was once plain, blue water?

Such strange days! Now it is tea again, afloat with sugar lumps and lemon peels. Wyverns and dragons and griffins and hippogriffs and Fairies dive and flutter down into the city like great bright feathery bombs, scattering to Pandemonium's four labyrinthine districts: Idlelily, Seresong, Hallowgrum, and Mallowmead. Though folk come and go, are coming and going even now, even as we come, something like ten thousand souls live in the satin and brocade and calico towers, walk the muslin alleys and cashmere boulevards, and cheer when the black lace streetlamps flare up with white oilskin lanterns at dusk. The highest point is Groangyre Tower, home of the Royal Inventors' Society; the lowest is Janglynow Flats. Some common imports include: grain, wishing fish, bicycle parts, children, sandwiches, brandywine, silver bullets—and Changelings.

All this Tom and Tam and Blunderbuss and Scratch saw as they left the Painted Forest—though not from an angle quite so wonderful as ours. Let us fold away our pterodactyl wings and hide them for a later evening—I promise we will strap them on again! No, Tom and Tam and Blunderbuss and Scratch saw Pandemonium from her streets, quite dwarfed by her shining, fuzzy, ropy buildings soaring up to tufted, ice-cream-colored cupolas in the sunshine. They walked very quietly, in the company of the King, for though they had grown up in Chicago, a very grand place indeed, Chicago does have rather fewer centaurs than Pandemonium, and no turquoise rhinoceroses at all. Blunderbuss capered happily through the avenues, giddy to find herself a scrap-yarn wombat in a scrap-yarn city.

It is very boring to follow people all the way from interesting place to interesting place. They do take so terribly long to do it, and we are important people with busy eyes, so I shall hurry our motley band along until they arrive where King Crunchcrab intended: Bespoke Espadrille's Shoe Imporium. The Imporium was a sweet little shop nestled in fashionable Little Buyan, in the Hallowgrum Quarter. It had just the sort of littleness and sweetness that whispers: *I am very expensive and exclusive; in fact, there is only room for yourself and Mr. Espadrille, for we do not want any gawkers peeking in at the wonders which are yours alone.* It whispers such things, but everyone in Pandemonium ignores it and piles into the Imporium till the windows are full of arms and stocking feet and the cash register quits in a huff.

But not today. Today only a few boys and girls in rags lag around outside the shop—though rags in Pandemonium are quite fine, cut sneakily with delinquent scissors from the back corners of buildings and dug up from the glimmering streets, leaving potholes like groundhog dens. The kids stood in front of the window, passing a bit of green Fairy flame from hand to hand, making it get up and dance in the shape of a ballerina, a witch, a gondolier, a toad. They giggled. One looked a little like Max, Tom Thorn thought. Taller, perhaps.

"Hullo," said Tom. He put out his hand to shake. "What's your name?"

The oldest girl flicked her eyes from him to the King. She curtseyed a few times, awkwardly, like a broken doll.

"You shouldn't be talking to us, Mr. Friendly," the boy who looked like Max hissed, snapping his hand shut and extinguishing the green flame. "We're Changelings. You don't want to be seen getting chummy with the wrong sort. Which is us." He curtseyed, too. But both of them were watching Tamburlaine as they spoke, as though they weren't talking to Tom at all. He felt quite invisible.

The boy who looked like Max started to say something else, but he was interrupted by a great lumpy shape in the doorway of Bespoke Espadrille's Shoe Imporium—that of Mr. Bespoke Espadrille himself. He was rather more walrus than man, with great long tusks carved with scrimshaw and long, shining quills of golden hair on his brown muzzle. But despite his great, drooping head, he had a man's thick arms and stout legs, and over his chest—which might have been walrus or human, for both can grow a majestic belly if they try hard and work at it every day—he wore a cuirass all of shoe buckles. The buckles shone, perfectly polished, silver, brass, ivory, gold, bronze, tin. Below this ballooned bright hot-green pantaloons, stuffed into the least interesting shoes. Mr. Bespoke Espadrille, the greatest cobbler in a hundred Fairylands, wore the plainest shoes imaginable. They weren't Fairy-like at all! Tom could not really hide his disappointment. His father might have worn such shoes and not counted himself the least bit unusual at the office. Yet even Tamburlaine could tell they were completely, breathlessly perfect. Their black leather gleamed softer than clouds, their laces braided from the hair of some exquisite animal that had never known a late fee at the library. Their heels looked as though they could stomp out injustice, no matter how great, and tucked into the top of each one gleamed a single blue-silver sixpence piece like a tiny mirror.

Mr. Espadrille let out a bubbling, grumbling, booming mutter of a grunt. The boys and girls by the window had not moved. They didn't look twice at Tom—what's another troll in Pandemonium? But their eyes had hit on Tamburlaine like darts finding home. Bespoke had her in his sight, too, and did not let her go. Tam blushed, a mahogany color moving across her dark, carved cheeks, and Tom saw in a moment that he was not strange in this place, not really. But she was. He put his arm around her. His troll-arm. His strong arm. His mother's jewelry tinkled comfortingly against her wooden spine.

"Well, don't stand there in the street," said Mr. Espadrille, who, Tom suspected, did not know how to curtsey. As they walked through his door, bells jingled, and buckles jingled, too, as King Crunchcrab corralled the walrus-creature into a rough hug, squeezing him fiercely.

"You moron," Bespoke scolded warmly. "Your boots are half worn through. Is that your third pair? If you don't stop it I'll beat you with my best stilettos. You know how dangerous a worn-out shoe is. Who brought you up?"

"I brought myself up, you pinheaded pinniped. Never you mind my shoes. I know what I'm doing. I'm here for my little friends. They'll need shoeing."

Bespoke disentangled himself and looked over Tom and Tam with his walrus-eyes. The shop was neat as can be, glittering single shoes on display, long blue and green and gold couches for trying things on, the walls decorated with thousands of shoelaces woven into a thatch.

"What are they wanting? Glass slippers? Red-hot iron oxfords? Flats to keep you dancing for a decade? Impertinent mules that think they know what's best for you? I've got them in ruby or silver. Winged slingbacks guaranteed to outfly good news and bad? Thousand-league galoshes? Steel-toed hip-waders made from genuine first-molt rubber-fiend skin? I've got them all, my lovelies. After all, what is a body without its feet? And feet, you must admit, are very poorly designed. Such little, soft things to carry you through your lives! Of course, all shoes are magic—they get you where you're going and tell you where you've been. They tell your secrets, can't hold their tongues a bit. A man in finery whose shoes are caked in mud and cracked with use"—Bespoke glared at King Crunchcrab—"is surely selling something. And a lady in rags with jeweled heels, her toes clad in sapphires with a silver tongue as curved as the lip of a sleigh? Well, she's probably a thief, but she might be a witch. Either way, best leave her be. My shoes, however, are better than the rest. I am a Skokhaz, and my people are great Wizards of the Wardrobe. My mother knew the devilry of dresses, my father the hocus-pocus of hats. And I am a sorcerer of shoes. My shoes are sought like talismans! And why?"

"Why?" asked Tom, quite caught up.

"Because they *know* that they are shoes, my boy. They know they have a purpose and they are eager to accomplish it. They have ambitions, aims, ardor! They are the most shoely shoes that will ever shoe, and as you are a friend of Charlie's, I shall shoe for you."

King Charlie looked at his feet. Even his wrinkles were embarrassed. "'Fraid not, Bessie, old boy. They're . . . they're Changelings. They just need their slips." He spread his hands at Tom and Tam apologetically. "It's the law, you know. *All Changelings are required to wear identifying footwear.* Didn't make it; don't like it. But if I don't abide I get . . . I get *ailments*. My fingernails turn black and my hair falls out and Simon gets to chain me in the basement until I come to my senses." He waggled his fingertips. Six of his fingernails were dark as spilled ink. "I try and all. I do."

Tamburlaine patted his shoulder. His wings fluttered weakly. "It sounds awful, being King," she said sympathetically. "I'm sure you do your best."

"Oh, that's not part of the King business." Crunchcrab shook his head morosely. "That's their bit of fun. My Parliament. To keep me in line. Rather have a Magna Carta, myself. They wouldn't have it. So last season."

And as they watched, his pinkie finger, nicely clean and pale, began to darken. "Oh, no, no, I've been away too long," Charlie Crunchcrab wailed. "I'm not allowed to wander. Bessie'll look after you, he will, I promise. I have to go, I have to go or it's the basement for me. You haven't seen it. I can't go back! Help me, kittens. Find the Spinster—she'll know what to do. She has to! I'm sorry! For everything that's bound to happen!"

The King ran from Bespoke Espadrille's Shoe Imporium with tears in his eyes, up the gabardine boulevard and away. Bespoke shook his walrus-head and bent behind his counter, rummaging in the shelves. He came up with four silver-and-black devices like fish on a string. Tom laughed. He knew those very well! It was the sort of measuring contraption he had to wedge his stocking foot into whenever he outgrew the shoes Gwendolyn bought him last month. It was called a Brannock. This one had curving silver wings on its sides and scalloped silver seashells on either end. The middle part was all shimmering black with silver writing on it.

"Don't even think about it," Blunderbuss barked. "Wombats don't need shoes! Or want them! My paws are too magnificent for your little machine, anyway." The walrus cobbler shrugged and put two of the Brannocks back under his counter.

"I don't usually do this sort of work," Bespoke sighed. "It's a dirty business. But if Charlie says I'm to look after you, I'll hold my nose." He laid down the Brannocks at their feet.

"But why?" asked Tamburlaine. "Why do we have to wear 'identifying footwear'?"

"My dear girl, do you recall that I said shoes get you where you're going and tell you where you are? It was only a moment ago, but there's been a spot of excitement since." Tom Thorn nodded. "Well, a Changeling's shoes . . . are the other way round. They make sure you don't go anywhere at all. Make sure you don't float off back to your own world or go gallivanting about kicking up trouble and stories and quests. Humans do have a hankering for that sort of thing. And so that no one mistakes you for . . . for one of us. But you! You're not human! You are one of us! I don't see why I should have to do it. Who ever heard of a troll in Changeling shoes? Or a Fetch." He said it as though it was a naughty word. "Forgive me, little sapling. I have a filthy old mouth, everyone says so."

Tam shrugged. "It's what I am."

Bespoke laughed. "I forget how plainspoken you hardwoods can be. Yes, dear, but in polite circles Fetches refer to themselves by the sort of wood they're chopped out of. You can call yourself Walnut if you like. It's a perfectly respectable species."

"You mean there are others? Like me? Fetches? Walnuts?"

"Of course—the spriggans make them by the cord every Autumn, which is every day in spriggan country. I had such a nice set of Tulip-wood twins in the other week for holiday clogs. Now, I *am* sorry, I am, but please put your feet here and here, my lambs."

They did, slotting their heels at the same moment into the shells of the Brannocks. "If your shoes are ambitious," said Tam thoughtfully, "and know where they're going, can't you make them so they know how to get to the Spinster? Whoever she is. I think the King forgot to tell us that bit."

Bespoke Espadrille adjusted the sliders. Tom looked down and read the silver writing on the Brannock. Curling letters arched over the toe slider, spelling out the Cobbler's Creed: *Wheresoever I Shall Go, Bear Me Thence Without Blisters or Sorrow.* Below this, he read the measurements marked out on the black footpad from smallest to largest: *Cloudcuckooland, Under Hill, Under Dale, the Road Most Traveled By, Through the Wasteland, After Love, Far to Go Before All's Done, Wanderlust, Around the World Seven Times, Back of Beyond, Never Resting Long.* Tom Thorn's foot, a troll's foot now, stuck out quite far beyond the end of the Brannock. He waggled his toes in his school socks, which were stretched so badly the weave had split in two places. Tam's feet just barely touched *Far to Go Before All's Done*. She fidgeted in her lap.

Bespoke walked over to the left-hand shoelace wall. He tugged on one of the laces and the wall popped open like a Summer window, revealing bolts of shining leather and goatskin and rabbit fur in every color. He stroked the golden quills on his great chin with one hand and tugged on his tusk with the other. "Can't do that if I don't know her address, my loves. I've never met the Spinster myself. She doesn't go in for fancy shoes. She's an old woman possessed of great powers—but aren't all old women possessed of great powers? Occupational hazard, I think. She's a Strega with a terrible gaze. I have heard through the textile underground that she always wears blue. Her curses are black and strong as bulls and they never end. Usually a curse gets bored and wanders off after awhile. But not the Spinster's hexes. They show up to work first thing and go home last. Used to see her in the city buying bread and onion dip and crow-eyes and whatnot, but she disappeared. Spinsters do that sometimes. Hole up with their cats and their knitting somewhere and complain about children playing on the lawn. Wearing *sensible* shoes, can you imagine? Poor Charlie. He must think she can curse him back to his ferry. But he doesn't want one of *her* curses. Not really. The last soul she slapped about never saw the light of day again. He asks everybody he meets, you know. Every new face. *Find the Spinster and I'll give you anything you want.*"

Bespoke Espadrille selected a bolt of deep, dark green leather and one of plummy purple, along with bright, puffy sky-blue rabbit pelt. "This one, this, and that," he said loudly. Perhaps there was an assistant in the back. Blunderbuss snuffled at the fur.

"We must find her," Tom Thorn said.

"We promised," Tam nodded.

But Bespoke was not listening. He'd sunk his head into his great chest, deep in thought.

"I can't let you leave without shoes," he sighed. "The Court would have my tusks. But I can do you something. I can. It's not much, but I'll sleep better."

The walrus-cobbler coughed. He coughed again. His throat rumbled, a deep, belly-cough, the kind you get at the end of a cold, the kind that means to bring everything up so you can be rid of it at last. He coughed one last time and up out of his gullet came a pair of pretty lavender tongue-and-buckle shoes lined with black fur and close behind them, two of spring green. They clattered onto the floor and Bespoke started up his rattly coughing again. This time, a pair of kelly-green wingtips popped free of his mouth, and then bright-violet loafers. They joined their fellows on the ground. With a final, satisfied cough, the great walrus leapt up—higher than they would have thought he could—and stomped on all four lovely shoes, splintering them to bits.

Then he knelt at their feet and tapped the Brannocks with his long brown fingers. "Up you get," he barked.

The silver Brannocks began to wriggle and writhe. They shaped themselves round Tom's and Tam's feet. The silver crawled up over their toes and clasped their ankles. The metal was cool and tingly, like soda pop. They squirmed and exchanged worried glances.

"No dawdling, now," admonished the cobbler.

And the silver settled down against their skin and became, as fast as you please, two pairs of sensible shoes with strong, flat soles, the deepest green and purple dyes can dream of. They were something like mary janes, except that they seemed to yearn to run, which yearning no mary jane would admit to.

Bespoke showed them a long mirror. Tom Thorn stared at himself. He hadn't seen his troll-face yet. He hadn't had a chance. He was glorious. Bits of amethyst and emerald showed through his skin at his elbows, his collarbone, behind his ears. His nose arched and jagged like a sea crag, his eyes had grown huge and deep and soft. His hair hung down under his knit hat, trailing over the jewels of his jacket, mossy strands against golden chains. He looked like himself.

Scratch shook his bell with delight and dropped his needle:

> *Those weary blues*
> *Can't get into my shoes*

"There," Bespoke Espadrille sighed. "Now they're the third pairs I've made for you."

"Why does that matter?" asked Blunderbuss, who had gotten quite bored, as she neither wanted nor needed such silly things as shoes.

"You're going to have to get your savvy on right quick, the bunch of you. Don't go around asking questions that make it perfectly clear you're tourists without maps. Haven't you ever seen a newsreel? Just last week some German milkmaid wore through three pairs of iron shoes trying to find the man she loved, and she didn't find him till the second-to-last pair fell apart. You have to wear through three pairs of shoes to get anything done. Everyone knows that. Once you wear through the third pair, whatever story you've got yourself into has to hurry up and finish its business so the next one can get going. Call it a head start."

He sniffed, and tears filled his great, liquid walrus eyes. "That's why my friend Charlie won't change his shoes. He's on his third pair, and when they're done, he's hoping he will be, too."

Tom and Tam left the Imporium. They looked north, toward the Financial District, and south, toward Riddle Row, though they had not the first idea what they were looking at.

"Well," Blunderbuss rumbled, "what about the Bingo parlor? Old ladies love Bingo. Do they have Bingo here? In the Land of Wom—"

"Psst," interrupted a little voice. One of the Changelings that had been playing with green fire outside Bespoke's shop whispered at them from an alley. She had warm brown eyes and red hair and wore fifty or sixty paisley cravats tied into a long scarf that turned into a dress somewhere along the way.

"I know," she said. "I know where you can find the Spinster. Give me something nice and I'll tell you."

"We don't have anything," Tom sighed.

But Scratch leapt forward, eager to please, to fix what he could fix. His crank spun and his sky-blue voice played softly:

> *Hush little baby, don't say a word*
> *Daddy's gonna buy you a mockingbird. . . .*

"Oh, that is nice!" cried the redheaded girl, clapping her hands. "Come on, then!" She took up Tamburlaine's wooden hand in hers.

"Where are we going?" said Tam shyly.

"Don't worry. I'm your friend. You're one of us." She glanced down at their shoes. "Sort of, anyway. So I can show you our secrets. I have to, actually. It'd be cruel to let Changelings loose in the city all alone.

Like letting puppies play in a fox den. We wouldn't do that to you. I stayed to collect you once you had your anchors." The shoes, again. The urchin was wearing rose-colored shoes not so different from theirs, though hers looked painfully tight, as though she'd long ago outgrown them. "Come *on*! Would it mean anything if I told you where I was taking you? I could say we're headed to Atlantis by way of Interstate 5 and that'd make as much sense as anything. I'm taking you to friends." She laughed a little. "You know what a friend is, right?"

"What's your name?" Tom Thorn asked, determined to get something out of her before they dashed off with another stranger.

"Penny," she said, and gave them a brilliant, dazzling smile. "Penny Farthing, at your service."

THE GIRL WHO LOST OMAHA

In Which Events Have Consequences

Far away from Pandemonium, a woman is crying. Her name is Susan Jane. It's a very Grown-Up name, and she's never liked it very much, but then, Susan Jane is a Grown-Up. I've not told you her name before now because most children who are not secretly trolls do not call their parents by their Grown-Up names. But you have met her before.

Susan Jane's sister and her husband make tea and hold on to her and then swap places. Their eyes are so red, poor dears.

"What's happened to her? Where can she have gone? It's been three days—where is my little girl? How can she just disappear like that? Just—gone one morning like the sun erased her?" Susan whispers. Her dog, a small, amiable soul who doesn't know how to make a single thing better but won't stop trying, licks her limp hands.

"She'll come home, darling," whispers her husband, who is called Owen. "She has to. She's so clever, you know. She's all right. Somewhere, she's all right. I came home, after all, against the odds. Remember?"

Susan Jane reaches out for her sister. Their dark eyes lock, the same eyes. The late afternoon Nebraska sun peeks in to see if it can be of any use.

"Oh, Margaret. Tell me September will find her way back to us. Tell me and I'll believe it."

Aunt Margaret drinks her tea. She can't bring herself to answer.

It's not always such fun, being a narrator. We must stand by and say nothing so very often, even when we know the very thing that would dry every eye and wake up the house again.

I'll put a new kettle on for all of us. Hold tight, Susan Jane. Don't cry, Owen. Hush, now.

CHAPTER XIV
THE CHANGELING ROOM

In Which Tom Thorn Meets a Certain Someone,
Finds a Secret Hideout, and Suffers a Calamity of the Foot

Penny Farthing led them through corkscrew streets the color of pumpkins and closes where tassels sprouted up in the dark like mushrooms. They ran past doors boarded up with bolts of sailcloth and windows both broken and whole. No one looked at them as they ran. Everyone seemed to try very hard not to look, in fact. A lady Fairy with long black wings spattered with colors like an opal whipped her head toward them once, and followed them with a hungry glare, but did not come near. They came nearer and nearer to the center of the city. Penny did not falter once, turning this way and that without once stopping to get her bearings. Finally, she brought them up short in a tiny dead-end cotton alley. The service doors of a little hotel would have emptied onto the pillowstones of the street, but they'd been covered over, rather sloppily, with taffeta bricks. A funny brass stump rose up in the middle of the street, a bit like a fire hydrant. It had big satin rope hoops hanging from it and said TIE UP HERE on its brass cap. An old nag horse with white fur and a black mane had been lashed to the hitching post and left blinking sleepily in the sun.

"All trails lead to ice-cold Coca-Cola," Penny whispered. From within the brass hydrant a voice whispered back:

"Are your whiskers, when you wake, thicker than a two bit-shake? Burma-Shave!"

Penny Farthing grinned again and, still holding on to Tam's hand, jumped up into the air—and straight into the ear of the old nag. Somehow, when Penny jumped, the ear got ever so much bigger, as big as a door, and before they could wonder at it, they were through, and standing not inside a horse, but in a cozy little room.

It looked like nothing so much as a dressing room in back of a theatre. Mirrors ringed with big lightbulbs dotted the walls, bright rags and feathers and coats and dresses and half-patchworked hats lay on tables and chairs everywhere. Nothing matched, furniture came from wherever it was found, a red carousel bench here, a polka-dotted fainting couch with one leg missing there, a striped writing desk in one corner, a glass sewing table in another. All over the walls were concert programs and menus and train schedules and angry, snippy notes in fine handwriting. *Anna, if you let the fire go out before dawn one more time I shall turn you into a musk ox! Bernard, you cow, can't you remember a simple thing like sparrow hearts at market? Report to the parlor at teatime for punishment! Delia, Master Bluebell demands that you dance for company this evening. Do try not to be awful at it.*

And sprawled on every bench and couch and stool and chair and scrap of floor were twenty or so human children, some, like Penny, older than Tom and Tam, almost grown, some much younger, laughing and whispering. Some even smoked odd little cherry-red cigarettes and drank green and shimmery things from square bottles.

Everyone fell silent when they saw the newcomers. One little boy, hardly old enough to dress himself, squealed in panic and hid under the fainting couch.

"Oh, Herbert, silly, don't be afraid!" Penny hushed the boy. "They're like us! Changelings! I know they look like Fairy folk, but the King himself brought them to Bessie for their shoe fitting. They're one of ours. They won't bite or tell on us."

"I bite," the scrap-yarn wombat said helpfully. "But only when I really want to."

At the sound of Blunderbuss's fuzzy voice, Herbert peeked out from under the couch. He took in her pea-green and tangerine ear, her blue-and-green striped belly, her mismatched eyes and squealed again. He barreled out into the open again and fell onto the wombat in joy, squeezing her and hugging her. Tom watched with some satisfaction, as she'd done much the same to him when they met—and a little sadness, for he'd been too busy trying his teeth on magic to give her the hugging he ought to have done. He would, when he got a moment to breathe, he promised himself.

"Easy on the squishables, little monkey!" the wombat huffed. "In the Land of Wom it's considered polite to challenge a wombat to a duel before you throttle them like that!" But she seemed pleased anyway.

"Welcome to the Changeling Room," Penny Farthing said, with not a little bit of pride. "We made it, it's ours. Of course Changelings made a lot of things in Pandemonium, but this one is our favorite because it only loves us. Fairylanders aren't allowed. Bayleaf—the tall chap there? Remembered some old nonsense from before he was taken and made us great beefy passwords that Fairies could never guess. This is where we come when we're not . . . occupied."

"But they *are* Fairylanders," said Bayleaf. "That one's a troll. And the other's a . . . matchstick girl or something. But they're not Changelings. Did you hit your head?"

Penny squared her feet. "They are! Come on, don't be thick. Can't you guess?" But he could not. Penny Farthing, by great feat of will, kept herself from bouncing up and down and gloating out loud. "They're the *other ones*. Goods exchanged! Born here, dropped off in our cradles like the Tuesday post. We always thought they existed! Now we know! And *they* know how to get back where they came from! It's only the best thing that's ever happened, you know."

But the rest of the Changelings did not cheer. They stared at Tom and Tam—and it was not a very nice stare. It was the stare an urchin gives to a child with a fur hat in a sweet shop who has gotten to pick out a whole cake for herself every week of her life.

"Hullo," Tom Thorn said. No one answered. A little child not much bigger than Herbert reached up and poked Tom's arm as if to see whether he was real. He cleared his throat. "Where are we, actually?" Tom asked. "Can't Fairies go anywhere? It's their city, after all."

"That's the clever bit," Bayleaf piped up. He had a shock of dark hair that stuck up every which way and wore at least three waistcoats. "This is like . . . a hidden pocket in a suit jacket, or a hollow cane. It's in Pandemonium, but it isn't Pandemonium."

Scratch wound his crank and the room jumped at the sound of his scratchy, sweet voice:

> *I gave my love a cherry*
> *That had no stone*

I gave my love a chicken
That had no bone
I gave my love a story
That had no end . . .

"Yes, yes!" Penny laughed. "We took out the stone and squirreled into the empty space in the big cherry of Pandemonium. It's all on account of the hotel, see. The Grand Cookscomb Hotel—a thousand and one rooms, no two alike, and no one the same night after night! The lavish Marie Asphodel Suite becomes the chic, modern Antonia Hyssop Room at midnight! The Cat's Eye Ballroom becomes the kitchen! The kitchen becomes the telegraph office! But hotels, you know, even regular hotels, are not natural places. A hotel is one house with a thousand other houses inside it. The rooms are little bubbles of Hotel Physicks, boxes of time where folk live a miniature version of their whole lives and then dash as quick as they came. A hotel room has to learn how to be home for anyone—and in all that learning they wake up a little. In fact, the best way to build a hotel is to round up a few rooms where secret things have happened. A hotel will bloom up around it like a dandelion. So when Old Lady Cookscomb was sprouting, we just . . . *popped* one of the bubbles free and coaxed it into a sympathetic horse. We fed it with all the things hotel rooms like to eat: tears and jumping on the bed and mints and empty room service trays and secret meetings and ugly mismatched furniture and individually wrapped soap and too many guests crammed in at once. So we're really in the Hotel, but not *inside* it. When the big hotel closed down, our bit stayed, and no one would even think to come looking for it. Hotel Physicks is complicated! But here we are."

"And you were all human. Born human. And brought here when you were babies," Tom Thorn said softly.

One of the others nodded, a girl nearly grown, with a big thick auburn braid and a long velvet dressing gown on, who was called Sadie. "All of us. Some ages ago, some yesterday. You'll remember—we all chose. We all took one look at Fairyland and said, 'Yes, please!' And when I came, I did whatever I liked! I ate so much splutterscotch grass I got drunk as a goblin and I slept under puffball parasols in the Darkest Fungal Fathoms. I befriended the great Hagfish who lives in Milkboil Lake, and she taught me to hold my breath for a year. I rode with the Mushroom Hunters of Brittlegill upon a Giant Jackal of my very own—and with my comrades I slew the Ancient and Carnivorous Crumblecap when I was but eight years old! I rescued four maidens from towers, beat twelve were-salamanders at riddling, and turned six separate reptiles back into minor aristocracy—one of which was a small dinosaur named Spearmint. I was Sour Girl Sadie Spleenwort, terror of the swamps! That was a Changeling's life! Adventures would just find you. You couldn't get away. I fell asleep in a pistachio grove when I was ten, and when I woke up I'd been given a cutlass called Hush, a ship made of jester's caps, and command of twenty levitating hyenas who couldn't say the word *yes* as they'd been cursed by the Khan of Zebras. Was that better than school and bedtime at eight and learning arithmetic so I could grow up and teach arithmetic? It was, it was!"

Tom's eyes shone. His heart banged a happy beat. He glanced at Tamburlaine, and thought his face must look much the same as hers. She grinned and held her hands to her chest. Yes, this, this! Giant Jackals and Zebra Khans and Mushroom Hunters with colors flying! That is Fairyland! That's what they'd come for!

"Even after the Marquess, it wasn't so bad," Bayleaf sighed. "We all had to come into the city from the country, even if we were quite busy planning an aerial raid on the Roc of Gristlethatch Manor." He coughed.

"For example. But she had a school built for us. We learned music and poetry and geometry and conversational Pookish. We got weekends free for Exercise."

A girl with round cheeks and several earrings in each ear, who was called Virginia, clapped her hands. "Oh, I miss Exercise! As much mischief as you could fit into—"

"The Grimnasium!" shouted several of the other Changelings all together.

"It was a secret. In Seresong District," Bayleaf went on. "Not so far from the Briary itself. She was a funny old thing, the Marquess. She put chains on us, but she seemed to feel bad about it every third or fourth Thursday. She made the Grimnasium for us. Blew it all in one go, out of a glassblower's punty as long as a whale rib: a great curved building as big as a roller-skating rink, as big as a circus, all of smoky glass and green lanterns and emerald trimming and a jade roof. The Marquess would unload every horned or scaled or winged or tailed creature she could catch in her nets into the back of the place. She dumped baskets of spindles and mirrors and straw and masks and stones and crowns and armor and knives and anything you like all over the staircases. Sometimes you'd go in and it would be a desert with ice-elephants marauding everywhere. Sometimes it'd be a huge stormy ocean with water like melon punch. We took our Exercise there, stretched our legs." His voice turned bitter. "You know, displayed our native behaviors in our natural habitat. Just like pet seals on a papier-mâché ice floe."

"It was so nice, though," sighed Virginia.

"She didn't do it to be nice. She did it so she could *say* she was nice," snapped Bayleaf. "And school was only so we could give geometry concerts every night and play the grumellphone in the Municipal Orchestra and steal the Pooka's shapeshifting recipe."

"I wish I had a grumellphone now, I'll tell you what," said Sadie with a harsh, short laugh like a hammer blow. She wrapped her braid around one hand nervously, as though someone might hear her.

"And if somebody wanted us, we could go away with them." Penny Farthing's lip quivered. "They asked nice and everything back then. I had a Fairy mother. We rode wild bicycles every day and ate tire-jerky round the campfire and she loved me till she wasn't allowed to love me anymore."

"Nobody wants to hear about your stupid mother!" cried Herbert. He had big blue eyes, the kind that are made primarily to fill up with big, blue tears. "Nobody else got one! It's not fair! I hate your mother!"

"Shut up," hissed Penny.

"I get it," growled Blunderbuss, who was at that moment nearly having her ear wrenched off by the distressed Herbert. "The Fairies came back and now they're in charge and they're nobody's mummies and once a kidlet lands here they're good and owned by one beastie or another. Yes? Am I right?"

"There's waiting lists," Sadie whispered. "You can put in for one of us at the Office in Idlelily. We cost the same as a carriage horse in good health. A little cheaper, even." She looked up to the peeling ceiling and gritted her teeth. "I'm Sadie Spleenwort," she hissed. She thumped her fist against her chest. "That's *me*. I'm worth more than a horse!"

"And it's like . . . like being in service?" Tamburlaine asked gently, trying not to offend. "Like in books they have in England. Butlers and maids and stables and things."

"That, too," nodded Bayleaf, and everyone suddenly got very quiet.

Penny Farthing started to speak, but Sadie interrupted her. "I'm sorry, Penn. I love you, but you can't tell them. You don't *know*. Your house works you, but you don't have to . . . to do *it*. Calpurnia would never make you. You're lucky. You're so lucky."

"Don't tell me what I know," Penny cried. "Do *you* know what Calpurnia Farthing had to do to keep me when the Fairies came back? She did used to have two hands, Sadie *Spleenwort*. You're not the only one who used to be brave! I rode at the head of a Bike Gang and even the bulls came when I called! Cal and I were the first in Fairyland to cross the Perverse and Perilous Sea by velocipede! They threw us a parade in the Antipodes when we kicked our stands down on dry land at last! Tell me again how much more you know than me!"

"They'll find out soon anyway," piped a boy with great brown eyes like hard toffees. "They've got their shoes. The Office will be coming for them soon. They'll have to Stand in the Corner like we all do!" And he burst into tears.

At that moment Tom and Tam doubled over, sank to their knees, and cried out together. Their stomachs burned, their hair felt as though it were falling out all at once, and their teeth ached as though they wanted to fire from their mouths like ivory bullets. Blunderbuss bellowed, her mustard-colored mouth showing as she roared. Static flew from Scratch like awful, screaming smoke. The wombat leapt out of Herbert's strangling hug and jumped this way and that, trying to stand between her troll and whatever was biting him. Scratch screeched, his needle flying, his crank whirling wildly. Tom and Tam held on to each other desperately. A sickening crack snapped the air. The wood of Tam's left foot split open and gold began to pour out—gold like maple syrup, oozing and hot and glittering. Tom Thorn looked down at his own foot; his shoe was already spilling over with the same sticky, dripping gold.

They were not the only ones—the girl with round cheeks and

earrings screamed along with them, clinging to the side of a mirror to keep from collapsing on the floor.

"That's the work bell," said Bayleaf, who looked a little glad to see the newcomers suffering as the rest had done. "You have to go. It'll only get worse if you shirk." He pulled up his trouser-leg to show them— one of his feet was solid gold from the knee on. "Some of us do try to say no. Run off."

Penny Farthing hooked an arm under each of Tom's and Tam's elbows and pulled them up. Tom thought his arm would come off in her hand—his bones burned.

"The Office! The Office!" wept the littlest children.

"Come on," Penny said. "I'll go with you. The Fairies can't really tell us apart. They call off the gold as soon as someone shows up. Ginnie?" The girl with round cheeks nodded gratefully and dragged herself over to Penny. They held hands, and Penny's red hair turned into Ginnie's brown curls like ice melting. "We swap a lot. When one of us is just too tired. Or when it's a Laundry Sabbat. You rest, Gin. Sleep. I left some cocoa in the sink."

Tom Thorn could hardly see. His foot felt so awfully, horribly heavy. "The Spinster," he gasped. "You said . . ." But he could not finish.

"What do you want with that dried-up old tragedy?" Sadie Spleenwort, lately of the swamps, scoffed. "You'd best look to your own business or you'll find yourself with a golden head. She's with the Redcaps. Holed up fast in their rum cellar and they'll never let her out, so you just keep your head down and learn how to say *yes, sir,* like it was your first word."

CHAPTER XV
THE LAUNDRY MOOSE

*In Which Tom and Tam Go to the Office, Meet a Humble Public
Servant, Fight Several Albino Moose, and Do a Spot of Laundry*

The Office had come to collect them.

The Office towered over their heads, blotting out the sunlight
and puffing little white cards into the air like smoke. It was a man taller
than a tannery, wearing a sweeping dark robe stitched with all the symbols on a keyboard that sit lonely, used but rarely, ampersands and per-
centages and brackets and *at* signs and carrots and asterisks. It glowered
at them with scalding red eyes.

"IN YOU GET," it bellowed, and opened its robe to reveal its chest:
a barrel-shaped card catalogue. Brass handles were bolted into its long
drawers below little cream-colored cards with addresses printed neatly
on them.

17 *Love-Lies-Bleeding Lane* rolled smoothly toward them, as spacious as a coffin.

"Hullo, Rupert," sighed Penny Farthing with a weak smile. "Doing well?"

"FINE," thundered the Office. "MISS MY GNOME. WAS A CUSHY GIG, THAT. I GET A SORE THROAT SOMETIMES BUT WHAT CAN YOU DO."

"Comes with the job, I imagine," she agreed. Tom and Tam tried vainly to stand on their own. They left gold footprints where they'd come running. "All that hollering takes a toll."

"I'VE A KNACK FOR IT," Rupert roared. "GOTTA TAKE WORK WHILE WORK'S TAKING, YEAH?"

"Yeah," Tam offered weakly. This seemed to snap the Office back to the task at hand.

"COME ON THEN, NO MOANING, I HAVEN'T GOT ALL DAY."

Their little wretched band climbed up the card catalogue as best they could. Rupert boosted Scratch up into the drawer first, then popped Blunderbuss, squealing woolly protest, after. Penny got Tom and Tam halfway up to 17 Love-Lies-Bleeding Lane before Rupert hoisted them up the rest of the way with a surprisingly gentle hand.

Tom and Tam teetered on the edge of the dark drawer. Nothing lay at the bottom of it. Nothing at all, except darkness. But Penny gave them a shove and they toppled ungracefully into the depths of the Office, dripping gold all the way down.

Let us say a house is a world. Its hallways and landings are rivers and seas connecting the great continents of living room, parlor, kitchen, library. We sail down them, dropping anchor in the port of breakfast, the harbor of bookshelves! Great mountains of stairs lead up into the alpine country of bedrooms and washing rooms and sewing rooms and linen closets. Let us say this is true—for it is just exactly what Tom Thorn and Tamburlaine saw when they passed through the little door at 17 Love-Lies-Bleeding Lane, a handsome tweed brownstone sandwiched between two others just like it on a broad and pleasant street lined with poplin poplars.

Tom Thorn pushed open the door—an oval velvet elbow patch with a brown-button knob. The horrid pain in his bones and his skin and his teeth and his feet went up like steam and vanished back to wherever it had come from. He stepped into a wide green meadow studded with wildflowers. His friends crowded in behind him, all but Penny gawping at the sloping hills, the bright violets and dahlias and tangled bittersweet berries racing one another across the sweetgrass. Little groves of almond and tangerine and breadfruit trees sprouted up in the most perfect places, where the nooks of hillocks met or where one might most want shade if one were walking through the countryside. The sun gushed light like a burst grape; four happy trickling brooks full of smooth round stones darted through the rich black soil. The clouds blossomed in a very strange shade of eggplant, but it somehow looked lovely and *right* in this particular sky. They had stepped, not out of the oval velvet door, but out of a very neat groundskeeper's hut, walls whitewashed and roof tiled in blue.

A lady came striding out of the nearest copse of tangerine trees. Penny stiffened; Tom Thorn and Tamburlaine gawped. She was the most perfectly beautiful person he had ever seen, so perfectly beautiful that she looked entirely wrong, precisely because there wasn't the tiniest thing wrong with her. She looked like a drawing or a sort of architectural plan for a lady—except she wasn't really a lady, but a Fairy. Her hair swept up into a wild mob of wine-grape-colored ringlets clasped with live black starlings clamping her curls in their beaks. Her wings folded decorously against her long, slim back, nearly black, so thick and dense were the colors of them. Her skin was pale and ageless, the color of copper gone slightly green with age. Yet she wore the most upsetting dress—a short tea gown made all of iron, from the shoulders to the fringe. It had been hammered together out of horseshoes and wheel hoops and hammer heads and ax blades and manacles. Where it touched her delicate skin it left red welts and tiny blisters like dewdrops, but the Fairy did not seem to mind them in the least; rather, she wore them like proud rubies.

"I thought Fairies were allergic to iron," Tamburlaine whispered.

"Quite," said the Fairy curtly. Her voice collided with them and burst into a shower of dark honey. "But that's an absurd reason to be afraid of a thing, don't you agree? I wear my day dress from nine in the morning to four thirty in the afternoon faithfully. I used to bleed the whole while. Oh, you never saw such a mess! But I am ever so much stronger now. I can put on my crinoline in the evenings and handle a hobnail without the smallest wince. It makes *quite* the party trick, I can tell you. But enough about my personal regimen!" She clapped her hands together. Her saffron eyes sparkled. "I may just have a *fit,* I am so thoroughly delighted to make your acquaintance! I asked for the two of you specially. I do so enjoy a spot of the unusual in my house. And folk have a charming habit of doing as I say. Very useful indeed. You may call me Madame Tanaquill. Your . . . animals may sleep in the stables with my own." She gestured toward an outcropping of blue rock to the west. A willow tree was trying valiantly to grow out of it. "Go on, my little pups!"

"I'm no one's pup, Miss Rustybritches, and I don't sleep in a stable, thanks much!" snapped Blunderbuss. Scratch stubbornly refused to sing for this person calling him an animal. He stared down with the mouth of his bell. But Madame Tanaquill positively rippled with calm uncaring.

"I shouldn't like to call my sheepdogs, but I shall," she said in a sing-song voice.

Scratch and Blunderbuss went, furiously, the gramophone's crank winding up indignantly tight. Now he did want to sing—or spit—at her! But he could not seem to find a thing to say or sing, for no song has yet been written that goes: *I love Tamburlaine and if you take me away from her I shall play John Philip Sousa at top volume till I explode or you do.*

"Now, that's all sorted! How nice. Let's get you started on the laundry, shall we? And after supper I am having an Affair. You will be expected to dress appropriately and present yourselves at the Cranberry Bog at one quarter past nine. I do not abide tardiness, children! Ginnie knows the way to the Laundries. My regular boy is already at his post, so don't make him labor alone longer than you must."

"Tanaquill," said Tamburlaine slowly. *"The Faerie Queene."*

Tom Thorn nodded and squeezed her hand. "Yes! Spenser! I knew it sounded familiar! You're the Queen of the Fairies!"

An impossibly pretty blush rose up in her high cheeks. "Certainly not, child. You embarrass me. Goodness! That was so long ago! Who can remember? Having spent some centuries as a preposterous four-armed statue in a field will do dreadful things to one's mind. No, Miss Toothpick, I am not the Queen of anything. Once, in my youth, perhaps, I carried the thistle and the fennel. Perhaps I wore the Hungry Crown. Who can say? I may have commanded bullfrog battalions and rode in a silver walnut shell drawn by eleven mad peacocks. But it becomes no one to dwell upon the past! I serve but humbly, at the leisure of the King, without ambition or thought of myself." She tilted her chin down demurely. "A throne is nothing but an ostentatious bit of chair that matches nothing and ruins the room. I am but a mild and hardworking soul, a simple Prime Minister. A humble public servant, devoted to service and sacrifice. Charles Crunchcrab"—she could not quite conceal an exquisite grimace of distaste at the name—"is my sovereign, and he is . . . well. He is a *charming* man. If you are lucky, perhaps one day you will meet him." She smirked. "Unless King Goldmouth comes back!"

Did she know? Tom had never been good at guessing when folk meant the opposite of what they said. He always said exactly what he meant—why would anyone say otherwise?

"Come now, the laundry won't wait! Let us see how my backward, upside-down Changelings handle a little honest work."

And Madame Tanaquill swept away, her iron dress clunking and clinking and clanging behind her. She disappeared back into the tangerine trees as the starlings sang in her hair.

Penny rolled her eyes. "That's about enough of that, I think. It's worse than scrubbing floors, having to listen to her! She's really the worst of them, just an insufferable bag of donkey hooves. And *such* lies!" She began to walk down toward a fold in the meadow where the four brooks met and tumbled into one another. Hibiscus and orchids rouged the mouth of the gully. Tom and Tam jogged after her. "I should have known she'd want you. Don't swallow a teaspoon of her bunk; she just wants to keep an eye on you, make sure you're not going to make anything *happen*. The Fairies are very concerned with nothing *happening*. Have this as your first bite of Fairy logic." Penny made her voice high and sweet and teasing and fancified, a fair impression of Madame Tanaquill's. "'Things used to happen, and that was fine as ferns until they started happening to *us*. Oh, wasn't that just *beastly*, Mr. Butternut? Undoubtedly, Mrs. Henbane! Why, I was a dung shovel for five whole minutes! Can you imagine? That's nothing, Mr. Butternut, I was a *priceless* idiot, so I spent my holidays as hat! I shall never recover! Oh, Mrs. Henbane, never you fear, we'll make good and sure nothing goes mucking about with *happening* at all anymore, won't that be nice?' That's what they call it! Our Holiday! A hundred years as garbage and they're worse than ever. They always say that ugly little mess about King Goldmouth, too. He was the big man when they were strong as gravity. Some whip of a girl with a needle for a sword stomped him flat and good riddance. Now they all hate King Chuck and it's *till Goldmouth returns* this and *if King Goldmouth could hear you he'd smack the sass off your wings!*"

Down in the gully, a herd of white moose splashed angrily in the cold water, hoot-roaring in rage, vicious blue eyes rolling, their hooves churning the water white. Their tails snaked up behind them, barbed with brilliant red thorns. A boy dressed rather like Robin Hood brandished a black oar in each hand, whacking their flanks whenever he could.

"Laundry day," Penny Farthing chuckled. "Aren't you glad you came all this way to be a washboard?"

"Stop jawing and help me!" hollered Robin Hood as he smacked another albino moose with his paddle.

They scrambled down through the orchids to an icy pool that was quickly becoming moose soup.

"Get the crossbow!" he panted. Tom looked about and saw one laying on the grass. Its arrows stunk of lye, but though his eyes stung, he managed to string it, remembering his Great Battles of Britain and hoping he'd done it right. Tamburlaine and Penny had got hold of several oak branches and were giving the front-most moose a good thrashing.

"In the eye!" urged Robin Hood, and Tom Thorn wrenched the crossbow up toward the frenzied blue eye of the biggest bull. He closed his eyes as he fired—he couldn't help it—and it struck the beast in the forehead. But that appeared to be close enough, as the arrow burst into streamers of wet green light and the moose crumpled to his knees.

The other moose realized their danger and lashed out with their red tails. Wherever the barbs sunk into the water they sizzled, dark red stains spreading through the streams. Tam and Penny and Tom dodged them—Tom felt quite sure they were poison, and one strike would be the last laundry he ever did. He ducked under one brutal, quick tail and rolled through the water, shoving the crossbow up into moose-belly and firing again. He looked over—Tam had somehow gotten on top of one and was beating it about the head frightfully with her branch, nearly crying in fear and confusion. The tail came up to stab her shoulders and he yelped to warn her—but Penny reached up with a knife and cut the tail off at the moose's rump. It shrieked and fell with a tremendous splash, Tam and all. Robin Hood tossed him one of the black paddles; Tom whirled around and caught the last moose square in the skull, knocking it up onto the dry grass. All four of them stood in the moose wreckage, panting and shaking.

And then the moose stood up, one by one, quite calm, and wandered off over the green.

"What was that? What? How was that *laundry*?" Tamburlaine's fingers rattled together like winter branches.

Penny looked at them oddly. "You can't see? Oh . . . that's . . ." And she had to sit down, she was laughing so hard. Robin Hood shook his head while she explained. "Well, you wouldn't, would you? We all get a gob of gnome ointment in the eye first thing, but you came round the back way. I bet this all looks like a lovely countryside to you, doesn't it? Pretty enough to pitch a village in? It's just a house. That's the parlor, where we were talking to Tanaquill, her dressing room in the tangerine trees—she's got a bedroom in the white hill up there. It's all just a

Fairy's idea of interior decorating. They make us dress like milkmaids and noble thieves so we match the draperies. If you could see clearly, you'd know we're in the laundries now."

"So that was just a lot of bedsheets and petticoats? That's what you saw? Bedsheets with poison tails?" Tom huffed.

"No, actually, that *was* a lot of white moose with poison tails," Robin Hood cut in. "That's just what Fairy laundry looks like. It hates us and wants us to suffer. It's not like they wear clothes, really, or sleep in beds that would look like beds to us. Their laundry is . . . . it's their insides, see? Rage, mostly. A little bitterness and gluttony and power-hungry jealousy thrown in with the delicates. They use it hard all week, and on the Sabbats we get it ready to wear again. But anyway, we still see the meadow and the hibiscus and the gully. We just see the washboards, too."

"Don't people get stuck with those tails?" asked Tamburlaine.

"Sure. I know a girl who lost an arm," answered the young man. He took off his Robin Hood cap, which even Tom had to admit looked silly. "Sorry, I didn't introduce myself. You sort of lose your manners around here, like old socks." He held out his hand and smiled a strange, horribly familiar, lopsided smile.

"I'm Thomas Rood," he said.

THE CRANBERRY BOG

*In Which a Troll Meets Himself, a Changeling Hides a Ferret in His
Pocket, a Girl Made of Wood Says Quite a Lot Concerning the
Emperor of Turkey, and a Fairy Ball Commences in a Cranberry Bog*

"N o, you're not," Tom Thorn insisted.

"I am, though," replied Thomas Rood.

Tom Thorn stared at the boy in his absurd green hose and doublet
and cap with a long pheasant feather sticking out of it. He could see it,
almost. His own face, his human face, as it would have looked if he'd
grown up with a smile other than Gwendolyn's to imitate, a glare other
than Nicholas's to learn. If he'd hardly ever had a haircut and had worked
so hard he had muscles before he had a beard. If he'd spent half his life
with his head bent and his jaw clenched. Though, Tom supposed, they'd
both done a little of that. He remembered what Sadie had said—a

Changeling couldn't get away from stories in Fairyland. They ran straight at you like dogs that missed you while you'd been gone. *Well, I'd better get in on the joke if I'm going to make my way here,* he thought.

"Pleased to meet you," Tom said, and put on his best grin, trying to make it a grin the other Thomas Rood would recognize. "*I'm* Thomas Rood."

"No," the other Thomas said, and to him it was not a joke at all. "*You're* not. You're not!"

Tom Thorn stepped back a little. "No," he said softly. "No, you're right. I'm not. I'm not. I'm Tom Thorn . . ." But he stopped. Shook his head. The time for that was done. "No, no, I'm not either. I'm . . . my name is Hawthorn." He had never said it out loud, not since he remembered it for the first time in the Painted Forest. "I'm a troll and my name is Hawthorn." He couldn't help it; he laughed, and felt tears swell up in his eyes. "I'm a troll and my name is Hawthorn," he shouted. A flock of flamingos startled from a swamp in the distance. Probably they were really a piano, he thought, and giggled again. "I'm sorry, I'm not making sense. It's just that you're me, you see. Or I'm you. We're us! Tom, we're us! Isn't it marvelous to be us?"

"I don't care for Tom," Thomas Rood said. "Shortening things makes them less interesting."

Tamburlaine glowed like a polished bannister.

"We're us. We're Changelings, Thomas. But we're each other's Changelings. You got traded for me like a stupid baseball player and you should have grown up in Apartment #7 and gone to Public School 348 and been friends with a boy named Max and written essays for Mr. Wolcott. Our mom should have made a yarn animal for you. Our dad would have . . . I think Dad would have liked you better. He'd like anyone better, is what I really think. He'd have carried you on his shoulders down on Navy Pier and won you a catcher's mitt at the shooting range. And you'd probably have known what to do with one! And I'd have done . . . whatever a troll does. And nobody would have had to do rage-laundry with moose. But it didn't go that way. So you're you and I'm me and you've never met the girl with the orchids in the hallway painting or hated the stove that wouldn't light. Do you get it?"

Thomas Rood was crying.

"Yeah," he choked. "You stole my life."

"I was terrible at your life, if that helps any."

Thomas wiped his nose with his Robin Hood hat and tossed it on the ground. He clenched his fists and unclenched them. His face colored darkly and he rushed at Hawthorn with an awful, bloody look on his face—and caught him up in his arms. Thomas Rood hugged Hawthorn so tightly he yelped—not an easy task when one is hugging a troll. Boulders rarely yelp when snuggled.

"It's okay," Thomas said into Hawthorn's ear. "It's okay. I stole yours, too. Nothing in Fairyland belongs to you unless you steal it. I don't know what a catcher's mitt is, but I bet you don't know how to turn invisible, so probably we're even. No grudges among Changelings, brother." He pulled away. "You really are my brother in a funny, mixed-up way. Never thought I'd have a brother. Feels weird. Like a new horse. Hullo, Thomas."

"No, no. You keep it. It wasn't ever mine. I was just . . . sitting on it," Hawthorn said. "Keeping it warm."

Everyone stood affably still, not having the first idea what to say next.

"They're looking for the Spinster," Penny Farthing said suddenly. "At least, they were when the Office came knocking."

"She's in the Redcaps' cellar," Thomas Rood shrugged, as though he were saying nothing more complicated than *It's awfully sunny out today, isn't it?*

"Yes, dear, they know that now."

"Then what's to talk about?" Thomas shrugged. "We'd better get ourselves powdered for the Bog tonight. Our room's a patch of desert just over that rise. Servants' quarters. It has a palm tree and a tent and some nice stars over it. Not bad. I've slept in worse."

"What do you mean what's to talk about?" Tamburlaine said, narrowing her eyes. "There's rather a lot to talk about."

"There's nothing to talk about because you can stop looking." Thomas Rood was already up and over the edge of the gully, heading for a low, shadowy hill. "Have you ever met a Redcap? You know why they're called Redcaps in the first place?" Hawthorne scrambled after his other half. Redcaps! That boy had seen Redcaps! And murderwives too, probably! "They don't get those hats red with beet juice, they soak them in blood. They eat hearts. *Hearts.* It's disgusting." Rood went on, hardly even out of breath. "A Redcap is a blood tornado with a bonnet on. They tried to eat the Spinster when she started meddling with the Fairies' business, trying her old curses on them, making all sorts of trouble. Tanaquill told them to have her for a midnight snack, but old Spinny was too quick for them. Redcaps don't like taking orders anyway. So they've got her locked up, guarded with a fearsome, fire-breathing something-or-other and a loyal warrior who never sleeps. Pretty standard situation when you poke at Fairies with all ten fingers. But that was ages ago. Everybody thinks the Spinster can do whatever they can't do themselves. We're hungry! Oh, have you heard? The Spinster can spin gold into wheat. We're sick to death of Fairies? Well, the Spinster can kill ten of them by blinking.

Poor old cow. I think she's just a sad old woman who'd like to see the sky again. But she won't. Not ever. Fairyland is like that sometimes. It just . . . doesn't play nice."

They climbed up over the ridge. A little round patch of golden-orange desert stretched out below them. A camel with three humps and blue fur munched on the fronds of a small palm tree. A tent of rich tapestries waited for them. Thomas Rood ran down the hill and jumped up to grab coconuts off the palm tree. The camel spat.

"Crack it open on the ground," he urged them.

Tam smashed hers hard against the rocky desert floor. Out spilled a hunk of moist dark bread, a rind of cheese, a flask of water, and three peppermints. Hawthorn gave his a good whack: a leg of chicken, black grapes, cold cider, and a pot of gravy.

"We're going to try to get to her anyway," Tamburlaine said, looking at her meal. How quickly she'd stopped being surprised at strange things like this. "Even if we hadn't promised, even if we didn't get a thing out of it, how can anyone let a nice old granny rot away like that? It's supposed to be good here. Better here. This is supposed to be the place where if a maiden is stuck in a prison, by god, you go and get her out. That's the whole point of having a Fairyland as far as I'm concerned. Fairyland is the place where nobody is left to their fate. Where you can always be rescued. And rescue someone who needs it. And if it isn't, I think we ought to make it that way. Tamburlaine—the real Tamburlaine, the one I'm named after—was a great King, you know. Christopher Marlowe wrote a play about him. He kept the Emperor of Turkey in a cage. Well, I turned a bedroom into forest. I bet we can make Fairyland a Fairyland. And no cages for anyone."

Tam seemed to suddenly realize that she'd said more in a go than she had since they leapt through the wall and clammed up. Thomas Rood stared at her with his big gray eyes. Big gray eyes Hawthorn had had not so long ago.

"You have storybooks in your world," he said. "Storybooks with stories about us in them. Changelings and things. Right?"

Tamburlaine nodded.

"Is that what Fairyland is like, in those books?"

"Not really," she admitted. "But sometimes. There's usually a lot of cutting off toes and dancing to death before everything gets right."

"There's four of us, a wombat, and a gramophone. That's enough for anything, I should think," Hawthorn said. He put his huge hand on Tamburlaine's knee. An amethyst glowed in the pad of his thumb. *Huh,* he thought, *hadn't noticed that.* Her knee was warm.

"I've stolen some things," Thomas Rood said slowly. "Nothing as big as a Spinster."

"But you know how to get onto the Cellar Steppes." Penny cracked her own coconut and looked very pleased with herself. "As soon as I saw the Office address I knew Pandemonium was setting a nice fat meal for us. Tanaquill always lets you bring up slow-gin and cornflower champagne for the Bog. I bet she already gave you the key."

Thomas Rood pulled a sleeping ferret out of his pocket. It curled up contentedly in his palm, snoring lightly, its little pink nose tucked into its white tail.

"But how does that help?" Hawthorn scratched his mossy hair. "Does your pet know where the Redcaps live?"

"Fairy Cellars all know each other socially," Thomas explained. "There's not really just the one per house. They're all connected together like a big old octopus sleeping under all the Fairy mansions. They talk to each other and gossip and trade vintages and pickles and hoard potatoes. When the Fairies have their balls, you have to bring up the gin and the champagne and the jellies and the rum right away because the Cellars run off from the houses and hold their own dances outside the city. Rolling oak barrels and copper pipes back and forth like toes tapping. It's *very* odd. So, you know, if you can get into one Cellar, you can get into all of them, except not, because they don't look like Cellars any more than laundry looks like a moose. They look like a wild Steppe, going on forever and ever. And there's Scythians on it. And once I saw a manticore. And remember the part about the fire-breathing guardian? If all you needed was a key, the Spinster would be sitting pretty in the Briary by now. Cellars are jealous; they hide all the water and the wine under glamours even we can't peer through. We'll die of thirst, or Scythian, or manticore. Or just get set on fire. That's likely the best we could hope for, being set on fire."

"Then what's there to talk about?" grinned Tamburlaine.

"Lots, really," Thomas Rood sighed. He kicked the golden sand at his feet.

"During the Bog, as soon as we can slip away," Hawthorn said eagerly.

Penny and Thomas Rood clammed up. They looked pleadingly at each other, and then at the ground, daring the other to speak first. Penny did it, in the end. "Oh . . . no . . . no, Hawthorn. We can't slip away. That's the whole point. If we slip away, the Bog is over. The Bog is for us."

Thomas Rood lifted the flap of the tapestry tent. Four suits of clothes lay waiting for them on four bedrolls.

"What's a wombat?" Thomas Rood asked suddenly.

They presented themselves as ordered at quarter past nine at the Cranberry Bog. A wide, crystal-dark lake flowed over the land, stars spangling in the water like chandeliers. Bright scarlet cranberries floated by the thousands, as lush and vivid as jeweled party balloons. Tiny diamond fish with fluttery veil-fins leapt out of the water and dove back down again at graceful, elegant intervals.

Fairies cavorted everywhere. They splashed in the Bog, their fine gowns and suits splattered with midnight mud. They scooped up cranberries to throw at one another, shrieking laughter, drawing stripes on their faces in the muck, diving into each other's arms, whirling up to the starry sky and crashing back down in the water all tangled together. The ladies' hair was nothing but lake-weed and crushed cranberries and that same inky black mud, but they wore it all like Parisian models.

Hawthorn and Tamburlaine wore the clothes that had been laid out in the desert tent for them, just the same as Penny's and Thomas's. The clothes were thin paper, barely thicker than newsprint, printed with pleasant farm scenes, as though someone had thought they might as well make an effort. *It doesn't matter what they're made of,* Penny had said darkly. *They're going to rip apart either way. Why waste good wool?*

Scratch and Blunderbuss had been allowed to join them—just this first time, Madame Tanaquill had relented. Blunderbuss idly chewed a corner of Hawthorn's suit. It had a shepherdess on it.

"Never. Again." Blunderbuss locked eyes with each of them in turn, so she could be sure she was understood. "No stables. No barns or petting zoos or pastures or nothing like that. Not for Scratch, either. We're not *toys*." She spat the last word so bitterly Hawthorn could not help but feel ashamed at all the times he had squashed and folded her in half to make a better pillow. She winked her brass eye at Thomas Rood. "A wombat is me, funny face. Aren't I grand?"

Scratch stepped gingerly in the water of the bog, lifting his long legs out of the water distastefully.

"What is it really?" Hawthorn asked softly, his feet already cold and wet in the muck.

"An empty room with an earthen floor and plain wood walls. The moon is coming in through three windows," Penny Farthing whispered back.

"How awful," Tamburlaine breathed.

"Not really," said Thomas. "Why would it be awful? Fairies make everything out of glamour. It's as good as wood and stone and mortar to them. Why force some poor soul to spend a life as a bricklayer when you can make a different universe in your parlor every hour on the hour, anything you can think of, with just a wink and a kiss?"

The Fairies burst into the Bog like a flock of wild parrots. They whirled and danced so thick and fast Hawthorn could not tell if there was a thousand or a million of them. They were a wheel of color and sound, their wings glittering, their feet invisible, their laughter like the bonging of bells where no bells should be. Out of the thick of them, Tanaquill came floating, her black-opal wings flared out wider than the most impossible bird, her face streaked with grime and mud and cranberry guts. Yet on her perfect face it looked like the season's best makeup. Her eyes burned like a wild animal, but when she spoke her voice still hummed and curled round their ears like a happy cat.

"Don't you all look splendid!" she cried. "And your livestock looks very well fed indeed."

"If you call a bucket of old *scientifick* journals a good feeding, and I don't," snarled Blunderbuss.

Scratch stayed stonily, stubbornly silent. It was a good weapon when he felt snubbed. His only weapon. He'd had nothing at all, since the stablegirls had not seemed to know, as Tamburlaine did, that a gramophone eats sheet music salad on a vinyl plate, and nothing else will nourish it. Scratch hated the Fairies, all the worse because they insisted on dancing with no music that he could hear, which to him seemed much the same as using the best and most comfortable armchair in the library as an outhouse. He stared out of his bell at the Prime Minister of the Fairies and hoped she'd choke.

"Take your places, darlings!" she trilled. "One to each corner, please, there's a lamb. Chocolates for all afterward, I promise! I've even set aside a bit of slow-gin for those special children who do an extra-good job." She clapped her hands twice and laughed all the way back into the mad throng.

"What's going to happen?" Tamburlaine trembled.

Thomas Rood squeezed her shoulder. "Nothing, matchstick girl. Nothing's going to happen to you."

He pulled the sleeping white ferret out of his pocket and tucked it carefully into her hard, wooden palm. "When the music starts, run. Run as fast as you can, over the crags, to the patch of snow with the skating pond in the middle of it. Then wake her up." He shuffled his feet. "You never know. Maybe the Spinster *can* do anything we need her to."

"Tanaquill will notice we're gone!"

"Not for awhile. Slow-gin's a bear of a drink. Besides, they don't even really watch anymore. We're like poor fellows playing fiddles in a pub while all the patrons try to ignore the racket."

"But *you*. What's going to happen to you?" Hawthorn suddenly could not bear the thought that Thomas, the boy who was himself, himself as he should have been if he had not been the boy he was, might be hurt, might go somewhere he could not and suffer there.

Penny smiled. She touched the tip of Hawthorn's nose with her finger. *Magic,* he thought. Just like Gwendolyn. "To us? We'll do what everyone does. We'll do what we are. We're Changelings. We change."

Penny Farthing and Thomas Rood ran to the near corners of the Bog, dragging their legs through the water and the berries. Hawthorn and Tamburlaine splashed through to the far corners, dodging Fairies, Hawthorn carrying Blunderbuss like a football, Scratch lifting his brass legs delicately as a heron. Wings brushed their faces as they passed; it felt like brushing against fish accidentally when one is swimming in a deep river. They had only just reached the little stone pedestals where they were meant to stand when a broken, disjointed music kicked up. Hawthorn could not see instruments; the song seemed to come out of the cranberries, a song as tart and sour and crimson as they.

Hawthorn began to run. Tam was running beside him, she was—he didn't look, he just chose to believe he wasn't leaving her behind. Thomas said run; he ran. Scratch loped beside him, shuddering in the face of the wild, uncouth music. The wet grassland squelched under his feet. The stars overhead bored into his skull and the jewelry on his coat jingled in terrible time to the Fairy waltz.

It was Blunderbuss who looked back. Once she did it, they all had to. They had to see. The wombat stretched her woolen neck round and Hawthorn followed her gaze, trying to run and watch at the same time. Tam was there, just behind him, and she looked, too, though she thought perhaps she didn't really want to.

Penny Farthing and Thomas Rood were gone. In their places crouched two snarling panthers, green eyes glowing in the dark. Then the panthers vanished and they wriggled into two tall, graceful giraffes— then they began to change too fast to stay together. Thomas flashed into a wild horse, Penny a basilisk, then a minotaur, then a boar with bloody tusks. Thomas shrunk down into a beetle, then swelled into a buffalo, a hydra, a griffin, a black donkey. For a moment they were both Wyverns. Then reindeer, then elephants, then two blue lions roaring up at the night.

• • •

They could still hear the music as they skittered onto the snow and ice of the pond. What was it really? A party? A secret bookcase? Tamburlaine held the little white ferret out in her hand.

"Hey," she whispered at it. She tugged a bit at its tail. "Upsie-daisie?"

The ferret's eyes blinked sleepily open. She yawned. She slithered off Tam's hand and hopped down onto the ice. She sniffed at it—and then with a ferocious appetite she chewed into the ice, sending up shavings like woodchips from an ax. Around and around she gnawed until there was a hole big enough for a body in the pond. The ferret looked at the hole expectantly.

"Nothing for it," Hawthorn said. Lights had appeared over the snowy ridge behind them. Voices. The stink of crushed cranberries.

The troll held his enormous nose, jumped into the slushy water— and came out in sunlight as hot as a slap.

JUMPING BEAN LIFE BY WOMBAT AND MATCHSTICK

*In Which Hawthorn Writes a Letter, Tamburlaine Paints a Redcap,
Blunderbuss Grows Up, and an Old Friend Pops in, Very Slightly Late*

The Cellar Steppes stretched out under an infinite sky. Hot orange grasses as tall as Tam's waist moved in great oceanic waves around bald spots of cracked cobalt earth yawning wide. The sky blazed deep, bright red, the bloodiest sunset a sailor ever shuddered to see. There were no trees and only a few stones, buttes towering up in spindly blue rock columns like forks stuck in a roast. The wind smelled like good, wholesome potatoes put away against hunger.

"How do we know where Tanaquill's Cellar ends and another

begins? Or where to find the Redcaps' Rum Cellar? It just goes on and on forever!" Tam scratched the back of her neck in the heat.

Hawthorn looked round. The Steppes lay empty and quiet. He saw nothing but sweet orange grass. But Thomas Rood had said everything Cellar-like would be well hidden. It wouldn't be anything so obvious as the blue buttes knobbling up toward the cloudless sky, or the cloudless ceiling, if only he could see it right, see it for what it was, and not just the Fairy wallpaper. It just looked so big. It went on forever. And trolls are not quick creatures.

Blunderbuss was looking up at him. She was grinning and waggling her rump, her scrap-yarn mouth a little ragged with running, stray bits of worsted popping free of her lips and catching on her cloak-clasp teeth.

"Go on," she rumbled. "You've still got your pencil, dimwit. And I'm bored with being little. Why are you still living like a seventh-grader who's late for class? The likes of us don't walk to school, we *ride*."

Hawthorn scrambled his pencil and notebook out of his satchel. He hadn't thought, he just hadn't thought. When you spend your whole life as a monkey who uses his hands to do things, it's a hard job to stop thinking you're that same clever monkey and switch over to being mostly mountain. He spread out the last page of Inspector Balloon's paper on the cracked cobalt dirt and wrote in his very best penmanship:

Dear Blunderbuss:
Please be as big and strong and thundery as a
rhinoceros so you can carry us. Please also be
armored and protected like a rhinoceros because
when you are big people will be more afraid of you,
and yarn never stopped so much as a pinkie finger.

I don't want anything to happen to you. Remember to have an extra-strength spine because I am much heavier than I used to be.

"Pssst. Put in that I can fly now," whispered the wombat. "Also that I can be invisible if I want."

"I don't know if that'll work, Buss. I don't even know if I can make you big. All I've done is make lamps and stoves and baseballs come to life so far. Besides, if you were invisible, you'd just use it for biting and you know it."

"Just the flying then. In Wom only the green parrots can fly and they're such rotten snobs about it. Next time they dive-bomb my ears I'll just blast off and roar until they drop dead of little parrot heart attacks. Flying! Me! Yes! Do it!"

Please be able to fly, but only if it is not too hard on physics once you're a rhinocerwombat and weigh a thousand pounds.

Thank you,
Hawthorn

He crumpled up the paper into a ball and tossed it into the air. Blunderbuss leapt up on her stubby legs and caught it in her mouth like a retriever, chewing ferociously and whooping with her mouth full. Before she landed, the steppe-grass lashed upward like fiery whips and caught her paws, her throat, her tail. The grass wound round and round her in pumpkin-colored ropes, braided and winding tight. The grasses formed themselves into bright greaves on her legs, a belly-breastplate on the underside of her tummy, a curling orange saddle on her back with long, wheat-sheaf stirrups hanging down round her ribs, and a helmet over her head, with grassy nubs of wombat ears and several wonderfully vicious-looking spikes. And as the grass-armor wove itself, it pulled. It pulled at Blunderbuss's skin, her bones, her insides, even her button eyes, kneading her like dough, stretching her up and out and sideways and diagonally.

"YES!" the wombat roared in a new voice, one that came from a much bigger chest. "I AM THE WOMBAT PRINCESS OF PANDEMONIUM! EAT MY SPIKES!"

Blunderbuss landed with a terrific thud and shook her head like a happy horse. "GIDDYUP, TROLLDOOFUS! ALL MATCHSTICKS AND MUSICAL DEVICES ABOARD THE STUPENDOUS SPLENDID AMAZING FANTASTIC COMBAT WOMBAT!"

"We still don't know where we're going!" Hawthorn held up his hands, laughing despite himself. His wombat, the old stuffed thing he'd begged Gwendolyn for, was standing before him, bigger than City Hall, doing a stumpy-footed dance of joy.

"I have an idea about that," said Tamburlaine. She held up her paintbrush. "Rip up some grass?"

Hawthorn yanked up fistfuls of the wheat.

"Now, Bussie, how about some of those passionfruits you were lobbing at Thom . . . at Hawthorn's baseball? Or . . . maybe just one, now." Her mind was suddenly filled with the vision of herself crushed beneath a giant passionfruit.

"Well, I'm not angry, really. I can only do passionfruit when I'm angry." Her armored ears lowered, embarrassed.

"Still can't turn invisible," Hawthorn said helpfully, knowing just what would set her steaming. "And you had to sleep in a barn."

The enormous armored combat wombat bellowed and hacked and fired a passionfruit the size of a small terrier onto the pile of steppe-grass. It bounced a little.

"Can you chew it all up for me? And just . . . spit it up again when it's good and mushy?"

"Disgusting!" nodded Blunderbuss approvingly. "I'll be Tobacconist next, you watch! I'll call this rule: *Barns are the worst and shall all be banished from the Land of Wom*." And she gobbled up the fruit and grass and gnawed it in her yarny mouth till her cheeks bulged as though she were blowing bubblegum. She retched up a great puddle of greenish-orangish-red goop and waggled her tail for praise.

"Perfect!" Tamburlaine scratched the wombat's stop-sign-size nose. "You and me, we'll have a show at the Met one day. *Still Lives by Matchstick and Wombat*."

"Still life is boring. Never stand still! Jumping bean life!"

"Jumping bean life." And Tam took a deep breath. She dipped her brush in the drooly muck and began to swipe long, bold strokes into the air. The vomit-paint stayed put, glistening in the breeze. "It's not really air, see. It's a wall or a staircase or an onion-box or something," she explained.

"But what are you painting?" Hawthorn asked.

"Well, I know what a rum cellar looks like, you know," Tam laughed. "It's worth a try."

She worked quickly. Greenish-gold rum barrels floated in the air, reddish rafters and flagstones. Finally, she put in a Redcap, or at least what she remembered a Redcap looking like in books. Hers leaned against a rum barrel, sleeping. The only safe Redcap is an unconscious Redcap, she figured. *Dear Wombat Puke, please be a door,* she thought hard. *Please go straight into the right rum cellar. Please don't just be a mess.*

"Ready?" Tam put her hands on her hips. "I'm either going to be very proud of myself or very embarrassed in a moment."

Everyone climbed onto Blunderbuss's broad, grassy back, Hawthorn in front, Tamburlaine behind, and Scratch, delicate as he was, sandwiched between them. His crank spun excitedly:

> *Ain't we got*
> *Ain't we got*
> *Ain't we got fun?*

With a valiant snarl the likes of which no basement has ever heard, Blunderbuss leapt toward the passionfruit painting. They collided wetly and with much gurgling. On the other side, the smell of molasses and yeast and good greenwood greeted them like a fine hello.

The Cellar Steppes had got bored of grasslands and become a long salt flat, red crystals crunching underfoot. The sky flushed a proper daytime blue again, but now there were a hundred moons in it, all shaped like stony white rum barrels with starry spigots hanging off them. Barrels great and small dotted the salt flat, too, red rock banded with red gold and sloshing with red rum inside. Thick liquor dripped now and again from the stone slats onto the desert. Nestled in a circle of particularly robust barrels were several rich red velvet armchairs and red lanterns and red tables, with red glasses set for tastings.

An incredible din filled the air. Hollering, ululating, bleating, laughing, whooping—and a gnash of metal and stone bashing one against the other.

The Redcaps were coming.

They poured in a scarlet screech through the Steppes, some running pell-mell on foot, others mounted on pigs and toads, their spurs and saddles as red as their long, billowing caps, tassels flapping in the air. Hawthorn squeezed his own knit cap, still stuffed into his coat pocket. Their little gnomic faces were transported in joy, their feet sending up clouds of blue and orange dust.

Behind them rolled a bicycle bigger than any Hawthorn and Tamburlaine had ever seen, a bicycle like an elephant, one of the old-fashioned sorts with the front wheel like a giant's dinner plate. On top of it a woman in blue hollered along with the Redcaps. She raised her fist in the air and barreled down mercilessly upon them.

The Spinster came riding down the Steppes with an army before her.

"Out!" she cried. "Get out! Leave me alone!"

White-and-black-streaked hair flew out from her brownberry head. The wheels of her velocipede spun savage and fierce.

"How did you get in here?" she yelled down, pedaling backward and forward powerfully to keep her steed in place. "Can't you leave an old woman in peace?"

"King Charlie sent us!" Hawthorn yelled as loud as he might, through two cupped hands.

The Spinster put her head to one side.

"You want we should make kebabs out of 'em, ma'am?" A large Redcap with a mushroom-shaped cap like a chef's hat, so red it was nearly black, twirled a long scarlet spear in her fist. She smiled broadly and cheerfully, without the smallest flutter of malice in her round face.

"You know very well today is Vegetables Only Thursday, Sir Sanguine. Now, put your armor away, I don't think we'll be needing it. Hold on, you lot, I'll be down presently."

Sir Sanguine scowled miserably. A little of her fight seemed to leak out. And very suddenly, Sir Sanguine was the only Redcap in the Cellar.

The wild throng simply popped out of the world when the Redcap put down her shield.

"*Jolly* good armor!" the combat wombat squealed. She was suddenly very interested in armor.

The Spinster unhooked a grappling claw and line from her belt and rappelled neatly down the side of her velocipede, which snorted and shook its handlebars as it jutted its kickstand into the salt with a spray of crystals.

"She seems quite spry for an old granny," Tam whispered up to Hawthorn.

"You're not such a dry old bird after all," Blunderbuss bellowed, much more loudly, having no particular manners about much of anything. She peered down at the figure in blue striding toward them.

The Spinster was not wearing a dress, but billowing azure trousers like a djinn, long midnight-colored sleeves like a kimono, and a bodice that seemed to be having trouble deciding whether to be a corset or a blue steel breastplate. Her face was wide and kind and sun-browned, full of the lines of living at her eyes, her mouth, between her stubborn brows. She was not ancient at all, but the sort of age people often call *hale* or *hearty*.

"What are you doing here?" the Spinster demanded. "I'm busy— you have no idea how busy I am! I've nearly got it figured out. You can't go interrupting me like this. I don't have the time for this nonsense."

"We came to rescue you," Hawthorn said, not at all sure that they were, now.

"As you can see, I'm quite all right. I've never needed a rescuing I couldn't whip up myself faster than the cavalry could get out of bed."

"But the Redcaps . . . they're horrible monsters holding you prisoner. . . ."

"Oh, Sir Sanguine? She's such a sweetheart! We get on famously. I've always had a way with red things, you know."

Tamburlaine spoke up. "We came to rescue you so that you can come and rescue the King."

"Now what," the Spinster sighed, "does Charlie need rescuing from today?"

"He doesn't want to be King anymore."

"I don't see what that has to do with me. He's never wanted to be King."

"Well, he feels pretty confident that you can help him abdicate without having to be assassinated by Simon," Hawthorn ventured.

"I see."

"Can you?"

"I have no idea."

"Then why's he so bloody sure you're the gran for the job?" cried Blunderbuss.

The Spinster smiled up at the wombat and her riders. The sun glinted on a mole on her left cheek.

"Because I've done it before," she said. "Twice."

A peal of indigo fire exploded through the air above them all, boiling and popping a trail through the sky. Something hurtled toward them at breakneck speed, something huge and bright and winged. A colossal red Wyvern beat his wings against a hundred rum-barrel moons. A man all of blue and black clung to his long crimson neck.

"Are we late?" the Wyvern called. "We came as soon as we heard footsteps but we *are*, aren't we? Oh, I'm just hopeless! Late begins with *L*!"

CHAPTER XVIII
SOMEONE COMES TO TOWN

In Which Much Is Revealed

"Want to know a secret?" the Spinster said, leaning forward in one of the plush red chairs. Red rum filled the red crystal glasses on a little carved table by her side, but she had not touched hers. None of them had. Her eyes twinkled in her sun-bright face, the tiniest of lines at her eyes crinkling as though she was about to play an extraordinary trick.

"Yes," Hawthorn said. "I always want to know. If there is a choice between knowing and not knowing."

"Well said." She laid her finger against her lips like a librarian. *Shhhh.* The Spinster looked one way, then the other. "I'm fifteen years old," she whispered, and giggled just like a schoolgirl.

"You're not," scoffed Blunderbuss.

"If I'm a day."

The scarlet Wyverary nuzzled her with his scaly, bearded chin, which meant nuzzling most all of her armchair, too. If we are all very quiet, perhaps we can sneak in and nuzzle him a bit, too. How he has kept us waiting!

"It's true," the Wyverary haroomed. "You can't lie once you've been to the Moon. That's just a fact."

The blue-and-black man, whose skin glowed like the ocean, all covered in swooping dark smoke-like tattoos, squeezed the Spinster's hand. "It's a funny thing," he said. "I'm both older and younger than she is, and she's both younger and older than I am. Time cannot bear boredom."

"But how can you be fifteen?" Hawthorn said. "I don't mean to offend you, ma'am, and I know we are only twelve, but we have both seen a number of Big Kids in our time, and few of them look like you."

"I'd wager few of them have ever spent quality time with a Yeti," the Spinster said quite proudly. The blue-and-black man whispered something to Sir Sanguine, who tipped her hat off her head and drew a large red box out of it, much, much larger than her hat.

"If we're going to talk about Grown-Up things like monarchies and Yetis and Big Kids, we ought to make friends properly. And there's nothing like a game for making friends out of nothing at all," he said. His long black topknot slipped over his shoulder. "Do you know how to play brownie backgammon? We've . . . well. We've been down here for a little longer than we planned, and you never play a game so hard as when you're in jail. We should know, Ell and I." He knocked his head cheerfully against the red beast's great flank. Ell and Blunderbuss were sniffing at one another curiously, being nearly the same size. They took turns raising eyebrows and stomping feet in the wordless greetings of very gigantic creatures.

"I do," Hawthorn said, and once he had said it, he was sure of it. He did know. He had played it! He remembered his mother's troll-hands on his, showing him how to move the pieces. He remembered how she smelled—like limestone and snow. It wasn't much. But he seized hold of the memory for dear life. The Spinster opened the red box into a board and set out the pieces along the points.

"The trouble with Yetis is how abominably quick they are," she mused, tossing a round glass die and pushing one of her copper pips across the board, where it promptly turned into a djinn's lamp. "They can move time around like checkers on a board, just by waving a paw. I suppose you could say I was queened before my time. But I get ahead of myself." She nodded her head gracefully. A lock of white hair tumbled down her cheek and for a moment she did look every inch a teenage girl with a wonderful, rich, gossipy tale to tell out of class. "My name is September. I'm a human girl. This is Saturday, who is a Marid, and A-Through-L, who is a Wyverary—that means half Wyvern and half Library. You've met Sir Sanguine, and this beautiful Dodo is Aubergine."

Hawthorn rolled two dice in his turn—it wasn't a good roll, but not embarrassing. He slid one of his bone pips toward September. It shimmied, flipped over, turned into a tiny brontosaurus, and stood on its head.

"I'm Tamburlaine. This is Scratch, he's a gramophone, though I guess that's not really a species name."

"I'm Blunderbuss!" roared the combat wombat who had not quite yet learned to keep her new voice down.

"You begin with B!" crowed A-Through-L, who decided at that moment she was quite all right in his book.

"I do! With gusto!"

September smiled at her friends. She rolled her dice and before he could hiccup, Hawthorn was a raccoon. He rubbed his nose and thumped his striped tail. What was it you were meant to do to get out of raccoon? He couldn't remember.

September sipped her rum. "I am a professional troublemaker. Actually, my official title is Professional Revolutionary, Criminal, and Royal Scofflaw, but that's rather a lot to hold in the mouth all at once. I don't mean to, really, I don't, but I just go face-first into mischief the minute I wake up for breakfast in the morning. A year or two ago I was Up to No Good (as the Fairies would have it) on the Moon. The Moon was having a baby, you see, only nobody knew that, they just knew there was a Yeti prowling around and terrific moonquakes and one thing lead to another and we ended up spending a bit too much time with that Yeti while he was midwifing the new Moon." Hawthorn rolled high this time. He pushed his pip with his tiny bandit hands. The pip spun on its side, faster and faster until it looked like a moon itself. The tiny brontosaurus jumped up and squashed the djinn's lamp underfoot. It burst—and Hawthorn the raccoon went up in a bristle of fur, leaving him all troll once more. Tamburlaine clapped her hands. But September didn't pick up the dice. She was looking down at her weathered hands. Her voice was very quiet. "Far, far too much time, really. I didn't think about it then. There was only the Moon and the other Moon and a big black dog and a monster and blood and soda pop everywhere and I tripped and fell—that's all I did, tripped and fell, and I brought the Fairies back. One of them had me in her hand like a little fly she meant to pull the wings off of. She kept me anchored, pinned in place when I was meant to go home, back to Omaha and my mother and father and a lot of washing up to do. I think she really meant to kill me—but then she saw. The Yeti ran off and she saw what had happened to me."

"Darling," Saturday said softly, and put his hand against her face. "It's not so bad. It's not." September went on. "I'd been standing right next to the Yeti while he moved time along so the little Moon could get big enough to live on its own. And time moved along for me, too, and all of the sudden I was forty and not fifteen. The Fairy laughed—it *is* a good joke by their standards—and dropped me onto Fairyland's belly again. Ever so much funnier." She covered her face in her hands for a moment. "But I don't *feel* any different! I'm still September, I've still only barely learned to drive. It's only that one day I was somebody else in the mirror and there was no getting it back!"

Oh, September. My best girl. I shall tell you an awful, wonderful, unhappy, joyful secret: It is like that for everyone. One day you wake up and you are grown. And on the inside, you are no older than the last time you thought *Wouldn't it be lovely to be all Grown-Up right this second?*

September sniffed, wiped her nose on her sleeve, and tossed her dice. She pushed three pieces forward all at once. They flapped copper wings and became three angry condors. "But the Fairies knew about me. All about me. And they figured it was safer to lock me up with a Redcap in full armor than to let me wander around tripping and falling into trouble. I've faced down two monarchs—they don't like their chances with me around."

A-Through-L leaned his great scarlet head down to their level. His eyes danced orange and winsome before them—but worried, too. "That's why they have their little parties," he confessed mournfully. "With the Changeling children. See, there's a Law. And though Laws begin with L, they're not really anyone's friends. It's not a Law like Don't Steal, but a Law like for every action there is an equal and opposite reaction. The

Law says Every Story Begins with *Someone comes to town*. Sometimes it's a Something rather than a Someone, but if Something and Someones and Septembers and Hawthorns and Tamburlaines and Blunderbusses and Scratches and Ells and Saturdays and Gleams and Aubergines didn't keep turning up in new places, everything would go along as it's always done. But the Changelings have to keep coming; that's a Law too." Saturday nodded. Scratch had settled in at the Marid's side. It liked him very much. To the gramophone, Saturday looked like music, if music were blue. "The mass of Fairyland must remain the same. So when a human comes here, somebody from here must go there. Changelings keep Fairyland level. But they bring so much trouble. They bring stories. Fairies only like the stories they get to tell. So they . . . bleed all the Changing out of them. Make them turn into a thousand things until there's not much left in them to go changing Fairyland. It's dreadful. They love it."

"We saw it," Hawthorn whispered. He clutched the dice in his hand but he'd forgotten the game. "Penny and Thomas. We saw them."

September winced. "I'm sorry. I'm sorry you did. The Fairies put me here, along with a good number of my friends, and trapped my car in a junkyard, so we wouldn't fix them and make them go back to being pots and pans—because just whacking me a good one on the head would most certainly start a new story that they couldn't control." The Spinster smiled. A long, slow, glorious smile. A smile she'd been making since a day long ago, the day she saw a leopard for the first time. Tamburlaine loved that smile. She wanted to learn to make one of her own. "Only all they did was give me a lot of time to figure out Laws and Theorems and try to understand just exactly how Fairyland works, the way my mother understands an engine. Oh, Sir Sanguine wanted to eat me at first. But I drive a hard bargain. It was ages ago now that I made my promise: Just as soon as I finish my equations you can eat me all up. Yes, Sir Sanguine?"

"I have the braising pot ready, Miss September."

September's eyes sparkled. "Science first, supper second! See? We're quite good friends. We've got a poker game going and we're working on a war-quilt together."

Tamburlaine took a long while to work her thought from her heart to her mouth, so long that it had fallen behind September's story by quite a way. "You're a Changeling," she said. "Just like us. Only you got swapped with yourself."

The Wyverary snorted. "You're not Changelings. I know all about them—they begin with *C*. Changelings are human. All squishy and small and stubborn and they never stop talking."

"We're the other kind," said Hawthorn. "We grew up in Chicago and we came back."

September looked sharply at them. "You came back? When? How long ago?"

"About three days now, I think. A lot has happened."

September, Saturday, and A-Through-L furrowed their brows all together, identically.

"I think," said Saturday, "it's time to go and see Charlie."

THE SPINSTER AND THE KING OF FAIRYLAND

In Which an Egg, a Crown, and a Small Bird Decide the Fate of a Very Large Number of People

September threw the backgammon dice up in the air and caught them in her mouth. She spat them back onto the board with terrible force, so terrible that the glass burst up into a great glass hand reaching out of the points and the pips—and in the hand squirmed Charles Crunchcrab the First, King of Fairyland and All Her Nations, in his nightclothes.

Our September has learned a thing or two while we've been away.

"You're here" the King cried when he saw them all. "I knew you wouldn't forget your old Charlie, who helped you across the water when you were just a little thing."

September shook her head. A-Through-L growled in his throat, and if there was to be a good growling, Blunderbuss would not be left out. Their rumblings harmonized nicely. "Is that all you can think about, Charlie?" the Spinster sighed. "When Fairyland is shaking itself apart? You're King! Can't you feel it in your kneecaps?"

"I'm six hundred years old, I feel everything in my kneecaps!"

"A King feels thermo-narrative mass disturbances in his kneecaps," snapped Saturday. "We have a whole diagram in the Rum Cellar that shows where a monarch feels the twitches and bellyaches of Fairyland. Maybe you ought to take a look sometime!"

September dragged the King of the Fairies out of the glass dice-hand. He brushed himself off, sheepishly, a child who knows he's broken a cup and there's a lecture coming he can't get out of. "The Gears of the World are coming apart! And all you can think about is quitting your job and settling into some cozy hole in the Summer Country. It took me months, months, but I've finally figured it out. It's all mass. Two Changelings came back, and the mass of Fairyland is greater than the mass of the human world. It's *wobbling*. And if you listened to your kneecaps instead of your own moaning, you'd know that!"

"So we'll send them back," groused the King.

"No!" cried Hawthorn and Tamburlaine together. "We only just got here. This is where we belong. It's not fair," Hawthorn finished for the both of them.

"You can't make us," Blunderbuss whispered, though her whisper wasn't soft or small anymore. "I'm not supposed to live in an Apartment #7. I'm supposed to run and bite and fly. You can't make me be a pillow anymore. I'm bigger than you. I don't have to do what you say."

Scratch spun his crank, warbling out:

Buy me some peanuts and Crackerjack
I don't care if we ever get back!

"Nothing's fair," September said softly.

"I won't do it," the troll insisted. "I'll run, I'll fight, I'll bite, but I won't go back."

Blunderbuss blinked back wombat-tears. The Wyverary lifted her woolly chin with his long red tail.

"Me neither," said Tamburlaine softly.

A great Quiet filled the air. Hawthorn and Tamburlaine would never have thought a Quiet could be so loud and strong, but so this one was.

"Er," said Hawthorn. "There's a dodo behind you. Has there always been a dodo behind you?"

A quite large and bright purple dodo, in fact. She stared at the Changelings with Quiet eyes and nudged September with her round beak.

"Aubergine!" September's face opened into a map of joy. "I didn't hear you come in!"

"That's the idea," the Night-Dodo demurred in a whispery, feathery voice. "I was thinking. I was thinking because I know something, something you don't know, but I couldn't decide whether I wanted you to know it, because I don't want anyone to know it, but I think you need to know it."

"It's all right, Aubergine," Ell crooned Quietly. "We'll take good care of it, whatever it is."

The Dodo bent her head and worried at her feathers. Gingerly, she pulled out a steely-bluish violet ball whose skin swirled like oil. She laid it at the Spinster's feet, and the feet of the King, and the feet of four other people she didn't know at all, which made her feathers fluff with nervousness.

"I never told you what a Dodo's egg does," she clucked. "Why everyone wanted them. So when Dodos roamed wild over Fairyland. Wanted them enough to drive us to the end of the world just to hide and have our chicks in peace."

"Well, I do." King Charlie was staring hungrily at the egg. "I know. I just didn't know there were any left. It restores what's lost."

Aubergine glared at him. "Only for the person who cracks it. And it rarely goes to plan. But yes. Don't you touch it, Chuck."

Hawthorn remembered how carefully he'd written his notes. And he'd still gotten kidnapped by his baseball. The egg lay in the middle of the rum cellar like an unexploded bomb. No one went near it. Tamburlaine squeezed his hand.

September wanted awfully to open it right then, to grab it and hold it tight and open it for herself. She would be herself again. She would restore what was lost and be fifteen, with school in the morning and her mother making oatmeal and her silly dog yelping at the sunrise and her father, her poor father, just waking up and looking for his glasses. She could deal with the wobbling of Fairyland in some other way. She had earned this. Hadn't she?

But September's heart had got quite Grown-Up (and at least a little bit Yeti) and it moved faster than her hands.

"Together," she said. "The Changelings and Charlie and me. All together." The Dodo began to protest, but September knew she was right. "Don't you see? It won't work for all of Fairyland if the King doesn't do it, too. If his kneecaps aren't connected to his country and the egg. He won't tell. He doesn't ever want to tell anything again."

"But we don't want to be restored!" Tamburlaine plead.

"No, Tam. It'll be okay. We weren't lost. We were never lost. We've lost plenty, but we aren't going anywhere. We restored ourselves."

They knelt, the four of them, round the purple egg. Blunderbuss couldn't watch. Her yarny heart thundered in her armored chest. Scratch wound his crank gently and bent his bell over Tamburlaine:

> A cherry when it's blooming
> It has no stone
> A chicken when it's piping
> It has no bone
> The story that I love you
> It has no end . . .

The Night-Dodo tapped the top of the egg with her glossy beak. The cap of her egg shattered. Quietly, and after a long moment, an answering beak poked out of the cracks in the shell. A tiny Dodo, this one all black with a long white beak, shook off ropes of glowing yolk and burst up to the warm blue sky of the rum cellar. It let out a piercing cry and soared up into the rum barrel moons with their starry spigots. For a long moment they all watched it spiral up and up toward the distant glamoured ceiling they could not see.

One of those pale rum barrel moons shattered. Shards and slats rained down to the ground. A great pale creature leapt through the ruined ceiling and screamed as he fell—a creature in a long, white fur coat with terrible black runes scribbled all over it, with a huge bald head and a golden mouth. He hit the royal floor and sent Crunchcrab and September flying with one fist. Saturday and A-Through-L ran to the crumpled pair.

"I am Gratchling Gourdbone Goldmouth," the giant bellowed, "King of Fairyland and All Her Nations, and I will eat you whole!"

"You're not," huffed Blunderbuss, scratching one haunch with her claws. "You're a baseball."

"Silence, rodent!" he roared again. "I am King!"

"I think that's *very* unlikely," said Hawthorn. "I've hit you with a bat ever so many times. I don't think you're meant to hit Kings with baseball bats."

"Also it says Spalding on your back," Tamburlaine added.

Goldmouth twisted round to get a look at his gigantic back, yanking his cloak up. Among the fell runes and occult seals and ancient, demonaic tongues written over every surface of him, was the unassuming word *Spalding,* in elegant, fey calligraphy.

Take me out to the ball game, Scratch played merrily, his brass legs skipping in the mud. *Take me out to the crowd . . .*

"Silence! Be silent! You will bow! You will crawl!" But they did not. They could not. They giggled helplessly, rolling in the brilliant, many-colored dirt of wherever they had got themselves to, afraid and exhausted and excited and at the mercy of Hawthorn's baseball.

"Don't be so cross," Hawthorn laughed, holding his stomach—which was rather a larger stomach than he had carried about before. "If you're good I'll bat you again! As many times as you want!"

"Shut up, shut up, SHUT UP!" Gratchling Gourdbone Goldmouth screamed. "I will never forget that, you little stump," he snarled. "I'd have taken you with me, all of you, to be my seneschals in the Bonecask, my grand palace in the Brasspot Mountains. I may have been helpless, once, in the dread despairing swamp you call a washing machine, but there is a throne here that belongs to me and I will have it again. I'd have made you princes and princesses. I'd have thanked you for bringing me out of my miserable sportsman's prison. You could have swum in emeralds and eaten swan's eyes every night of your life until you died fat and ancient and drunk. I'd have let you watch while I ate every one of my enemies, a few of my friends, and whole countries of no-one-that-matters. And I'd have spared you. I'd have *spared* you, because without you I could never have come back to the country I own. But now you will have nothing—"

"What's a seneschal?" Blunderbuss chirped, wiggling her purple nose. "Is it delicious?"

"A SENESCHAL GETS EATEN LAST!"

A second tornado split the seams of the Briary ceiling-sky, which was beginning to lose its grip on the glamour and flicker into dark stone. And then another. And another. The world was raining bodies like horrible comets. A tangle of iron and lovely limbs hit the Steppe grass with a screech and a crunch. A heap of snarling teeth and black plumage made landfall in the distance. More and more came hurtling down, and finally a black ball of fur and lace and silk and bright, bloody magenta curls slammed through the stone and the sky. Halfway through its fall, the ball stretched out and flexed its paws, as though it had only been napping all this while—which, of course, it had. Iago, the Panther of Rough Storms, yawned and arched his silky spine and flew down to the now-quite-crowded floor, bearing the Marquess and her son, Prince Myrrh, on his broad, dark back. She was still asleep, her hair mussed, skirts tangled. She had lines on her face, not unlike September's, only these were from her bed linens, where she had lain dreaming for five long years. Prince Myrrh cradled his mother's head protectively in his lap. He opened his mouth to protest at the abomination of being tossed like a playing-ball across the whole of Fairyland, but he did not get the chance, for it is very hard to talk over the whole world changing just below you.

Hawthorn and Tamburlaine could not hope to know who all these creatures might be. September knew one very well, of course. They were coming to, here and there, brushing the dust and bruises off—all the lost Kings and Queens that ever called Fairyland theirs and lost it, awake and alive and restored. Goldmouth, Madame Tanaquill, Titania, Hushnow the Raven Lord, Anise the Gnome Princess, dozens of them, already eyeing each other warily, searching in their clothes for weapons.

"Better climb on," Blunderbuss said. "I know lions round the watering hole when I see them."

King Charlie stumbled to his feet. His hands went to his head—and found nothing. The crown of Fairyland had rolled off his head and was at that moment, that awful moment full of yelling and thundering, full of fallen monarchs and history roaring back from the dead, spinning like a dropped coin, like a backgammon pip, toward Goldmouth. But September was coming awake herself. She moaned and swayed upward, her eyes blurred, touching her own head, her own hair. She touched her face—and there were no lines there any longer. No creak in her bones. But she could not quite stand. She went to one knee to steady herself—and the crown stopped. It rocked back and forth for a moment, as though it was looking at her.

"Don't you dare," hissed Goldmouth. "You're mine, you've always been mine, you disloyal slattern of a piece of junk! Come here right this instant!"

But crowns rarely listen to the one that claims them loudest. It rocked forward, backward—and clasped September's bent head in its circle of golden crab claws. The claws melted like old ice, and when the gold was gone, in its place a circlet of jeweled keys remained, glittering on her thick, curly dark hair, without a single strand of white.

"Oh, September," cried A-Through-L, wrapping her up in his wings. "Say you're all right!"

"All hail September!" whispered Saturday. "Queen of Fairyland!"

The Marquess's eyes fluttered open. She held one graceful hand to her forehead and put the other to her great cat to steady herself. She looked all round at the many impossible things sharing her palace with her.

"What's happening?" the Marquess gasped.

CHAPTER XX

THE BOY WHO WAS LOST, THE GIRL WHO WAS FOUND

In Which Thomas Wakes Up

Gwendolyn and Nicholas Rood returned home from their rally late, tired circles round their eyes, coats slumped over their arms. The house was top full of quiet, almost as though it were holding its breath as hard as it could. Gwendolyn put her umbrella away—wasn't the umbrella stand on the other side of the door when she left? *Don't be silly, Gwen,* she thought. *You're just dead on your feet. A little sleep is all you need.*

But she went to check on her son before she went chasing that little sleep, for no mother can rest until she knows that her child, if not her umbrella stand, is mostly how she left him. Gwendolyn pushed open the door of Thomas's bedroom, trying not to make a peep. She looked to his bed for that familiar shape beneath the covers.

But Thomas was not there. He was standing in the middle of the room, dazed, as though he'd been sleepwalking. Moonlight trickled through the window. He must have been playing dress-up in his old costumes, for he was dressed, absurdly, as Robin Hood. He looked up at her, startled, as though he'd only just woken up. He seemed to drink up her face like water after years in the desert with only dew to treat his thirst.

"Hi, Mom," he said, in the very smallest of voices.

And in another city, not so far away from Chicago, just over the prairie and down the rivers, another mother and another father sat in another living room. They rubbed their eyes and squeezed each other's hands and made toast, because we've all got to eat something. The dusk glowed so very pink and red that strange night in Omaha, round Owen and Susan Jane's wooden table. The shadows played in every corner. The moon was already out, in a hurry to get on the scene.

Once September's father had fallen asleep on the sofa under his plaid blanket, their small dog curled up on his chest, Margaret drew her sister aside. They stood together in the kitchen, so very alike, as they had always been, even as children. The same dark hair and dark eyes and fierce set of their jaws. September's eyes and hair and jaw, too. Margaret touched her sister's cheek gently. She smiled, a smile that startled and teased and danced.

"Listen to me, Susie," Aunt Margaret whispered, so that only they two could hear. "I know where September is. And I can take you there."

Crowned the Queen of Fairyland, September has a lot on her hands, especially when the magic of a Dodo egg brings every former King, Queen, and Marquess of Fairyland back to life. They all want to claim their own right to the throne, so A-Through-L and Saturday devise a clever scheme to determine Fairyland's next ruler. Who shall win the Royal Race, a chase across the nation for the Stoat of Arms, to rule all of Fairyland?

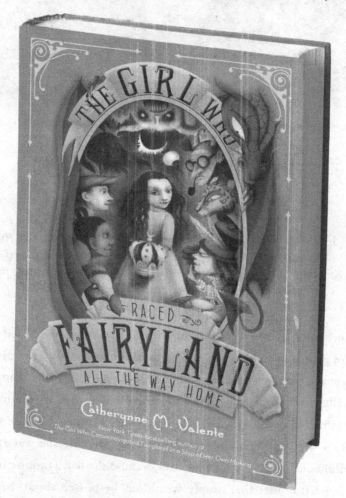

Read on for a sneak peek.

CHAPTER I

THE QUEEN OF FAIRYLAND AND ALL HER KINGDOMS

In Which We Begin Just Precisely Where We Ended, Far Too Many People Talk All at Once, an Emperor Gets Himself Stabbed, Queen September Makes Her Inaugural Speech, and a Wondrous Race Is Scheduled for Thursday Next

Once upon a time, a country called Fairyland grew very tired indeed of people squabbling over it, of polishing up the glitter on the same magic and wonder and dashing dangers each morning, of drifting along prettily through the same Perverse and Perilous Sea, of playing with the same old tyrants and brave heroes every century. Because she was quite a large and opinionated country, and because she was as old as starlight and twice as stubborn, and because she had a mountain range on her left border that simply would *not* be bossed about, Fairyland decided to do something about it one day in March just after her morning tea.

A vast and hungry country takes tea somewhat differently than you and I. Fairyland's teatime consisted of a dollop of rain in the Autumn Provinces, a particularly delicate icing of clouds over the Painted Forest, a healthy squeeze of blazing sun in the Hourglass Desert, and a fresh, green wind blowing wild through the streets and alleyways and secret corners of Pandemonium.

The Green Wind sailed through the tufted wool cupolas and brocade bridges and taffeta towers of the capital city. He banked off felt and bombazine memorial statues, twirled on his left toe on the copper silk tip of Groangyre Tower, and stopped to kiss every black lace gargoyle on every rooftop and balcony in the place. He was a handsome thing, with a neat little pointed green beard and dancing green eyes. He was dressed in a green smoking jacket, and a green carriage-driver's cloak, and green jodhpurs—but he had left behind his green snowshoes in his flat in Westerly and swapped them out for green winklepicker boots. Fairyland is warm in March, which is not called springtime, but Bideawhile, for Fairyland has not four seasons, but five and one quarter. In Bideawhile, the bare winter trees put forth tiny paper buds, and on these buds are written secrets, memories, tales only trees can tell.

The Green Wind finished freshening up every curtain and front stoop in town. He straightened his green cravat and soared over the Janglynow Flats, through Hallowgrum and Seresong, stopping only for a short coffee at his favorite crinoline café, and then, without further dawdling, straight through the satin green of Mallowmire Park, to a certain window in a certain palace. The certain palace was called the Briary; of all the lovely towers and castles in Pandemonium, it alone was not made of silk or wool, but of living vines, briars, trellises, and flowers that bloom all year long. The certain window belonged to the Queen of Fairyland.

Pink and yellow peonies chased each other round the window frame. A bluish yellow light fluttered over the walls of the Queen's bedroom, where wild dahlias of every color crowded together, as close as wallpaper. The light came from a hard-working hurricane lamp on the Queen's table. The room stood quite bare except for that humble table, two armoires, and the Royal Desk. The Royal Desk was carved out of a single enormous crystal tree that some brave window-maker cut down long ago in the Glass Forest. It still glowed with fiery hot colors though it was a thousand years old and counting. Rich green and violet and scarlet and orange blankets towered on a small thin bed like an embroidered mountain, for the work of a Queen often takes all night long, and even monarchs need naps, from time to time.

But the Queen was not asleep in her bed or at work at her desk. In fact, the Queen had not yet even seen that bed, nor jumped up and down on it even once. The room stood quite empty and prim and full of anticipation, waiting to be useful. The Green Wind made his apologies and sailed out into the sunny sky. He swirled down the buttercup and begonia walls of the Briary, past the tearooms and the coffee-rooms and the saucer-rooms, to quite another window.

This window was round the back, very tall and thin and serious, like a church window, but it offered a far more interesting view than an empty desk and a hurricane lamp at the end of its oil and its wits. The Green Wind put his green eye to the window and saw several alarming things inside: a broken Dodo egg (along with its Dodo), an enormous scrap-yarn wombat, a talking gramophone, a great red Wyverary, a Marid, a Troll, a girl carved out of wood, a Redcap, and about a hundred people, animals, fairies, and other assorted creatures with the power of frowning and shouting, all drenched in jewels and velvet, all expressing those powers of frowning and shouting as hard as they could. In the midst of it all stood the Queen, looking as baffled as a goose in calculus class.

And so the final dish in Fairyland's tea was a heaping, hideous, unruly platter of shouting, stomping, and rather unskilled fisticuffs.

"*You* shut up!" screeched Hushnow, the Ancient and Demented Raven Lord, who collected all the bright and shining things from all the worlds and hoarded them in Fairyland before the days of the week had names. Warm sunshine danced through the blooming walls of the Briary's great hall. Light bounced off the Raven Lord's onyx-armored wings.

"Emperors do *not* shut up!" roared Whipstitch, the Elegant Emperor, who ruled Fairyland with a silken fist five hundred years before your grandmother learned to dance. The golden buttons on his peacock-blue cloak trembled in fury.

"Has anyone got a rowan branch?" trilled Titania sweetly—and I'm sure I needn't tell you who *she* is. She stared down a certain pale giant by the name of Gratchling Gourdbone Goldmouth, with angry red stitches running all up and down his tattooed skin and SPALDING written on his back in a lovely hand. "It's *just* the thing for giving jumped-up sporting equipment a good hiding."

Goldmouth bellowed rage at the palace hall.

"And you I'll have for a coat," Titania purred to Reynaud the Fox, a King so old the word hadn't been invented when he pounced upon the crown.

"*What* did you say to me?" the fox snarled, his tail puffing up ferociously, the smell of his wrath filling the crowded room. The room was so crowded, in fact, that some kings and queens and duchesses and lords and presidents and empresses and sultans and ancient foxes from before a noun was a noun had begun to spill out into the street. They all wore such fine clothes and finer voices and the very, very finest of tempers that it hurt to look at the great, rude, noisy lot of them all crammed together like a pack of businessmen trapped in an elevator. Everyone who had ever ruled Fairyland, even for the littlest moment, poured into the grand hall of the Briary. More and more came all the time, some still wearing the robes they'd been buried in, others, respectably retired, caught in their dressing gowns, still others, like Reynaud and Horace the Overbear wearing no more than their own good fur.

"You are all despicable fools and if you do not cease your whining I shall cease your faces," seethed Madame Tanaquill, Prime Minister of Fairyland, and, to her mind, the only one in the room with half a right to speak. The buckles and horseshoes and blades of her iron dress clanked against one another.

"Please!" cried a girl in a blue dress, wearing a crown of glittering jeweled keys. "Everyone please be quiet!"

We know this girl awfully well, you and I. She was born in May, and she has a mole on her left cheek, and her feet are very large, but no longer ungainly at all. Her name is September. She is seventeen years old. She was born in Nebraska, she has not seen her parents in ever so long, and she rather wishes her dress was orange.

She is the Queen of Fairyland and All Her Kingdoms.

In short, everything was just as you and I left it not so very long ago. The world had gotten itself turned on its ear and couldn't hear itself think for the braying and honking and *see here, young goblins* of the royal mob.

The trouble was, only a few moments ago, September had been a stately middle-aged woman languishing in a prison that looked very much like a rum cellar. A Moon-Yeti had taken the years of her youth from her. A Dodo had given them back. And somewhere between the Yeti and the Dodo, she'd forgotten what it was like to have a seventeen-year-old voice, a voice that didn't know its own strength yet, a voice that Grown-Ups felt very safe ignoring completely. No one paid her the mind they'd pay a bus ticket.

"A-Through-L, would you?" September said, looking up, with the impish sort of love that occurs between a girl and a reptile, into the shimmering orange eyes of a towering scarlet Wyvern.

"Oh yes!" A-Through-L cried. After all, he was aces at *shhh*ing, being only half Wyvern. His father was a Library. A powerful *shhh* is the final test of any Great Librarian, and Ell had been practicing.

The Wyverary opened his long red jaws and roared fit to deafen the moon. A stream of indigo fire erupted from behind his wicked teeth, twisting and crackling over the heads of the furious Kings and Queens of Fairyland. Thrum, the Rex Tyrannosaur, roared right back in Ell's face. But as he was merely an extinct lizard and not a Wyvery, his roar had no fire in it. No one else so much as took a breath between insults. Half of them had gone red in the face, the other half green, and at least a third had begun to cry.

A great stone strode up to the rear of the crush of fairies and foxes and gnomes and ravens. It had legs and fists but only the barest beginning of a face. It did not even have a name. It was the last to arrive, but the oldest and strongest of them all—the First Stone of Fairyland, laid down before one seed of glowerwheat, before the first luckfig root went searching in the soil for water.

"HELLO," said the First Stone politely. It sat on the grass, carefully trying not to crush the violets.

September, Queen of Fairyland and All Her Kingdoms, waved back shyly. She hadn't the first idea how to be a Queen. She could be a Knight, or a Bishop, or a Criminal, or a Spinster, but what could she possibly do with *Queen*? She thought of the Marquess and Charlie Crunchcrab. She thought of the Whelk of the Moon. She thought of everyone she'd ever met who was in charge of anything. She thought of her mother bossing around her engines, of her father keeping peace in his classroom—and September knew what to do. After all, in chess, the Queen does whatever she wants.

Queen September put her hand straight up in the air as though she meant to ask a question in class. She waited. It always took a while when her father did it. The Changelings Hawthorn and Tamburlaine understood right away, having been in middle school only last week. They raised up their hands immediately. Hawthorn's huge, mossy troll fingers and Tamburlaine's dark, slender wooden palm shot up into the air. Saturday extended his long blue arm. Scratch and Blunderbuss, being a gramophone and a wombat, respectively, could not quite work out how to manage it. They sat up as straight as they could instead, stretching scrap-yarn nose and gramophone bell toward the ceiling.

It was no good. September was not as tall as the First Stone or Gratchling Gourdbone Goldmouth, or even the Quorum of Quokkas wrenching their tails in anxiety.

"May I?" she asked Blunderbuss. The scrap-yarn combat wombat was nearly the size of A-Through-L, made of a hundred different colors of leftover yarn, and, September judged, quite comfortable for standing on. A Wyverary's back is rather knobbly and pointy—good for riding, but a terrible podium.

"You'd do my fuzzy heart happy," chuffed Blunderbuss, and got down on her huge knees to let September up. Saturday thatched his fingers together to help her hoist herself. He kissed her cheek as she put her toes into his hands. "Ha!" barked Blunderbuss, when September was safely aboard. "I always thought a Queen would weigh more! I could carry a hundred of you, if you'd all sit still, which you wouldn't, but I'd make you!"

Once again, Queen September put her hand into the air. She did not say a word. And now, slowly, the others began to notice September and her friends and their funny fingers pointing at the sky. A duchess here, a pharaoh there, a brace of congressional banshees in the corner.

"What's she doing?" asked Pinecrack, the Moose-Khan. "She looks quite, quite stupid. I shan't have the first pang of guilt about impaling her with my doom-antlers."

"Perhaps it's some new gesture of power at court. We had many in my day," considered Curdleblood, the Dastard of Darkness, a shockingly handsome young man dressed like a minstrel, if only minstrels wore all black and had long, sharp teeth hanging from his hat instead of merry bells.

"Your day was a thousand years ago," snapped the Headmistress, who had ruled only a short while before King Goldmouth swallowed her whole, and was extremely unhappy to be teleported from her tidy ghost-crosswords into this intolerable clutter.

"And it was a *wretched* day, I must say," said a sweet young lady with candy-cane bows in her hair and a dress all of butterscotch and marshmallows. When she conquered Fairyland, folk called her the Happiest Princess, though at the moment she felt quite cross. But she didn't stop smiling, even as she spat at Curdleblood: "You painted the whole country black! I was still scrubbing behind the mountains when I lost my crown!"

"Still," the Moose-Khan mused, "we shouldn't like to appear *ignorant*. Much may have changed since the age of hoof and snow. I don't want the Queen to think me old-fashioned."

Pinecrack sat back on his haunches and lifted one hoof into the air. The Headmistress, ever conscious of manners, followed suit.

"Her?" snarled Charlie Crunchcrab, who had been King Charles Crunchcrab I only ten minutes ago. It's very hard to make such a quick adjustment, and we ought not to think too harshly on him for behaving as poorly as he is surely about to do. "*Her?* She's not the Queen. That's just September! And that name is a Naughty Word, you know. She's the Spinster. She's a troublemaker. She's a revolutionary and a criminal and a dirty *cheat*. She's a human girl! She hasn't even got wings! If she's the right and proper Queen, then my hairy foot is the Emperor of Everything!"

"Sir, I beg your foot's pardon, but *I* am the Emperor of Everything," a young boy in a dizzying patchwork suit interrupted. Though he was a child, his voice rolled deep and sweet across the floor, like cold chocolate poured out of a dark glass. "At least I was," he finished uncertainly. And he raised his hand in the air.

"Oh, I see, you're trying to show me up!" cried Cutty Soames, the Coblynow Captain who sailed Fairyland across the Sea of Broken Stars to its current resting place. He stuck one sooty, filthy arm up with a sneer.

Others did the same, one by one, more and more, paw and hand and hoof and talon. No one wanted to be singled out as a country rube or an unfashionable cretin who didn't know the wonder and mystery of the Raised Hand. Finally, the grand hall stood quite silent, filled with all the kings and queens of history politely waiting, like schoolchildren, for the teacher to be satisfied with their manners.

"Thank you," said Queen September, lowering her hand. "Now, you must stop behaving like a stepped-on sack of scorpions or we'll be here till Christmas, at least! And I don't think any of us would really like to holiday together, so let's all serve ourselves a nice big plate of hush."

"HELLO," said the First Stone from the long lawn of the Briary.

"Hello!" answered September brightly. "See, isn't it nice to act like somebody raised us well?"

"Who the devil are you?" hollered a mermaid soaking in the Briary's saltwater fountain, resting smugly in the arms of a silver statue of herself.

"You're a human being! You're not even allowed to look half of us in the eye!" howled a man in a waffle-cone hat and doublet and hose made all of mint ice cream. Have a care not to laugh—once, centuries ago, every soul in Fairyland feared the Ice Cream Man. "Get down off that wombat so I can break your neck, there's a good girl."

Madame Tanaquill swept through the throng, her head held high, striding forward with the sure knowledge that the sea of kings would part before her. It did. The train of her iron dress steamed and sizzled behind her, burning the floor of the Briary and several unfortunate toes, any Fairy thing it touched, for none could bear iron but Madame herself. She glared at Hawthorn and Tamburlaine as she approached, but turned her sweetest smile toward September. And it *was* a sweet smile, the sweetest since the invention of kindness, full of patience and love and understanding. It chilled September to her toes. Madame Tanaquill put a hard, cold, possessive hand on September's foot.

"My dear friends!" she sang out. "Most beloved and respected jewels of Fairyland!" The way she said *beloved* and *respected* sounded very much like *rotten old rubbish* and *not worth the rust on my décolletage.* "May I present to you this marvelous morning, the brave and bold September, our darling monarch, our hallowed Queen! I'm sure you will soon come to love and admire her as I do."

September wondered if every word Madame Tanaquill said meant just the exact opposite of what actually came out of her rosy, prim mouth. The Prime Minister did not love or admire her any more than she loved or admired a glass of spilled wine in her dancing hall. This same woman had dropped September and Saturday and A-Through-L in prison and promptly forgotten about them. But just now the great Fairy was looking up at her with every ounce of affection and joy a face could wring out, her wings fluttering demurely, a blush riding high on her glorious cheeks.

"You needn't worry," September said flatly. She didn't like to say things flatly, but sometimes it is the perfect antidote to someone trying to convince you the noose in their hand is a lovely silk ribbon for your hair. "I don't want to be Queen. I didn't ask to be Queen. I shan't be Queen any longer than lunchtime if I can help it! I daresay a kitchen chair would make a better Queen than me."

Madame Tanaquill's smile grew even deeper and more genuine, even more like a mother filled to bursting with pride. But the bottom fell out of her dark eyes; hateful lightning flashed within.

"I don't have a care what you want, you horrid little insect," she hissed through her smile. "The Crown chose you. You *are* Queen of Fairyland. It's about as appetizing to myself personally as a pie full of filthy, crawling worms, but it's a fact. You can pull and pry and blubber, but that Crown won't come off until you're dead or deposed. I could cut you down in a heart's-breadth, but the rest of these ruffians would have my head. They take regicide *terribly* personally. Make no mistake; this present predicament is *entirely* your fault, you and your wretched Dodo's Egg. You will want my help to sort it limb from limb. You are a stranger in Fairyland—oh, it's charming how many little vacations you take here! But this is not your home. You don't know these people from a beef supper. But I do. I recognize each and every one. And if you show them that you are a vicious little fool with no more head on her shoulders than a drunken ostrich, they will gobble you up and dab their mouths with that *thing* you call a dress. You may not like me, but I have survived far more towering acts of mythic stupidity than you. I am good. I know what power weighs. If you have any wisdom in your silly monkey head, from this moment until the end of your reign—which I do hope will come quickly—you and I shall become the very best of friends. After all, Queen September, a Prime Minister lives to serve."

Madame Tanaquill turned her shining face to the assembled kings and queens of Fairyland, some of whom still had their hands up.

"You must forgive her. She is only a new Queen, and new Queens are like baby horses: They do not know what their legs are for yet, but they are perfectly adorable while they try to work it out! All of us remember our first days in the Briary, I'm quite sure. We were all then grateful for the patience shown to us as we searched for the necessaries and put down rebellions and turned our enemies into flamingoes. Ah, memories! Let us now extend that patience with both hands to the newest member of our very exclusive club."

She clapped her shimmering hands together—and applause filled the hall.

"It's perfectly clear what's happened—an illicit Dodo's Egg was brought onto the premises by persons of dubious intent and cracked open on the floor like the world's worst breakfast. Some of you may recall that a Dodo's Egg restores what was lost. This is a very dangerous magic, for it can get rather overexcited and run wild where other magics would sit nicely with their eyes on their own paper. This is why we Fairies only used them privately, in the safety of our own homes, and after working hours. But some people haven't got the class a Fairy holds in her handbag, and so, here we are. All the lost kings and queens of Fairyland, dead and alive and other, found and rounded up and come round for supper with no notice at all. It's *very* awkward for all of us, I'm sure! But we must make the best of an absurd situation." Madame Tanaquill held one hand delicately to her forehead, as though all that had thoroughly tired her out. "Goodness! There's enough out of silly old me! You'd think I had the Crown! I shan't say another word until we've heard from the lady in question."

The Prime Minister looked expectantly at September.

In chess, a Queen can do anything she wants, September thought. *No one else is going to come and tell me what to do, so I had better get on with doing for myself.*

"Good afternoon!" September cried out in her best Queenly voice. "I'm very pleased to meet all of you, even though I can tell by the fire coming out of a few of your noses that almost none of you are pleased to meet me. Except the big rock in the back, and I've got to tell you: At the moment, he is by far my favorite. Um. I think, for my first decree, I had better insist that no one maim or murder anyone else for at least a week. You can all hold out that long. I know better than to ask for longer. Some of you have *very* sharp claws." September took a deep breath. She remembered the Blue Wind—she who blushes first, loses. If she let them think they awed her, she was lost. "For my second decree, I shall have to ask that you all wear name tags. I know you were all very important once upon a time, but you might as well be portraits in a museum to me." September thought she'd done that quite well. Having spent a little time being forty years old helped a bit, when it came to scowling down Grown-Ups and saying wicked things so that they didn't sound wicked, only a bit bored.

A young girl in a black dress and a black hat as tall and tiered as a wedding cake looked up at September from the throng. Her hair glowed deep, angry red.

"You know me," said the Marquess softly—oh, but how sound carries in the Briary! Her hand fluttered to her fine hat, as if everything might be all right, might be just as it was, if only she still had it.

"Yes," answered Queen September. "I know you." A look both dark and bright passed between them. "Perhaps you'd better stay where I can see you."

Photo © Winter Tashlin

Catherynne M. Valente, the acclaimed author of many books for adults, made her children's book debut with *The Girl Who Circumnavigated Fairyland in a Ship of Her Own Making*. She lives on an island off the coast of Maine.